THE SMAL
GENERAL

A NOVEL BY

ROBERT STANDISH

9624

1945
THE MACMILLAN COMPANY · NEW Y

PREFACE

It would be possible, I suppose, to write about events in China in the same restrained and conventional fashion appropriate to the more prosaic events in Europe, but I would not care for the task, even supposing I were competent to perform it. The Chinese scene itself, the characters who flit across it and the—to Western ideas—grotesque and sometimes ludicrous situations which recur, all conspire to suggest the somewhat fanciful, but none the less faithful, method I have adopted.

Things Chinese defy accurate measurement by Western foot-rules. There is much loose talk these days, for example, about Chinese "unity" as though such a state had been achieved. I saw the beginnings of Chinese unity a long while ago, which means at most that I saw emerge from hopeless and chaotic disunity the dawn of a belief—never before entertained widely or seriously in China—that if unity of a kind could be achieved, there might be a way of holding at bay the predatory forces throttling the ancient Flowery Kingdom, lately turned Republic.

Under General Chiang Kai-shek, and with the richest part of China in Japanese hands, there has been an acceleration of the move towards unity, but no more. It means little more than that a few more millions of Chinese regard unity as their goal. They will achieve it, but not yet. If there were unity, Chiang Kai-shek would not have divided the forces at his disposal, fighting the Japanese with one part and using the other to watch the Chinese Communists, whom he fears only very slightly less than he fears the Japanese.

The Chinese are far too intelligent a people not to realise that the word "unity" can be used to cloak other and uglier things. Slaves in a chain gang are united and much good it does them!

It is not lack of sympathy with the Chinese which prompts me to say what I have said. The reverse is true, for I have a great love and admiration for the Chinese people, an enormous respect for their fine qualities and a constant appreciation of their delightful

iii

faults. It is much more than a truism, I am sure, that we love people for their faults as much as, if not more than, we love them for their virtues.

The sketchiest knowledge of the Chinese people—and I claim no profundity in my own—reveals their intense individualism, wherein lies so much of their charm. It is proverbially harder to achieve unity among individualists than among sheep, which explains why almost the first act of modern European dictators on assuming power has been to kill or imprison all individualists. In fact, individualism and treason have become synonymous terms over a large—too large—part of the world.

In time of danger unity of a certain degree becomes a protective instinct: to that degree Chiang Kai-shek may be said to have succeeded. But when the Japanese danger has passed and the Japanese power for evil has been killed, it is my guess that the full flower of Chinese individualism will re-assert itself. I fancy it is Chiang Kai-shek's guess also, or he would not be keeping such a wary eye on the Communists, whose fear of totalitarian Tokyo just about balances their fear of totalitarian Chungking.

Unity may come to China's 450 millions, but when it comes it will be the kind of unity which is founded on intelligence, not the kind of so-called unity which turns the masses into screaming robots.

Meanwhile, because I have laughed with and at good Chinese friends without losing their friendship, I do so sometimes in these pages. There was no malice then; there is none now. Nor did I detect malice behind their gusts of laughter at Western inconsistencies.

There is not, I feel sure, any situation conceivable from which the Chinese could not somehow derive food for laughter. Because stark tragedy has never been far away from China, its people have always sought refuge in laughter. It is this ability to laugh when lesser peoples would weep which has enabled their civilisation to endure plague, famine, flood and war, all on such a gigantic scale that the imagination rebels against such horrors. Instead of giving up the fight and reverting to savagery, the Chinese have pursued their calm assured way. Against such a background their philosophers and sages have climbed the topmost peaks of human intellect; graceful poems written before Rome was a city still sound as music to the ears of tens of millions, their pristine beauty untouched; workers in lacquer, silk, jade, ivory and silver have given to the world the most beautiful objects ever fashioned by human hands dedicated to beauty for its own sake; and, lest one is ever tempted to feel sorry for the Chinese people, they have achieved a way of inner life so supremely satisfying to them that their attitude to other races is not, as so many believe, hostile so much as pitying—sorrowful that others have not yet reached the same lofty plane of thought.

There may be some force or personality which I am too ignorant to envisage, which will succeed in killing the vividly coloured pattern of Chinese life, creating from it the soul-destroying monotone of Hitlerised savagery, but I do not think so. The sort of men who were my friends in China would never have submitted to the dragooning which in some lands is called unity.

Unity will come in China smoothly, naturally and because it is good sense, or it will not come at all. In the meanwhile there will always be food for mirth at the antics of silly little men who will doubtless try to implant strange new ideologies into the beings of those who already know The Way and have learned to rank patience high among the virtues.

R. S.

v

PART ONE

⤳ I ⤳

THE Small General was weighed down with a sense of the great responsibilities which had been thrust upon him. He was nine years of age, almost a man, while his army numbered several thousands. The army was hungry, too, as the shrill piping from numberless throats testified. Not even the fact that his army consisted almost entirely of ducklings made the Small General less conscious of the burden which had been thrust upon him. He found himself wishing that the ducklings would make less noise so that he could think while performing his very necessary preliminary tasks.

First in order of importance was to drag his *sampan* off the mud bank, where it had lain since the previous evening out of reach of any storm which might have come up in the night. In the bow of the *sampan* the Small General stowed the bowl of rice, flavoured with fish and vegetables, which was his provender for the long day which lay ahead. This done, he went to the pen where, eagerly awaiting their release, were the subordinate officers of his command, quacking loudly in their impatience. With the opening of the bamboo door they emerged, a dozen or more ducks, led by a self-important Mandarin drake who wore the unmistakable air of authority.

Speed was now necessary, for the ducklings, chafing under their confinement, were eagerly pressing forward, anxious to be out of their dismal night quarters and off to the feeding grounds. If their release were delayed much longer there would be casualties among those crowding against the doors. Already, the Small General's quick ear detected, there were notes of distress coming from the piping eager throng. Meanwhile, with much of the bored air of a drill sergeant taking over a squad of recruits, the Mandarin drake had disposed his adult ducks in a wide semicircle, large enough to enclose the army of ducklings which at any moment would come tumbling across the foreshore to the

3

lake edge in a torrent of pattering flat feet, wriggling bodies and futile flappings of tiny half-formed wings.

The Small General flung wide the bamboo gates of the pen, running as fast as his legs would carry him to the *sampan* which was to be his headquarters for the day. Speed was very necessary in this last manœuvre. Otherwise, in his haste to reach the *sampan*, he could not avoid treading on the stampeding ducklings as they made their way to the water.

A bare minute after being released, the army of ducklings was afloat, paddling for dear life off-shore in the wake of the veteran Mandarin drake, with the flanks covered by fiercely quacking mother ducks, who threatened stragglers with unimaginable ferocity. The Small General brought up the rear in his *sampan*, which he propelled expertly by means of an *uloh* in the stern, the traditional Chinese boatman's oar. On a flimsy wooden perch athwartships were two patient cormorants, one on either side of the *sampan*, watching with a somewhat contemptuous air the efforts of the ducklings to keep pace with their elders.

An opalescent haze was lifting from the placid surface of Lake Ta Hu, cutting down visibility to a few hundred yards. When his island home became engulfed in the mist behind him, the Small General was more than a little conscious that the real general was the Mandarin drake, who did not rely upon sight for his sense of direction. The old drake was almost eight years of age and he knew with unerring instinct the position of all the feeding grounds within miles of his island home. On this lovely spring morning he was leading his charges towards a long mudbank which extended for some miles along a promontory which jutted out from the Soochow side of the lake. On this mudbank, as he knew from long experience, were rich and rare delicacies to be found, such as delight the heart of a duckling. If he had known the purpose for which the ducklings were being fattened it is doubtful, or at least debatable, whether he would have given his tail just that exact ecstatic waggle which the duck family uses to express supreme satisfaction. From time to time, more as a gesture than for any solid purpose, the old drake looked over his shoulder in the direction of the *sampan*, as a sheep dog looks to his master for orders. The Small General, as the drake well knew, was the master, but it did not alter the fact that until the mist lifted he was by way of being a blind master. It was the way of

4

China, the vast and sprawling Celestial Empire, to give obeisance where obeisance was deemed due, even though it became at times an empty gesture. In his *sampan*, rowing slowly to keep pace with the slowest and smallest of the ducklings, the Small General carried a very long and thin bamboo, at the end of which was a bundle of rags. This was, so to speak, his baton, the symbol of his authority. When the mist lifted he would only have to wave and point with the bamboo to be obeyed instantly, but until then he was very well content to leave the real leadership to the old Mandarin drake, who was very old indeed when one remembered that one year in a duck's life was roughly equivalent to seven or more years in a man's life.

Just as a year is a very long time in the life of a grown duck, so a mile is a very long distance in the life of a duckling. By the time they had arrived on the mudbank some three thousand ducklings were very tired and hungry. But it was well worth the long paddle, for there were succulent worms and grubs, weird insects without stint and tender young reeds and marsh grass. These were no pampered ducklings such as might have been seen in a rich man's garden, fattening for the table, whose food was laid conveniently in a trough every few hours. On the mudbank was food in plenty for those who would find it. As is the way of the world, the most delectable morsels would go to those with the quickest eyes and bills, while the weaklings would perish.

The mist lifted just as the army of ducklings reached the feeding grounds. The old Mandarin drake, hungry though he was, disdained to eat until his charges were spread out over the mudbank in a line some four hundred yards in length. The mudbank itself was some five hundred yards in width and a little over a mile in length. The sun would be low on the western horizon before the three thousand odd ducklings had swept it clean of everything edible.

The cessation of the plaintive piping, while three thousand little bills delved ecstatically into the slimy ooze was fully as startling as a great volume of sound which suddenly breaks a silence. The Small General, seeing that his charges were happily occupied, remained some fifty yards off-shore, following them in his *sampan* as they worked slowly along the mudbank. As the sun grew warmer he hoped it would turn out to be one of those very clear days when it would be possible to see the Great Pagoda at

5

Soochow. It would not be possible from the lake level, of course, but by noon he would be abreast of a small island on which grew several tall trees. By climbing up one of these he had twice been able to catch a glimpse of the famous edifice, a full twenty miles distant. These occasional glimpses meant a great deal to the Small General. Thus far his world was bounded by his island home and the immediately adjacent islands and mudbanks. Lake Ta Hu, as he knew, extended more than twenty miles northwards and half as far to the south. To the east was Soochow, while to the west were wild mountains where, so it was said, bandits lurked to intercept unwary travellers. There were even tales of pirates on Lake Ta Hu itself. He had never seen them, of course, and knew very little about them, for it was generally understood by those who dwelled on the shores and islands of the lake that it was unlucky even to mention them. The pirates preyed on rich merchants, but never on the poor people who, in remembrance of this, always greeted the enquiries of soldiers and officials with blank looks.

"When the pirates become as greedy and as dishonest as the soldiers and officials," the Small General was told by his father, upon making enquiry, "it will be time to talk about them. Ten pirates commit less robbery than one official. Remember that!"

The Small General had remembered, for was it not known throughout the length and breadth of Lake Ta Hu, that Sung, his father, was the wisest and most astute of men? Important men came from as far as Soochow, Hangchow and even from Chinkiang, a hundred miles to the north, to consult Sung upon matters concerning silk growing. These last had come all the way down the Grand Canal in a vast houseboat, equipped with fine porcelain dishes, luxurious silk hangings. Servants waited on them and sing-song girls entertained them when time hung heavily. No man on all Lake Ta Hu had such a fine large flock of ducks, nor did any go to market in such excellent condition. The Small General reflected how very fortunate he was to have such a great and wise man for a father, known all over the world for his wisdom and greatness. Had not his fame spread even as far as Shanghai, whence had come rich foreign barbarians to seek advice anent silk culture?

The Small General had known when he awoke a little before dawn that it was a day which augured well. So it was turning out to be. Shading his eyes, while perched in a high fork of a tree, there stood out clearly against the eastern sky the thrilling outline of the Great Pagoda at Soochow. It was even more thrilling to realise that in a few months he would no longer have to strain his eyes to catch a distant glimpse of this wonder. He would see it every day, walk around its base and perhaps even gain permission from the officials to climb to the very top. He would not be like the other boys on the lake, unable to read and write. The Sungs had always been scholars. In Soochow's halls of learning there was always a place for the new generation of Sungs; for the sons, that is to say, for girl children were not deemed worth the trouble of educating.

At high noon the Small General's *sampan* floated over deep clear water. It was time to unshackle the cormorants, for he preferred not to think of what would be said if he returned home in the evening without a basket of fresh fish. There were many mouths to feed on Sung's island, as his home had been called for many generations. Indeed, the island's original name, if it had ever had one, had been lost in antiquity.

The cormorants were angry and hungry. They took to the wing eagerly, circling the *sampan* at a height of some two hundred feet, their sharp eyes searching for fish. They dived simultaneously, entering the water with closed wings, so streamlined that they scarcely made a splash, each emerging many yards distant from the point of entry and each greatly concerned with the disconcerting fact that he could not swallow the fish stuck in his gullet. Although it had happened a thousand times before, neither bird seemed to remember that its neck was encircled by a narrow bone ring, nicely calculated to prevent the swallowing of any but the most insignificant of fish. As always, they returned to the Small General for help. Obligingly, he disgorged the two fishes and sent them off to find more.

In the bottom of the *sampan* were three bottle-necked baskets. One of these was for the really choice fish, suitable for the evening meal of the great and wise Sung. The middle basket, the largest of the three, was destined to contain fish, good enough, but of a quality suitable for the female members of the family, the servants and the numerous Sung cousins whose status was barely distinguishable from that of servants. The last and smallest basket was, of course, for the small and not very appetising fish which, when

7

the other two baskets contained enough, would be given to the cormorants as their reward. When their day's work was done the bone rings would be removed from their necks and they would be allowed to eat their fill. Until that happy moment their angry squawks fell upon deaf ears.

By late afternoon, when the army of ducklings was approaching the end of the mudbank and three thousand small crops were filled almost to bursting-point with the rich food, the Small General observed with some consternation that, whereas the second and the last basket were well filled, the first was completely empty. His father had a somewhat caustic tongue at all times, but never more so than when the quality of his evening meal was below standard. After all, as his son was quick to realise, it was of little avail to be great and wise if this enviable condition involved being ill fed also. The poorest peasant was privileged to go to bed hungry, but it was unthinkable that this should be the fate of Sung, the undisputed master of Sung's island. Some ten generations of Sungs occupied grave mounds on the island, mounds which were, generation by generation, steadily encroaching upon the rich deep soil of the mulberry plantations where, as everyone knew, the rare qualities of the leaves grew more and better silk per *mow* * of cultivated land than anywhere in all China. Already more than seven *mow* of mulberry land had been surrendered by the living to the dead. These honourable ancestors, as the Small General knew, would be highly critical of a son who failed to provide his father with prime fish.

Reluctantly, for it was hard work and he was not very skilled, the Small General rigged a small trawl made of fine-mesh net stretched within a bamboo frame. Manipulating this with one hand and the *uloh* with the other, he drove the *sampan* through the water at a great speed, timing himself to reach the end of the mudbank at the same time as the ducklings. Once these had taken to the water, as he knew from experience, fishing was at an end. Hopefully, he hauled in the trawl. It was indeed a day which had fulfilled its hopeful auguries, for in the bottom of the net were two fine fat Mandarin fish, justly so called because they were fit for the table of a Mandarin. The Small General licked his lips with zest, for the larger of the two fish would surely suffice to fill even his father's capacious belly, and he was surely the logical

* Rather less than one-fifth of an acre.

recipient of the smaller. The Mandarin fish is a skin-fish. Beneath its skin reposes the rich fatty oil in which it can best be cooked. In the great cities there were rich men who paid large prices for such fish.

Bringing up the rear of the now replete ducklings, the Small General set a course for home, waving on the stragglers with his long bamboo wand. His thoughts dwelled luxuriously upon his twin longings: the evening meal was first, of course, for he was very hungry and not a little tired, but always in his thoughts there hovered the bustling life of the big cities which he had never seen.

The Small General had heard it said that so vast was Soochow, by no means the largest city of China, that sometimes as many as three thousand ducklings were sold and consumed there in one day. He was not, of course, able to count to three thousand, but his father had told him that this was, approximately, the size of his army. Now in the Sung household one duckling sufficed for many persons. Needless to say, the bird would never be served whole and recognisable in the manner of the foreign barbarians, but carved before coming to the table and disguised with rich sauces. The best pieces, naturally, went to Father Sung. By the time he had eaten his fill the remaining one-third of the duckling would suffice for the rest of the family, who found that their rice, flavoured with the rich juices of the bird, was delicious and nourishing.

A few days previously the Small General had seen with his own eyes (or he could not have believed that such depravity existed, even among foreign barbarians) a party of these light-haired strangers eating their noonday meal on a houseboat. The previous evening they had bought from Sung's island a small sucking pig. This had been cooked and served whole, even to the head. In its mouth had been put a slice of lemon and around its neck a pink paper frill. The Small General had watched in horror while a large red-faced man had carved the pig. There were three men and three women in the party and, although nobody at home would believe the story, the women had been served *first*. They were even allowed to sit at the same table as the men. From this and from the fact that they had paid for the pig some three times its value, the Small General reached the reasonable conclusion that foreigners were not only uncouth, but stupid.

9

With this conclusion the Small General had reached another: that since Soochow could consume three thousand ducklings in one day, it was simple waste of time to try to envisage anything so vast. Never in his short life had he seen more than about a score or two of persons together at one and the same time.

When the ducklings reached the end of the mudbank their little crops were so full that the Small General wondered how they remained afloat. They were desperately tired, too, needing much urging on the part of the older ducks for the long swim back home. Some of them, indeed, had to be gathered up from the water and given a ride home in the *sampan*, where they lay on the bottom exhausted.

Considerable skill was needed for the last manœuvre of the day: the round-up of the stragglers and weaklings. Here the old Mandarin drake showed a masterly understanding. When the convoy leaders were a bare hundred yards off-shore and the stragglers twice as far behind the leaders, the Small General gave a signal to the Mandarin drake and then, rowing as fast as he could, drove his *sampan* between the shore and the stragglers, leaving the old drake to round them up and keep them afloat until the stronger ducklings had reached the shore and the security of their pen. This done it became the duty of a watcher on shore to close the gates of the pen and open the gates of a smaller pen to house the weaklings. These last were then driven ashore by the old drake and into their less crowded quarters.

By this manœuvre it was possible to save the lives of hundreds of ducklings each year. The weaklings were hand-fed for a week or two and, when they had regained their strength, were allowed to join the main body of the army again.

Being an only son, the Small General was the apple of his father's eye. From a comfortable couch, out of reach of the light breeze which usually rippled the lake at sundown, the elder Sung lay watching his son approvingly, waiting for him to come to report the day's doings.

Sung was a portly man in middle life. His sober silk gown revealed him as a man of substance, which indeed he was. He would not have been called a rich man in Shanghai, Soochow or Hang-chow, of course, but here on Lake Ta Hu his wealth was almost legendary, as the wealth of the Sungs had been for many generations. Among those who dwelled beside or on Lake Ta Hu, to be as rich as Sung, or as clever as Sung, or as artful as Sung, were everyday expressions.

There were many things about the Sungs which puzzled their neighbours. Why was it, they asked themselves, the Sungs had become so rich? Sung's island was no larger, the soil no richer, nor was the land cultivated better than on a score of other islands, whose people remained desperately and miserably poor. Yet the grandfathers of the oldest could not remember a time when the Sungs did not live in a fine house, eat the best of food, wear better clothes than their neighbours. The Sung flocks of ducks were large, but there were others larger. To the sometimes jaundiced eyes of neighbours the Sung mulberry plantations and even the trees themselves seemed identical with scores of others. Nor were they particularly large. Yet somehow and for a long while more silk cocoons per *mow* of mulberry land left Sung's island for the filatures than, so it was said, any other spot in all China. In proof of this did not buyers come from every part of China where silk was grown to buy the famous Sung mulberry seedlings,.wherein it was assumed lay the secret of the great yield of silk, great only in proportion to the number of mulberry trees cultivated?

Even though from time to time jealousy was bound to raise its ugly head, there was no denying the fact that the Sungs were, as they had always been, kind and good neighbours, helpful and generous to those less fortunate and, as everyone was forced to admit, never allowing their material prosperity to make them haughty or condescending with their neighbours.

The portly Sung, who reclined comfortably while his son shepherded the last of the straggled ducklings into their pen, lived in the full tradition of those other Sungs who lay buried beyond the mulberry plantation. He had inherited the qualities which had made his line passing rich amongst poverty and important beside the obscurity of neighbours. He had achieved something more, perhaps, than his ancestors. Predatory officials and greedy tax-gatherers seldom came near Sung's island, and on the rare occasions when they came they were dined and wined well, treated with the utmost respect, but left no richer than when they arrived.

"Trust Sung to know where something is buried!" his neighbours said of him, interpreting rightly the surprising fact that officialdom found it the path of wisdom to leave Sung in peace.

11

How Sung knew where these venal officials had buried their skeletons was a mystery, but that he did know was painfully evident.

Sung in the ordinary course of events was deemed rich enough to become the prey of the pirates who infested Lake Ta Hu and the waters adjacent. But it was common knowledge that the door of Sung's house was never bolted and barred, night or day. Whether this was sheer foolhardiness, or because its owner knew he had nothing to fear, his neighbours were left to conjecture for themselves.

Nobody lived on Sung's island, of course, except the Sung family, but it would have been child's play for the pirates to have slipped ashore on a dark night undetected.

During all the years over which Sung had been shipping silk to the filatures in Soochow, his was the only boat which at one time or another had not been compelled to pay tribute to the pirates.

"The pirates would not find it worth while to molest a humble and unimportant person like myself," had been Sung's explanation of the phenomenon when taxed by a neighbour to explain his immunity.

"Then why should the pirates levy toll on me, who am very much more poor and humble than yourself?" was the obvious retort the neighbour might have made. That he did not do so was due to the delicacy which forbade such an ill-bred remark. But the neighbour was entitled to his own thoughts upon the subject.

"Your army suffered no misfortune today?" asked Sung, as the Small General laid before his father the two fat Mandarin fish which he had netted.

"The number which went out this morning returned this evening, my father, less three small and very weak ducklings. . . ."

"Three ducklings in one day lost!" said Sung in mock horror. "Do you realise, son, that if you were to lose so many every day the sum of them would be more than a thousand in a year?"

"They were very small and very stupid little ducks, my father. They were also very greedy, for they swallowed things larger than would pass down their throats. They lay upon the water for a little while and then, I think, a large fish came and swallowed them, for I saw them no more."

"Doubtless, son, you have brought these large fish for your father's supper? Fish which can engulf my ducks at one swallow should be most excellent."

12

"I ask my father's pardon, but I failed to catch the large fish. Perhaps tomorrow . . . also, my father, I am very tired and very hungry."

"Too tired, perhaps, to eat your rice?"

"I do not think so, my father."

"Eat first, son, and then sleep!"

The Small General, truth to tell, did not know which of the two was his more pressing need. He had been up and about since the first light at four o'clock in the morning and it was now past eight o'clock. The small bowl of rice he had eaten at noon had seemed very small indeed. As in a daze he went towards the kitchen where his mother, superintending the labours of four female cousins, was busily preparing the master's evening meal.

"What kind of a son is it who looks longingly at a Mandarin fish when his father has not yet eaten?" asked his mother rhetorically.

"Perhaps my father will require only one of the fish . . . ?"

"That we shall not know until your father has eaten his rice," * was the reply.

"I will ask my father," said the Small General. "I am growing old. I have caught many Mandarin fish, but never have I eaten one. I am not a cormorant with a ring round my neck."

This last was said so emphatically that the lad went off to his father with, ringing in his ears, a fearful mother's injunction not to speak with disrespect.

The Small General stood beside his father's couch, waiting for permission to speak.

"What is it, son?"

"My father," said the lad in a respectful but yet firm voice, "I am very hungry. My mother says that I may not eat the smaller of the two Mandarin fish, lest my father requires both. I am come to ask my father whether he will require both of them."

"It is customary for a dutiful son to eat with gratitude that which his parents give him, is it not?"

"That I do not know, my father, for I am an only son. Doubtless when I go to Soochow to learn wisdom I shall know of this and other matters."

Sung puffed his pipe meditatively, pressing down the tobacco

---

* To eat one's rice in China signifies merely to eat. A common form of polite greeting is "Have you eaten your rice?"

ash with the longest fingernail on all Ta Hu, the symbol of his material success in life. Here was proof positive that the owner of these writhing black fingernails demeaned himself with no toil, nor had these many years. Intelligence, as Sung saw things, was a gift from heaven which emancipated the recipient from all toil, marking him out as one of the elect. Toil was for the young or the foolish and, of course, for women. He smiled benignly on the Small General: the boy had poise and courage, both good qualities, and he combined them with respect, which was even better. The boy should, therefore, have the smaller Mandarin fish and for sauce he should have a little homily from his father.

"We Sungs are not princes," observed Sung.

"But we are very important, are we not, my father?"

"Yes, son, we are important. There is no family in all Lake Ta Hu more respected. But our lake is a small puddle beside all China. It is easy to be a prince, but not so easy to be born a Sung. A prince tries his first teeth on gold, while a Sung has to bite on a piece of bone. There was a time, son, when I too was called the Small General and when I rose before the sun to take my army out on to the mudbanks. There was a time, too, when my father ate fat Mandarin fish, while I disputed with the cormorants—I and my brothers—the contents of the third basket. It is in the memory of these things that I now enjoy my ease. I shall enjoy my Mandarin fish this evening with more zest than any prince. Do you know why, son?"

The Small General shook his head, hoping that he was not being disrespectful in thought by wishing that his father would come to the point and give his decision on the matter of the smaller Mandarin fish.

"The prince, who has known nothing but rich living all his life, and cannot look back on lean days, grows weary of rich living while he is a youth. You find it hard now to believe that you could tire of rich living, but it is so. Dawn is the sweeter because of the blackness of the night; rest and ease are only sweet to those who have known toil. You have much to learn, son, before you will be fitted to take my place; aye, and before I shall entrust you with the secret of Sung's island. . . ."

"The secret, my father? What secret?" This sounded so intriguing that the Small General forgot for the moment that he was very hungry.

14

"The secret why, son, this small island grows for its size half as much silk again as any. The secret which enables us to live well upon the sale of mulberry seeds and seedlings. The secret which brings rich merchants and even the foreign barbarians to this small island. When you have that secret, son, you will be able to grow a fat belly like mine and to wear your fingernails in a manner befitting the elder son of Sung. But until then, son, there are many things to be learned. . . ."

"And the smaller Mandarin fish, my father? I may eat it?"

"You may eat it. Go tell your mother to cook yours as she will cook mine, with a sauce made from the shrimps caught yesterday in the Chien Tang River below Hangchow and brought to me this morning by my friend Chang, the silk merchant. Go now and eat the rice of a dutiful son. I am pleased with you. . . ."

⋘ 2 ⋙

It is small wonder that many envious eyes were cast at Sung's island for, even in a lovely region of a lovely land, its beauties and attractions were known far and wide. They say in China: "Heaven lies far away in the sky, but Soochow and Hangchow are here below." There are even those who profess to believe that, knowing both Soochow and Hangchow, Heaven might well prove disappointing.

Now Lake Ta Hu lies roughly between these two great and lovely cities, nearer to the former than the latter, and was at one time without doubt the water link between the two. But that was many centuries ago, before the building of the Grand Canal, the southern end of which skirts Ta Hu to the westward on the last lap of the long journey from Peking to Hangchow.

Since merchants are notoriously insensitive to beauty and vastly more concerned with speedy transportation of their goods, the Grand Canal ranks as one of the world's busiest waterways, whilst the usually placid surface of Ta Hu is rarely disturbed by any other than the small inter-island traffic, or that between the islands and the mainland. The people on and around Ta Hu were well content with this state of affairs and content, too, that the bustle of the Grand Canal should leave them untouched by the multitude of new persons, new things and new ideas which, year in and year out, passed up and down. They knew nothing about Heaven, these simple people of Ta Hu, and very little more about Soochow and Hangchow. But they did know that life on Ta Hu was very pleasant and that nowhere on the lake, or for many miles around, was it more pleasant than on Sung's island.

Probably there had been a time when Sung's island was barely more than one of the mudbanks, whose slimy surfaces made such excellent feeding grounds for ducks. But generation after generation of Sungs, by dint of back-breaking and barely conceivable toil, had lifted the rich silt from the lake bottom and spread it

16

over their land, until the average height of the island back from the foreshores was some eight feet above the level of the lake. To prevent the result of all this toil being lost, there had been constructed some two hundred years before this story opens a fine stone holding wall, every stone of which had been cut by hand in the hills thirty miles to the westward and sailed across in flat-bottomed boats with high lateen sails.

It would seem, therefore, that those dead and gone Sungs, at rest beneath their grave mounds behind the mulberry plantation, had earned their long repose. But whereas these earlier Sungs had shown no mercy to their muscles and sinews, their latter-day heir and descendant, the father of the Small General, believed that brains were provided for the express purpose of easing the strain on those muscles and sinews. Although he was probably unaware of the fact, Sung's ideas were in tune with those of the twentieth century, which had just emerged from the womb of time.

It was a Sung tradition that each generation must carry on the work of raising the island a little higher above the lake level, enriching the soil with the rich lake silt. Hitherto certain days in the year had been set apart for this time-honoured toil. But Sung, although he had broken with the tradition, and had never made his back and thews ache with dredging and carrying baskets of silt, had in fact added more soil to his island home than any previous generation had added. More important still, he had achieved this without dirtying his hands.

Some ten years before this story opens there had arrived at Sung's island one hot summer's day a wealthy silk merchant named Lok-kai-shing, reputed to be one of the richest men in Soochow. Now Sung, although he was not in the least surprised to receive this call, expressed both his pleasure and surprise.

"I am overwhelmed with pride," he said courteously, "that the rich and mighty Lok should condescend to honour my poor home with his presence."

"On the contrary," declared Lok, "it is I who am honoured by your permission to moor my poor houseboat within sight of your ancestral home."

Now let us not fall into the error of supposing that Lok had made the journey for the sake of exchanging platitudes and courtesies with Sung, nor even that the latter supposed such was the case, nor even yet that Lok believed Sung laboured under any such delusion. But in China, even twentieth century China, the courteous host is expected to see these little comedies of ceremony through to the finish, and no less is the courteous guest expected to do his share.

The advantage of the meeting lay with Sung for, as soon as Lok's houseboat approached the landing place, he knew why Lok had come. For three or four years he had waited for the day when Lok's curiosity would master him. Now that the long-awaited day had come, Sung was in no hurry. On this day, or the next, with elaborate carelessness, Lok would broach the subject uppermost in his mind.

All through the heat of the day Lok and Sung sat together amiably in a small tea-house which Sung had constructed for his own pleasure upon the highest point of the island. Servants had brought tea and light food for them and hot steamed towels to wipe their hands and faces, so that even the burning heat of the day seemed cool by contrast. They had chatted lightly of this and that, interpolating here and there a well-rounded quotation from the Classics, with which neither of the two men was too familiar, but which helped each to convey to the other that he was a well-informed man-of-the-world. Sung knew that Lok came expecting to find a bumpkin, for these two had never met before. Lok's fame as a silk merchant had, of course, spread far and wide, but at that time the fame of Sung did not extend beyond the confines of Lake Ta Hu. It was merely as a buyer of silk cocoons that Lok had heard of Sung, as the latter had intended he should hear.

Once every year Lok's agent called at Sung's island to buy cocoons and, so pleasant was the spot and so good a host was Sung, that the agent usually remained two or three days. The buying agent for a silk filature is usually an observant man, or he does not long remain a buying agent. This agent of Lok's was no exception to the rule. While engaged in gentle strolls round the island, with or without his host, he had observed—counted in fact—the number of mulberry trees owned by Sung. He had also noted, with considerable surprise, the quantity of cocoons purchased from Sung, which was fully fifty per cent in excess of the quantity which might reasonably have been expected from the number of mulberry trees.

The following year there was the same proportionate excess

18

of silk cocoons and again the third year. Up to this time he had kept the information to himself, suspecting that he might have miscounted the mulberry trees. The third year he left nothing to chance and, while Sung was busily engaged elsewhere, strolled through the plantations making a very careful count of the mulberries, which confirmed the accuracy of his count two years previously.

Now in silk-growing there is, depending upon the region, a fixed and very definite relationship between the number of mulberry trees a man may own and the number of silk cocoons he may reasonably expect to produce each year. There are, of course, slight variations due to weather conditions, but these would affect all growers in the same region. Sung, it seemed, had for three consecutive years produced half as much again by weight of silk cocoons as had been produced by any other grower in the same region and under the same climatic conditions, proportionate to the number of mulberries owned.

When he had checked this remarkable fact to his own satisfaction the agent, immediately upon his return to Soochow, informed Lok, his master, of it.

Lok, in addition to being a silk merchant, was the owner of extensive mulberry plantations, his chief source of pride and satisfaction. Nowhere in all China, he would assert proudly, was a stronger silk thread produced. The news that upon a small island in Lake Ta Hu an insignificant peasant was able to produce silk upon such a scale hurt Lok's pride and aroused his curiosity. It was possible that this Sung had stumbled by accident upon some secret which had eluded all the patient research of centuries and, if this were the case, he would take no chances of the secret falling into the hands of his fellow members of the Silk Guild in Soochow. Not only pride, but potential profits, were at stake.

When the cool of the evening came these two men, Lok and Sung, strolled around the small island in amicable conversation. Each of them took with him his favourite cicada, imprisoned in a small wicker cage at the end of a stick. The cicadas vied with each other in their strident tuneless song, which falls so pleasingly upon Chinese ears and so harshly upon those of westerners, providing one more example in a long list of the inability of the west and the east to see things through the same eyes, or as in this

19

case, to hear them through the same ears. The cicada is mistaken in turn for a cricket, a grasshopper and a locust, but it is none of these three. Foreigners in China, tortured almost beyond endurance by its deafening song, have aptly named it the scissor-grinder.

So, to the music of the cicada, these two men strolled gently around Sung's small domain, and at a pace which enabled Lok, while still maintaining his careless ease, to verify his agent's count of the mulberry trees. While Lok counted, Sung appeared to give his full attention to his cicada, talking to it softly in endearing terms.

"You send fine cocoons to my filature," observed Lok at last. "My workers tell me that none finer"—he swallowed hard—"not even from my own land, passes through their hands. I am happy that I shall now be able to tell them I have seen the famous island where they are grown. . . ."

"It gives me great pleasure that the humble product of my land finds favour in the eyes of such an illustrious person," replied Sung politely.

"To what do you attribute the excellence of your silk?" asked Lok, coming towards the point of his visit rather more swiftly than either prudence or courtesy suggested. But in a battle of wits, he was sure, he had nothing to fear from this amiable bumpkin who lived his lonely life upon a small island in the lake and had not, upon his own admission, visited Soochow for nearly ten years.

"That my poor silk possesses any excellence whatever," said Sung with becoming modesty, "must surely be due to the toil of my honourable ancestors, who carried the rich lake silt up on to our land. But these few *mow* of land are, if report be true, but a grain of sand compared with the magnificent mulberry plantations of the illustrious Lok . . . ?"

"Mine, perhaps, are somewhat larger," replied Lok airily, "but I had not mere size in mind. I was thinking more of quality and in this matter"—here he paused impressively—"my brief visit here has taught me that I have much to learn from the Sungs."

"Aye, and it may be that you will learn a good deal more before very long," mused Sung, waving away the compliment with a self-deprecatory gesture.

Meanwhile, in the Sung kitchens there had been tremendous activity ever since, a few minutes after the arrival of Lok's boat, the master of the house had sent word that the best of everything would not be too good for the evening meal.

Lok was a gourmet. His heart sank, therefore, at the prospect of the kind of peasant meal which he feared would be served to him, to refuse which would be an unpardonable discourtesy. At that time, which it must be remembered was a full ten years before this story opened, Sung was a lean and wiry man, who had none of the appearance of one accustomed to good living, so Lok may be pardoned for the error of judgment.

The two men, still chatting most amiably, their cicadas now silenced by the gathering darkness, took their seats at the table in a very comfortably furnished room. Lok's spirits rose upon the appearance of a platter of finely sliced chicken livers, served with a shredded sour cabbage and chopped celery. With this on side dishes were smoked eggs, pickled duck feet and delicate slices of a domestic ham, than which last Lok had not tasted better in Soochow's most famous eating places. With the arrival of thick flakes of Mandarin fish in a soy-base sauce, pork balls *sauté* with a highly-seasoned sauce and green peppers, Lok began to realise that the arts of good living were not confined to Soochow. By the time he had eaten with relish a dish of ducks' tongues, cooked with bamboo shoots, he realised that the country bumpkin he had come to patronise had given him a dinner which he doubted whether his own elaborate establishment could equal.

"I commend to you this poor wine," said Sung, to whom the effects of the meal on his guest were not being lost. "My revered grandfather sealed the jar with his own hand these seventy years ago. It should be passable, even though unworthy of such an illustrious guest."

Elsewhere the wine would have been called a *grand vin* for it was, as Sung had stated, seventy years of age, delicately flavoured with pomegranate and served warm, as is the Chinese custom. Like many of the world's great discoveries, the art of wine-making was an accident in China. Chinese wines are made from either rice or *kao-liang*. Many centuries ago a cook in the Emperor's kitchens forgot a bowl in which he had left rice to soak. Several days later, wishing to ascertain whether the rice was spoiled—for no Chinese will willingly waste one grain—he drank from the bowl. The fermented liquid pleased him greatly and, it

21

is recorded, life from that moment seemed easier and the world a better place.

By producing this rare wine Sung rose greatly in Lok's estimation, no less than Sung was made, by his guest's lip-smacking, glad that he had found one who appreciated the good things of life. Both men, under the wine's warming influence, shed some of their formal courtesy, dropping a little the mask of caution which each had worn through the long day. With gravity they began a game of forfeits, the penalty to the loser being the drinking of a cup of wine. The game they played was stone-paper-scissors. Two fingers extended represent scissors; the clenched fist a stone; and the outspread hand a sheet of paper. At a carefully synchronised moment each played offers to the other one of these three symbols. Now it stands to reason that scissors will not cut a stone, so stone is the winner. It follows equally that paper will wrap round a stone, and that scissors will cut paper.

Some believe that this simple game is one of pure chance, but those who know better have observed that some men always win, while others always lose. It has been noticed, furthermore, that the former are usually astute men, able to see a little further into the future than their fellows and able, also, a little better than most, to interpret accurately motive in others.

Sung and Lok began their meal at about eight o'clock in the evening. At midnight, still toying with a rich sweetmeat compounded of almonds, honey and ginger, the two men had emptied via the warming kettle a jar containing little short of two gallons of wine.

Each man looked now at the other with a new measure of respect, almost of affection, for in the game of forfeits neither was by more than a cup of wine the winner.

"He has kept his head," each mused of the other. "He has paid all his forfeits and yet, miraculous to behold, he is as sober as I am. This one is no fool. I am insane to believe that I could trick him. Why, it is obvious, he is as quick-witted as I am. This man will be far more valuable as a friend. Together we may do great things. Heaven must have decreed that we should be brought together."

"I dare not stand before you, so poor has been the meal I have offered you!" said Sung in the polite fashion of the country, when his guest indicated his intention of departing to his houseboat to sleep.

As though to prove the contrary, Lok replied with a great rumbling belch, so genuine of execution that it could not have been mistaken for one of those puny artificial belches which polite guests use to feign appreciation of a poor meal. Lok's cavernous belly shook and heaved with the sheer impact of it. They heard it in the kitchen as a pæan of praise.

"The master will be pleased with us," they assured themselves with satisfaction.

"I will not permit you," observed Lok, his voice dripping with honey, "to be so modest over such a feast, the equal of which has not been served on the table of the *Tao-tai* himself these many years."

Lok, with Sung to accompany him and a lantern-bearer walking ahead, staggered magnificently down to his houseboat. Each man knew, though nothing had been said, that with the morning's light they would reach agreement and understanding upon certain very important matters.

In a world perennially torn by strife is there not a lesson to be learned from the fact that those with well-filled bellies reach amity more quickly than the rest of their fellows?

"You have done well, woman," said Sung to his wife as he sought his couch. "If you will but bear me a son I shall esteem you as a good wife."

Thus encouraged, or so it would seem, the wife of Sung bore him a son some nine months later, the Small General of the ducks.

"Now it might be," Lok was saying the following morning, as he and Sung settled down to the discussion of matters, "that some excellence of the soil upon your island accounts for the great yield of silk."

"It might well be," agreed Sung.

"It might also be that a rare skill in pruning the mulberries is responsible," ventured Lok.

"It might be," agreed Sung.

"We must also consider," said Lok thoughtfully, "that you may have some special way of feeding your trees, enabling them to provide finer and more plentiful leaves."

"We must consider that also," agreed Sung.

"Then again," continued Lok, "the secret may lie in some special way of handling and feeding the silkworms, giving them greater happiness so that they reward you more lavishly than other growers are accustomed to expect. . . ."

"It is not for me, a humble and relatively ignorant person," said Sung, "to speculate upon these matters when in the presence of a known authority upon all matters pertaining to silk. All I can say with certainty is that with these few poor mulberries and this unworthy little island I am enabled, by Heaven's grace, to produce a few miserable cocoons more than other growers produce from the same number of poor trees."

Sung was happy in the knowledge that in one matter only— and that the most vital—had he deceived Lok: Lok did not know that he, Sung, had planned and engineered this meeting. He was able, therefore, to play convincingly the part of a man not very much impressed with his own small personal success.

"You do not seem to realise," said Lok, "that although the increased yield of silk here on this island is but a small matter, by virtue of the fact that the island itself is so small, an increase of fifty per cent in the yield of silk in the great silk-growing districts of China would mean fabulous wealth for all concerned. For you, too, Sung, it would mean riches, honour and fame, and also abundant honour to your revered ancestors who dug this small island from the very depths of Ta Hu, planted the mulberries and then went to their well-earned rest."

"But how, wise and learned Lok, could I profit from such a matter? I will not disguise from you the thought that a taste of riches would be sweet, although I am not so sure about fame and honour. These last sometimes prove embarrassing."

"You mean," laughed Lok, "that if too much fame attached to you, as well as the riches, the tax collector might think it worth while to come more frequently to Sung's island? Is that it?"

"Some such thought was in my poor head," agreed Sung.

"Then let us try to devise some method by which riches, but not too much fame, accrue to the eminent Sung," said Lok, beaming with pleasure at having taken the point so well.

"I am inclined to believe," said Sung more brightly, "that my small success is due to the rich mud which comes from yonder small bay." Sung pointed towards a mud flat which was enclosed

24

warranted. Somewhere within his grasp, Lok b
secret which would revolutionise an industry whic
of the chief sources of China's prosperity for n
ve thousand years. Riches he already had in plenty
d a long line of distinguished ancestors. Here wa
to become a distinguished man himself, to die ful
and to leave on earth successive generations of Lok
date their ancestry back to him. He wanted to b
ughout all China and beyond as "Lok, the man who
silkworms flourish where only two flourished before."
tial Lok houseboat, replete with every luxury, became
visitor to Sung's island at every season of the year, so
uld observe at first-hand how Sung handled every one
ltifarious processes between the pulping of the mul-
t to obtain fresh seed and the despatch of the cocoons
ture. Try as he would, he failed to find that Sung
any process which differed widely from those in general
region.

occasion Lok arrived at the island to find everyone hard
der Sung's supervision preparing a special manure for
rries. Over an area of more than one acre there was,
t in the sun to dry, a vast quantity of lake weed and
atic plants. In separate heaps nearby were large quanti-
ig dung, a huge pile of silkworm droppings, the ash
d from burned rice straw and a small quantity of crushed
eed.

tood by during a whole long day, making copious notes
tities. It occurred to him that there might be some special
es in the lake weeds, which he watched while they were
and mixed with the other ingredients. A few days later
coolies were loading barges with the weed and taking it
plantations.

neighbouring islet, which was the property of Sung, there
in great profusion a wild plant called by the Chinese
l-tsao, whose foliage resembled that of the bamboo. Four
ations previously a Sung had discovered that a liquid
ed by boiling the leaves of this plant was a most powerful
icide, being particularly deadly to an insect called sang-niao,
in the Yangtsze region of China caused great destruction
g mulberries. Lok arrived one day while these leaves were

by two arms of the island. "Would it be possible, do you think, that this mud, transported elsewhere, and placed carefully around the roots of mulberries, according to my own fashion, would achieve the same results?"

"That we shall soon find out, Sung, for within the week—and with your permission—I will have here a fleet of barges. The method shall be tried in my own plantations. Now doubtless, Sung, you will require some small compensation? What do you suggest? How much per barge-load?"

"I would not accept money from the wise and learned Lok for my mud," said Sung engagingly. "The coolies who come to fetch the mud for the Lok plantations need only spread upon my small island one barge-load for every barge-load they take away. That is eminently fair, for if indeed the mud be the secret and is of great value, I shall have received exactly equal value, whereas, if it transpire that I am wrong in this matter, and the mud prove worthless, I shall have received something worthless in exchange for something worthless."

Lok swallowed hard, but agreed, for expressed thus, the arrangement seemed very fair.

Barely two months later Sung, reclining at his ease outside the house, noted with great satisfaction that, without having soiled his hands, and without losing one drop of sweat, he had raised the level of Sung's island higher than any previous generation since the island first rose out of the mud.

Two thousand coolies, employed by Lok, had laboured for weeks filling the barges with mud, half of which went to the Lok plantations beyond Soochow, on the banks of the Grand Canal, while the other half had been spread where needed over the Sung land.

How true it was, Sung mused, that to have strength without brains was to be little more than a water buffalo.

In a mood of great thankfulness Sung walked across to the grave mounds of his ancestors to do obeisance to them and to inform them that, in accordance with the Sung tradition, his generation—as represented by himself—had raised the soil of the island by as much as the three previous generations combined. That this had been achieved so easily, and without the expenditure of Sung sweat would, he knew, gratify those stern forbears whose descendant was about to raise the name of Sung to an eminence of which they had never dreamed.

All this happened, as has been stated already, some ten years before this story opens and a little more than nine months before the birth of the Small General, who would one day fall heir to the island and everything on it.

IN THE years intervening betw
chapter and the time when the
self-reliant lad of nine years of a
esteem between Lok, the silk me

The vast quantities of silt an
bay of the island and taken by ba
tions upon the banks of the Gra
wonders which Lok had felt himse
was very glad to hear, the richness
beneficial to the yield of mulberry
by any appreciable sum the loser b

In the growing of silk, as become
of the matter, the yield of mulberry
in the ultimate yield of raw silk. T
relate, consumes during its short life
thousand times its own weight at the

When it had been demonstrated to
secret of Sung's island did not lie in the
to explore other possible causes. Perha
some special method of feeding the s
system of manuring or pruning the mul
be the secret, Lok was determined tha
determined, furthermore, that he shoul
claim which would attend his discoveries.
with a modicum of profit. It never crossed
as was in fact the case, Sung had all along
was exploiting it and Lok for his own sub
not made the error of believing that Sung
plenty of facts which proved the contrary.
made rich man, accustomed to bask in the f
and tending to believe, as self-made men wil
that he was more astute, more nearly infallib

than the fact
lieved, was a
had been on
far short of f
but he lacke
the chance
of honours
who would
known thro
made three

The pala
a common
that Lok co
of the mu
berry frui
to the fila
employed
use in the

On one
at work u
the mulbe
spread ou
other aqu
ties of
obtained
cotton s

Lok
of quan
qualiti
cut up
Lok's
to his

On
grew
pu-m
gener
brew
insec
whic
amo

being gathered. He remained to watch the process of boiling and spraying. Leaving nothing to chance, he bought from Sung a barge-load of the leaves.

On these visits Lok and Sung entertained each other alternately. Either in the Sung house, or abroad the Lok houseboat, they would eat Lucullan meals, drink wine and play stone-paper-scissors far into the night, with intervals of sober talk while Sung, tongue in cheek, entered into the spirit of Lok's restless curiosity to probe the secret of the island.

It was during the fifth year of their association that Lok came to the conclusion that if he were to solve the mystery which had so eaten into his being he must abandon the natural lines of research for the supernatural. He reached this conclusion on a day in early summer when he arrived at the island unexpectedly to find Sung at his devotions in the great shed where the silkworms were housed. It was the first day of the hatching of the silkworms.

Sung was prostrated reverently before the shrine of Yuen-fi, the Empress of the Emperor Huang Ti, who has long been deified as the Goddess of Silk. It was she who in 2600 B.C. first reared silkworms and founded thereby an industry which for so many centuries brought prosperity and world-wide renown to the Celestial Empire.

Now Sung was a great lover of flowers and, despite the smallness of his island and the high value of land, had set aside a small area as a pleasure garden. In China very rich men have flower gardens for their pleasure, but these are relatively few and far between, for the rich soil of the land is consecrated to the growing of food for the teeming millions of people who have never been able to grow food as fast as they have been able to reproduce their species.

On this day Sung, in absolutely sincere adoration of the Goddess who had brought a small prosperity to the line of Sung, had cut a basket of superb golden-yellow roses as a small offering before the shrine. The basket was festooned with a quantity of golden silk floss.

Lok, who had entered the silkworm house very softly, because silkworms hate noise of any kind, stayed where he was and did not reveal himself. He watched Sung make the offering of the roses and listened while he prayed for a bountiful silk yield. Lok

29

noticed in detail the arrangement of the shrine, memorised the words of the prayer, resolving at the earliest opportunity to instal just such a shrine in his own establishment and to use the same forms and ceremonies in his own prayers.

The realisation came over Lok that it was many years since he had personally offered a prayer at his own shrine. Being a rich man, he had deputed this and other ceremonies to underlings. Perhaps, he mused, the Goddess was offended with him and resented such careless treatment.

While Lok was musing thus, believing that he had solved the secret of Sung's island, Sung caught a glimpse of Lok in a mirror which hung beside the shrine. The flowers were on one side of the shrine and the mirror on the other. The Goddess thus was enabled to see double the actual number of flowers donated, a most excellent and economical arrangement. On catching sight of Lok, standing there eavesdropping on his devotions, Sung became very angry in his heart. He had been about to rise to his feet, but with a mind which worked quickly, he decided instead to offer the Goddess a short impromptu prayer.

"Most excellent and benevolent Yuen-fi," he prayed, "the humble and adoring Sung desires to know what is the secret of the beneficent yield of silk on this insignificant island. At the hour of sunset I will come here alone and burn much silk. I will leave here paper and brush. At the hour of dawn I will come again to find words of wisdom. I go now to see that my workers are at work."

This last was, as Sung had intended it to be, Lok's exit cue. When he rose to his feet and walked slowly and softly towards the door, he saw, some fifty yards distant, the portly form of Lok.

"The portents were good this morning," said Sung, going forward to greet his guest. "When I rose from my couch I saw a heron perched on the eaves of my house, which I always find is a bringer of good fortune. Now behold! the heron did not lie to me. The happiness of the day is now complete, for has not the day brought the illustrious Lok to my humble home. It is a doubly fortunate day for me as, at an early hour this morning, a passing friend brought me as a gift from the Whangpoo River, hard by Shanghai, a most noble *sam-li*.* At noon we shall eat lightly under the trees and my friend Lok will tell me all the news from Soochow."

* A rare and delicious fish, kin to the American shad.

Lok beamed amiably upon Sung. Indeed, he felt amiable. There had been moments during the preceding months when he had doubted Sung's good faith. But having been a witness of the scene before the shrine, he no longer entertained doubts. It was a double relief to him, for was he not known far and wide as the astute Lok? He was not called astute for nothing and it was inconceivable that a man who could hold his own in the silk markets of Soochow, Hangchow and Chinkiang, and who was held in high esteem by the export merchants of Shanghai and Foochow, could be duped by a country bumpkin lording it on a tiny island in Ta Hu. He had, he realised, been foolish to entertain the thought. This Sung was a very worthy man, beyond doubt, a pleasant companion and a good host. Shortly, although he did not know it, the said Sung would pass on the secret of his high yield of silk. When the Goddess wrote her reply to Sung's prayer, Lok intended that somehow, by hook or by crook, he would see that answer before Sung saw it. By exploiting the secret properly Lok knew he could become a great power in China.

After their noon meal Lok and Sung, with two of the latter's poor relations to do the rowing, seated themselves comfortably amidships in a wide *sampan*, protected from the hot sun by a matting awning. With them for their pleasure they took Sung's two favourite cormorants, while Lok with pride produced a new cicada, of pre-eminent vocal powers, which had been sent to him as a gift from a fellow merchant in Foochow.

They talked little, these two. They drowsed gently in the heat, occasionally stirring themselves to release the shackled cormorants, watch their swift upward winging and their sudden stone-like dives. It is a wonder that the intensity of each man's thoughts did not burn into the consciousness of the other.

Lok was thinking, gloatingly, of how he would intercept the Goddess of Silk's message to Sung, while the latter was chuckling inwardly at the trick he intended to play upon Lok. Sung justified himself and his contemplated action by remembering with a certain high moral indignation the perfidy of Lok who, coming upon his host during his prayer, had been deceitful enough not to disclose his presence.

Towards the hour of sunset Sung excused himself. Lok, who knew full well the reason, made no demur and absented himself upon the houseboat, dallying awhile with a pretty sing-song girl he had brought with him from Soochow.

Sung, of course, kept his promise to the Silk Goddess, burning a large pile of silk floss outside the building where the silkworms were hatching, choosing a spot where the fumes of the burning would not irritate the silkworms. It would not have been the prudent thing to have broken his promise to the Goddess. When he had done this he left beside the shrine a brush, inkpad and a sheet of paper for her use, as he had promised. But an hour later, making sure that he was unobserved by Lok, Sung returned to the shrine, whence he removed the blank sheet of paper, substituting for it another sheet which was not blank. On this he had written:

> The ancestors of the worthy Sung have blessed the mulberries of Sung for his piety in sparing their graves. His trees will yield abundantly wherever they may be planted, so long as every year a handful of soil from beside the graves of his ancestors is scattered among them. So is a good son rewarded.

Sung then sought out three cousins, strong men who worked for him.

"Until two hours after midnight," he enjoined them, "stand guard beside the shrine of the Silk Goddess and let nobody approach. Two hours after midnight go to your beds, see and hear nothing."

Sung felt that he could trust to their discretion since none of the three could read or write. All through the long evening Sung amused himself with Lok's impatience.

"You are such a magnificent host," he said to Sung at about ten o'clock, "that my full belly makes me very sleepy. With your permission I will retire to bed."

"Your wish is my command, illustrious Lok!" Sung answered in polite acquiescence, conducting his friend as far as his houseboat.

It was an unhappy night for Lok. Across the path which led from the houseboat there chanced to be a trip-wire, causing Lok to fall heavily.

"Who is there?" called Sung, as though just awakened.

"It is I, Lok. I could not sleep, so I took a stroll and I have fallen. My regrets that I have disturbed you."

For three long hours Lok prowled around the island until at two o'clock in the morning he saw the three watches leave the shrine and go to their beds. He had no suspicions, believing that the three men were very devout.

Lok crept silently into the building. Happily for him, a patch of moonlight illumined the shrine of the Silk Goddess. He peered eagerly downwards to learn whether the Goddess had answered Sung's prayer. Lok's pulses beat more quickly when he saw what he fondly believed to be the writing of the Goddess upon the blank sheet of paper which Sung had put there with writing materials. The Silk Goddess, protector of the poor silk-grower, had answered Sung's prayer. There was insufficient light to read what was on the paper. That would have to wait until Lok returned to his houseboat. Meanwhile the intruder hastily pushed the message of the Goddess up the sleeve of his gown and put in its stead an identical but blank sheet of paper, abstracted that same evening from a pile which Sung had with apparent carelessness left lying about the house.

Lok chuckled at his own astuteness and at Sung's discomfiture when, at an early hour in the morning, the latter would interpret the blank sheet of paper as a sign of the Goddess's displeasure.

Sung, who had watched Lok's movements from the recesses of a small summer-house, also chuckled, also at his own astuteness. But Sung was very angry. Lok's behaviour was quite scandalous in an honoured guest who had been hospitably entertained. Indeed, so indignant was Sung that, while Lok was stealing the sheet of paper from the shrine, he slipped quietly down to the wooden jetty alongside which Lok's houseboat was moored, arranging in neat fashion another trip-wire for Lok's discomfiture. Chuckling to himself, Lok walked gaily along the jetty, but after a dozen paces his merriment ended abruptly as the trip-wire caught him across the ankles and precipitated him into some three feet of slimy ooze, compounded of a liberal proportion of duck droppings and other horrors.

Before he was able to enter his luxurious quarters on the boat Lok's servants, awakened by their master's cries, had to cleanse him by throwing many pails of cold water over him. Clutching the written message from the Goddess, Lok made his way dismally to bed.

With trembling hands Lok lit a lantern beside his bed, reading by its yellow flickering light the message which Sung had so carefully prepared. In his triumph Lok forgot his discomfiture of the evening and remembered only that Lok-kai-shing was a very astute man.

Lok possessed a book which he hoped would one day be known by posterity as *Lok's Gems of Wisdom*. In this book the not over-scrupulous silk merchant was wont to indite brief quotations from his own remarks, little homilies on conduct and records of certain of his business and social triumphs. To these he added before he sought sleep a cryptic guidance to his descendants: "When the wise man seeks a favour from a Goddess, he spends the night beside her shrine lest another receive her favour."

Sung was an early caller at Lok's houseboat the following morning, enquiring politely whether the latter had slept well.

"I did not sleep at all well," said Lok most cheerfully, "but I am happy this morning for, according to my horoscope, I shall have a day full of success."

"Then I, too, am happy," replied Sung. "The good host is happy when his guest is happy, and you shall be my guest today. In my horoscope, also, there is good fortune. Let us, therefore, share it."

The two men, beaming beatifically, strolled easily through the lanes of young mulberries, admiring the effect of the golden sunlight on the fresh green foliage.

"I have a mind to buy a few thousand of your mulberry seedlings," observed Lok, apropos of nothing. "Make me a price, Sung."

"That, I regret, I cannot do," said Sung sadly, "unless I first secure the consent of the Silk Goddess. If it be her wish that I do so, I will make you a gift of them, my good friend."

"You sound somewhat old-fashioned, Sung," said Lok lightly. "I thought that in these modern days men paid more attention to good husbandry than to the Goddess."

"It is possible, my friend Lok, that an enlightened man such as yourself, accustomed to the life of the great cities, regards our small island observances as somewhat foolish. But have patience with me, for here in this quiet spot old ideas die hard. I will consult the Goddess at once and if it be her wish that you shall have these seedlings they are yours upon the terms she dictates.

34

Let us not quarrel about the price. Let us agree that we will abide by her terms, whatever they may be."

"It shall be as you wish, Sung," agreed Lok heartily, chuckling to himself when the idea came to him of repeating his performance of the previous night, but with the difference that this time he would leave a sheet of paper on which he would inscribe carefully the Goddess's wish that Sung should make a free-will gift of the seedlings to his friend Lok.

"In matters such as this," remarked Sung, "it is our family custom to consult the Goddess at noon. We receive her advice at sunset. Do not laugh, my friend, but have patience with my whim."

Sung left forthwith to consult the Goddess, or ostensibly so. Actually he went to his house and wrote for a few moments on a sheet of blank paper. This he handed to his wife's slave girl. "At one hour before sunset," he instructed her, "place this sheet of paper on the shrine of the Silk Goddess."

To his wife Sung said: "Prepare at once a light meal for me and my guest. Have it served upon the large *sampan*. We will eat out on the lake, away from this heat."

All through the long afternoon Lok was ill at ease. This meal served upon the water, pleasant though it was, prevented him from carrying out his intention of putting on the shrine instructions which would result in Sung presenting him with some ten thousand seedlings.

It was sunset when the two men stepped ashore.

"Let us go now to learn whether the Goddess has settled the small matter of the seedlings for us," said Sung. "Then we will feast and forget business."

They both bowed respectfully at the shrine. Sung then stooped down and picked up a sheet of paper which was lying there.

"For ten thousand seedlings," Sung read aloud, "Lok will give Sung his fine houseboat in payment. The one will bring much silk and the other much travel."

"It is a foolish, fantastic price to pay for a few seedlings," spluttered Lok angrily. "They are not worth one twentieth of the price of my fine boat, nor yet one fiftieth."

"Calm yourself, friend Lok," said Sung soothingly. "I will not hold you to such a hard bargain. I know that each of us agreed to abide by the decision of the Silk Goddess, but I release you

35

from your promise. There! It is finished. Forget it and come with me to the house where a poor meal is being prepared."

Lok gritted his teeth with rage. This poor fool Sung, who had allowed himself to be outwitted over the matter of the Goddess's answer to his prayer, still was ignorant of the great secret of his prolific mulberries. The ignorant bumpkin would have been delighted to have accepted a few cents per hundred more than the ruling price for seedlings. Now, by sheer blind luck, Sung was to have the benefit of the bargain. Lok was on the point of taking advantage of Sung's generous offer to release him, when he realised that here was the key to all his scheming. It was a fine houseboat, true enough. But he was a rich man and he could afford the price of a better one.

"You are generous, Sung, but I will not avail myself of your generosity. When Lok-kai-shing makes a bargain, whether his bond be spoken or written, he keeps to it. The houseboat is yours, Sung."

"You are too generous, Lok," protested Sung weakly. "I also do not like to take advantage of you. Let us forget the matter."

But within the hour Sung entered into possession of his new acquisition, graciously consenting to permit Lok to use the boat for the return journey to Soochow.

Before Lok-kai-shing went to his bed that night he and Sung had signed a paper whereby Sung agreed to sell to Lok all the mulberry seedlings the island could produce in the next five years. The price agreed was some three times the ruling market price of similar seedlings, but Lok was well content. Ten thousand seedlings would have been a mere drop in the ocean to him, for he had vast plantations. Now, with the hundreds of thousands of seedlings which Sung would grow for him, he could replant everywhere. All he would need to do would be to pay an occasional visit to Sung, carry off a few handfuls of soil from the ancestral grave at each visit, and the prolific yield of Sung's island would be reproduced on a scale thousands of times greater. But, Lok consoled himself, in a short while the price paid would seem very small in comparison with the riches and honour which would accrue from the transaction.

When Lok had sailed for Soochow, Sung went to the shrine of the Silk Goddess and meditated awhile. "Thus," he told his patroness with a certain unctuousness, "are greedy and dishonest men punished for their misdeeds. For it is very true that if Lok had not come here stealthily, like a thief in the night, seeking to secure an advantage over me by removing the sheet of paper, he would not have fallen into the trap set for him and I, an unworthy Sung, would not be the owner of his fine houseboat."

In this virtuous mood Sung felt generous and expansive, also very grateful for favours received. Going into his small garden, therefore, he picked a large bunch of roses, some yellow and some red, placing them before the shrine of the Silk Goddess. As a further token of his gratitude he burned before the shrine a bundle of silk floss which might have been sold for as much as eight or ten cents.

⋰⋰ 4 ⋱⋱

SUNG had travelled very little from his island home. The furthest he had ever been was to Soochow. City life was neither suited to his taste nor his pocket. A bad meal in the city was ten times more costly than a good one at home; people were noisy and rude; while to buy a little comfort and privacy meant the outlay of more money in a day than Sung was in the habit of spending in a month.

But with the acquisition of the Lok houseboat, Sung's attitude to travel underwent a subtle change. In this fine boat the comforts of home travelled with him. Mandarins enjoyed no greater comfort when away from their homes. Nor did Sung lack poor relations to do the hard work.

Courtesy demanded that if passing through Soochow Sung pay a call upon Lok-kai-shing who, in addition to a fine house in the city itself, maintained a country establishment on the banks of the Grand Canal. It was to this last Sung made his first journey, taking a route which skirted Soochow.

It was with mixed feelings that Lok saw one evening his own houseboat, now owned by Sung, moored at the private wharf of his country retreat. Sung was a very good companion on his own little island on Lake Ta Hu, but Lok feared greatly that he would jar on the more polished and sophisticated people with whom he was accustomed to associate at home. There was, also, the delicate matter of the transfer of the houseboat's ownership. Lok was most emphatically not prepared to retail for general consumption the story of how this had been brought about. A rich merchant with a reputation for astute dealing cannot afford to lose 'face' by admitting publicly that he had been outwitted in a deal. Lok was perfectly satisfied that he had outwitted Sung, but to those unacquainted with all the circumstances of the transaction, appearances were exactly contrary. Now in turning these matters over in his mind Lok did less than justice to Sung's *savoir faire,* and a very great deal less than justice to his astuteness.

Lok was on that day entertaining a number of fellow members of the Soochow Silk Guild who, upon observing a stranger arrive in what had once been Lok's houseboat, which now bore the 'chop' of Sung, were very curious, even though too polite to ask direct questions.

At the dinner-table that evening his guests were complimenting Lok upon the food and his cleverness in having settled, in his capacity of President of the Soochow Silk Guild, certain matters outstanding with the larger merchants of Shanghai.

"I know nothing of the Shanghai silk merchants," observed Sung with becomingly modest demeanour, "but it is in my mind that they would have to burn their lamps very late at night to outwit our generous host in negotiations. I have come here in what was once the famous Lok houseboat, hoping that thereby I may regain some of the 'face' I have lost at home. True, I have this fine houseboat, but I tremble for shame when I think what I gave for it. In matters of business, I now realise, I am but an infant in arms. I sit at the feet of the master. . . ."

As he said this last Sung lifted a wine cup towards Lok, who beamed happily towards his guest.

"What did our supremely clever host secure from you in exchange?" asked one of the guests, permitted to be thus direct by the fact that the subject had been opened in front of them all.

"That he shall tell you himself, if he so wishes," replied Sung, "and then, perhaps, I may persuade you, my fellow guests, to bring pressure to bear upon him to ease the terms of the bargain."

"Thanks be to Heaven," mused Lok, "that this Sung knows how to behave himself in distinguished company, though how he learned in Ta Hu is more than I can guess. If these guests of mine were to hear the tale of my agreement to abide by the written message of the Silk Goddess, the echo of their laughter would be heard throughout China. Now he leaves me to give them any explanation I please, or none at all."

Lok smiled warmly at Sung and at the expectant faces of his other guests.

"My friends," he said impressively, "I am only going to satisfy a very small part of your curiosity. My friend Sung has made a certain discovery. All I will tell you just now is that this discovery is not altogether unconnected with the shimmering produce of the mulberry which is the basis of our association. Let me tell you, furthermore, that my friend Sung is too modest. He would have you believe that in matters of business he is a mere child. I, who am in a position to know whereof I speak, tell you that Sung knows well enough how to protect his own interests. . . ."

Lok felt he could afford to be magnanimous after Sung's handsome behaviour. No man in China likes to appear a dupe.

"Let me tell you this, my friends," continued Lok, "that in a year or so every one of you sitting at this table should reap the benefit of the transaction which Sung and I have so amicably concluded. The well-being of the silk industry is very near to our hearts. Just now I will say no more."

Courtesy forbade questions and the guests were soon happily engaged in a game of forfeits, which resulted in the drinking of a prodigious quantity of a rare old wine, setting the seal of conviviality upon the gathering.

Sung, nevertheless, managed to inject into the conversation a modest reference to his own poor home, which beside that of the illustrious Lok-kai-shing, was a mere hovel, but at which any or all of his fellow guests would always find a warm welcome. It gratified Sung to observe that his companions were consumed with curiosity.

It was not necessary to tell them where his home was located, for every *laodah* * on the Grand Canal and adjacent waters would know by this time that the Lok houseboat had been acquired by Sung of Sung's island for some mysterious consideration. The more mystery the better for Sung's plans.

Lok-kai-shing was no exception to the general rule that men do not achieve great success without making their share of enemies. Among these he numbered a fellow silk merchant and silk grower named Chu-pao, who was eaten with envy of the successful Lok. The rights and the wrongs of their enmity are of less importance than the fact.

Chu was one of those who kept his mouth closed and his ears open, and little touching the silk trade could be discussed in Soochow without his knowledge, sooner or later. Chu learned before most people that the palatial houseboat of Lok-kai-shing was now owned by an unimportant person named Sung, who lived upon a small island on Ta Hu, and further that this Sung

* Boatman.

was on terms of intimacy with its former owner. Lok, as Chu knew very well, did not waste time associating with useless non-entities. It followed, therefore, with the certainty of night following day, that Lok-kai-shing had received some very valuable consideration for this costly and magnificent houseboat.

Then there came to Chu's ears the echo of what had been said in the presence of other silk merchants at Lok's country retreat. Veiled and ambiguous though this was, it enabled Chu to reach the conclusion that this unknown Sung had made some important discovery which touched the silk trade. If this discovery were valuable to Lok, it would also be valuable to Chu; which explains why, less than a week after the dinner at which Sung had been Lok's guest, Chu decided that his health would benefit by a short holiday breathing the pure air of Lake Ta Hu.

Chu arrived at Sung's island in time to see a barge-load of mulberry seedlings leave for Lok's plantations. A small bribe to one of the *laodahs* confirmed the destination.

Chu cruised about among the mudbanks, assuming a great interest in the feeding ducklings which, under the stern eye of the Small General, were busy fossicking in the ooze.

"Those are very fine ducklings," observed Chu amiably.

"They belong to my father," was the proud reply. "I am the son of Sung."

"Your respected father must have great confidence in you, son of Sung!"

"I am the Small General. The ducks obey me. Would you like to see my cormorants catch some fish?"

"Indeed, I would greatly like to see this thing. I have heard many times of cormorants which catch fish, but I have never seen it with my own eyes. I am always too busy with my affairs in Soochow. . . ."

"You come from Soochow?" asked the Small General eagerly. "That must be very wonderful. Soon I shall go to Soochow where I am to become a scholar. My father tells me I shall see the Great Pagoda every day. See! The cormorants return, each with a fish. . . ."

But Chu had a far-away look in his eyes. His mind was on other things. "I will go to pay my respects to your father," he said, giving an order to the *laodah* to row back towards Sung's island.

Sung chuckled at the thought that this fat fish was nibbling at the hook which he himself had so casually baited at Lok's table.

"I came," said the newcomer, "to ask whether you have for sale a few of the fine ducklings which your most dutiful son guards so faithfully over yonder."

"They are as yet too young, I fear," said Sung regretfully. "If you are passing this way in two weeks time I daresay there will be some then. . . ."

"Alas! Long before then I shall be back in the heat of Soochow," said Chu. "Pray forgive this intrusion, but I was greatly struck by the excellence of your ducklings and no less by the diligence of your son."

"I am about to drink a cup of tea," said Sung hospitably. "I would be honoured if the stranger will join me. I am Sung; this is my island."

"I am Chu, a silk merchant of Soochow. Your kindness overcomes me."

"In this quiet spot I seldom have the pleasure of entertaining a distinguished stranger," said Sung politely.

During the hour which followed, the two men talked of everything under the sun except of silk. They exchanged wisdom regarding the cooking of ducks; bandied sly remarks regarding the beauty of Soochow's women; debated the joys of urban *versus* rural life; and agreed that a ham cured in Hangchow was vastly superior to any other in the region.

It was left to Sung to broach the subject of silk. This he did at last because he did not wish to convey the impression that he was studiously avoiding it.

Sung's opportunity came when the calm of the day was rent by the clang of iron upon iron as a young man in his employ beat out a bent sheet of iron with a hammer.

"Cease that noise, idiot!" called Sung in a stage whisper. "Do you not know that my silkworms are in their first sleep?"

"You are a silk grower as well as a duck breeder?" queried Chu politely. "We have another bond, for I am a small and unimportant silk merchant."

"I have a few hundred mulberries, but my land is so small and inconsiderable that it is beneath your notice," protested Sung.

"I am sure that you are too modest," replied Chu, not to be outdone. "I beg you to allow me to see your trees. Their colour at this time of the year is so fresh that one forgets the heat."

Chu allowed himself to be pressed into staying for the noontide meal and then, because the afternoon heat was too great, postponed the inspection of the mulberries until evening, by which time Sung declined to allow his guest to depart until after the evening meal.

"I seldom have the chance to talk to one so distinguished as yourself," Sung explained, "so that I shall be forgiven if I try to prolong the pleasure."

"One day, I hope," said Chu, "you will be my guest at my entirely unworthy home in Soochow."

Late that evening Chu felicitated Sung on the excellence of his mulberries and the care in their cultivation. "It so happens," he told Sung, "that I have recently acquired a small mulberry plantation. It is in poor condition after years of neglect. I would like to buy from you a few thousand seedlings to replant it."

"It is a matter of deep regret to me," said Sung, "that I cannot oblige you, for I have already signed a contract for all my seedlings for several years in advance."

Chu looked very disappointed. "Today has been so very pleasant as your guest that I would have liked to keep the memory of it green always. In a remote spot such as this one does not expect to find such princely hospitality, nor such distinguished conversation."

"You are too kind," protested Sung.

"You are under contract to sell your seed, also?" asked Chu.

"No, there is no contract to sell seed, only the seedlings. I must retain enough seed, of course, to fill my contract."

"Then I would like to make a contract with you for all your seed," said Chu a trifle too eagerly.

"Let me make you a small gift of some seed," protested Sung. "Between friends—and I feel we are already that—let us have no question of buying and selling. Besides, there is another matter. You will laugh at me, of course, behind my back, but we have an old custom here and around Ta Hu old customs die hard. . . ."

"I consider it is good to hold to the old customs," said Chu stoutly. "They are a good brake on the impetuosity of the young."

The gift of a handful of seed was no good to Chu. Nothing less than a monopoly would suffice. If Lok-kai-shing were prepared to pay away a fortune for seedlings, Chu-pao could afford to risk contracting for the seeds. Nothing less than the prospect of a vast

43

fortune, he was sure, would occupy so much of Lok's time and energy. Chu trembled with his eagerness, fighting to conceal it. Here at one stroke he could make a vast fortune and revenge himself upon Lok. It stood to reason that this Sung had stumbled upon some valuable secret. If that secret were in the seedlings, it would also be in the seeds.

"Our foolish custom here," said Sung blandly, "is never to undertake any new thing without seeking the advice of the Silk Goddess. Nobody has ever wanted to buy my poor seeds until now. I will, therefore, consult the Goddess. If it be her wish to give you the seed as a gift I will do so; if to sell to you, I will sell at the price and under the conditions named by her. It is our old custom. My honoured ancestors would not approve if I were to depart from it."

Chu agreed with a smile. If this Sung were so simple as to be influenced by the outworn hocus-pocus of peasants who sought to placate their nebulous deities, it ought not to be difficult for a smart city merchant to drive a favourable bargain with him.

A few hours later, when the conditions under which the Goddess approved of the sale of mulberry seed were announced to Chu, he recoiled as though he had been struck.

"It is a ridiculous price, I fear," said Sung sympathetically. "You would be better advised to buy your seed from the north, from the mulberries around Chinkiang. I would feel dishonest if I were to sell seed to you at such a price. The Goddess, I fear, has an inflated idea of the value of my poor possessions. She has fallen into the error of believing that I am selling pearls. If it were not for our foolish island custom, my friend, I would willingly give you all the seed you require. . . ."

Chu thought hard and fast. He thought of how sweet it would be to profit at Lok's expense, to spirit away with him the secret which, he was sure, lay locked in Sung's mulberry seed. The price was fantastic, beyond all reason, but . . .

"I am a rich man, Sung," said Chu. "I can afford to gratify my whims. The price of the seed is, as you rightly say, absurd, but it is my whim to possess it."

They drew up the contract there and then and it is hard to say which of the two men who signed it exulted the more. But it is a matter of record that from the hour when Chu-pao's houseboat left his island, Sung decided that he would allow his fingernails to grow as long as they would, in token that he and menial work were forever divorced.

The Grand Canal might well be called Main Street, China, for a confidential whisper at one end of the great waterway becomes public property at the other end at a speed which would not disgrace the telegraph. On the entire length of the canal there were no sharper ears, or better tuned to catch the least whisper, than those in the employ of the great Fureno Trading Company of Japan, the famed House of the Three Bamboos, whose 'chop' was almost as well known in China as in the Empire of Japan. The Chinkiang office of the Fureno Trading Company, situated where the traffic stream of the Grand Canal's southern section merged with the noble flood of the Yangtsze River, soon heard that in the region of Soochow and Ta Hu something was afoot of vital interest to the silk industry. The Fureno office in Soochow, curiously enough, heard the same stories later.

Now among the multifarious activities of the Fureno interests were vast silk filatures in Japan, where the silk industry was growing apace, like almost everything else in the mushroom empire. Any new thing concerning silk touched The House of the Three Bamboos at one of its most sensitive spots, for huge capital sums had been poured into the silk ventures of this commercial colossus.

Unequivocal orders arrived from Tokyo to learn in detail what was afoot and to report in due course.

In Soochow the Fureno interests were in the very capable hands of a Mr. Kiyoshi Matsudara, a young man of pleasing manners, a distant cousin of the Fureno family, with high hopes of swift advancement in the organisation. He spoke Mandarin Chinese and the Soochow dialect fluently, had lived in Honolulu where he had acquired a working knowledge of English and prominent gold sheaths over perfectly sound front teeth, which a perpetual smile enabled him to exhibit. Matsudara suffered a few bad moments at being reminded by the Chinkiang office of events happening on his own doorstep, but recovered his balance quickly enough to report to Tokyo that he had already been working on the matter quietly for some time.

It is a tribute to Matsudara's efficiency that, within forty-eight hours of hearing the first whisper from Chinkiang, he had narrowed the field of enquiry to Lok-kai-shing, the silk merchant, and a certain obscure Sung, who lived upon a small island in Lake Ta Hu.

When Matsudara read his orders from Tokyo, signed by Baron Fureno in person, he realised immediately that he had reached a crisis in his life. He would either carry out his instructions with his customary efficiency, in which event the sun of head office approval would shine warmly upon him, or he would fail, in which event he preferred not to think what would happen. Head office was not unreasonable. It did not expect men to make bricks without straw; it did not split hairs about methods or ethics. To obtain the information required, Matsudara was quite aware that he might use bribery from the liberal funds at his disposal, and if successful there would be no cavilling about amounts. If plain thuggery were in his good opinion cheaper and more effective, then he might use thuggery, secure in the knowledge that so long as his thuggery could not be traced back to the House of The Three Bamboos, he would earn no disapprobation.

Head office wanted results. Methods were the affair of the man on the spot.

The most careful enquiries through Chinese intermediaries revealed merely that some important new discovery had been made. For a small consideration Matsudara was able to secure a more or less verbatim account of what Lok-kai-shing had said over the festive board. The fact of Lok's interest being established, it followed that the richest silk merchant in Soochow would not trouble himself over trifles.

It is almost axiomatic, and most certainly logical, that to bribe a rich man is more costly than to bribe a poor one. Matsudara, therefore, concentrated his attentions upon Sung. Armed to the teeth, so to speak, and accompanied by two clerks who had just completed their military training in Japan, together with a large bag of silver Mexican dollars, he set out one fine morning for Lake Ta Hu in the firm's houseboat, bearing on its bows the 'chop' of The Three Bamboos. The purpose of the armament was for protection against the real or mythical pirates of Ta Hu. The bag of silver dollars was for Sung.

The usually placid surface of Ta Hu had been whipped all night by a wind off the mountains. The shallow lake, aroused quickly to fury, was at dawn still too rough to permit the army of ducklings to go off to their usual feeding grounds. They remained, therefore, in the shallows on the lee side of the island under the vigilant eye of the Small General, who hoped that before noon the water would be smooth enough for his charges to venture out on to one of the larger mudbanks.

Sung, who awakened sleepily some two hours after dawn, was surprised to see his son running up the pathway to the house.

"My father," the Small General gasped, for he was much out of breath, "there is a man with shining teeth in a large boat who asks if this is Sung's island."

"What did you reply?"

"I did not tell him anything, my father, for I do not like his face. Also, he wears the clothes of the foreign barbarians."

"Is he a barbarian?"

"He is not the same colour as the barbarians, my father, but I think he must be, for he talks our tongue strangely."

"Then tell him, son, that this is indeed Sung's island, but that Sung is taking his rest and may not be disturbed until noon."

A flat-bottomed houseboat in choppy water is inconceivably uncomfortable. On top of this was the fact that Matsudara could not reconcile his dignity with awaiting the convenience of a Chinese peasant farmer. When at noon, therefore, he set foot upon the narrow wooden jetty of Sung's island, he was too shaken and irritated to be his usual suave self. In the dawn of history it was common knowledge in China that an angry man suffering from injured dignity seldom retains calm judgment and poise. Sung, who was a most observant man, had noted in his rare and brief contacts with persons of other than Chinese blood, that their poise deserted them for surprisingly small reasons. While the strange houseboat spent the morning crashing to and fro in the choppy water of the lake, Sung had lain at ease listening to the sweet music of a cicada, which the Small General had the previous day captured for his father's pleasure. At noon, therefore, he was soothed and entirely master of himself.

Before Matsudara had arrived within speaking distance of him, Sung was pleased to find that his judgment of the stranger coincided with that of the Small General. Aside from wearing the hideous clothing of the red-haired barbarians, the man was too jaunty and pleased with himself.

"I am addressing the respected Sung?" asked the stranger.

Sung bowed assent without speaking and without rising from his lounge. As there was nothing to sit on, the stranger was compelled to remain standing.

For five minutes or so the two men exchanged platitudes and the flowers of indirect speech, but those uttered by Sung were so limp and perfunctory that they were almost insulting.

"To what, am I permitted to ask, do I owe the pleasure and honour of this visit?" asked Sung, several whole minutes before courtesy permitted so direct a question.

"The wisdom of the respected Sung has travelled far," said Matsudara, gritting his teeth and smiling at the same time, "and I am come to sit at his feet."

"It is a far journey from Japan to sit at the feet of one so humble and unworthy," replied Sung, which translated into colloquial English meant as nearly as possible: "Cut the cackle and get to the hosses."

"We Japanese have a small and inconsiderable silk industry. From China, the home of silk, we have much to learn. It has come to our ears that in all the land of China we could not seek advice from one more fitted to give it than the illustrious Sung. For this advice I have in my houseboat yonder a bag of silver containing some two thousand dollars. Will the illustrious Sung accept this as a small gift for his advice?"

Sung's reply was a gross breach of manners.

"As a gift," said he, "I am minded that the sum is too large, for I am not a prince sitting here to receive tribute. But I am also minded that if the sum be a bribe, I find it too small."

"Will the illustrious Sung deign to say more?"

"My horoscope tells me," said Sung with a small bow, "that today is inauspicious for the discussion of great matters. One week hence, when the stars are favourable, my houseboat will be moored beside the Fifty-three Arch Bridge, where the River Dai-dai joins the Grand Canal. Under favourable stars let us then renew the discussion."

"I will remember that the gift was too large," said Matsudara meaningly, thereupon taking his departure.

Sung had not had the smallest intention of going to Soochow, but he needed time to think. If this unpleasant Japanese person could so carelessly dangle bags of silver dollars before a complete stranger, it would be a pity to dismiss him too soon. In a week much might happen.

In less than a week much did happen.

On the third evening after Matsudara's call at the island there arrived from the western side of the lake a small sailing *sampan,* scudding before the breeze which came off the mountains. In the *sampan* were three men who, as soon as they were abreast of the island, ran down their sail, rowed in to shore and, hauling their boat into a thicket of reeds, made their way stealthily to Sung's house, where they were made welcome.

When tea had been served and the doors closed against sharp ears, much laughter echoed around the room where Sung entertained his guests. The leader of the three new arrivals was known by many names, one of which was Red Tiger. He was none other than the King of the Pirates, and a strange tale he related.

"I do not have to tell you, my friend Sung," he was saying, "that I do not molest the good people of Ta Hu, but it is against my principles to reject a piece of business unheard, especially when the sum I hear mentioned is one thousand dollars. The message was brought to me by a good friend, who in turn is a good friend of Li, the aged beggar who solicits alms by the Customs Bridge, who heard of the matter from the chief *laodah* of the barges which bear the 'chop' of The Three Bamboos. Someone, it seemed, was very anxious to cover his tracks. When the message reached me it was hard to conceal my mirth. For one thousand dollars I was to kidnap the Small General, son of my friend Sung, hold the boy in some safe place and then await instructions. . . ."

"The misbegotten spawn of a she-monkey!" exclaimed Sung. "Does he think that we people of the lake are cannibals that we prey upon each other? May the bones of his ape ancestors rot in the topmost fork of a stinkwood tree! May my right hand wither if I do not make this an expensive day's work for this imitation of a man with the golden teeth . . . !"

"I cannot stay long, Sung," said Red Tiger anxiously. "I have work to do on the far side of the lake and I must be there before dawn. What is to be done?"

"Send word that you have the Small General in a safe place," said Sung. "I will make sure that no stranger sees him. I will shed a few tears before the Japanese ape. These will convince him if

49

he has doubts. When I have a plan I will send word to you by a trusty messenger. You have been a good friend, Red Tiger. See that you keep out of the hands of the *tao-tai*, for it is said that in the yard of his *yamen* there is a special cage for you. He has sworn he will catch you before the year is out. He would enjoy watching his men cutting you into small pieces. Be watchful lest you fall into the hands of a traitor."

"Have no fear for me, Sung. Spare your pity where it will be most needed."

When Sung was alone he went into the room where the Small General lay sleeping peacefully. As he looked down upon his son he knew that he was become deeply and bitterly angry. A stranger sought to bring pressure to bear upon him through a beloved son—his only son. The stranger must be made to pay.

Before he left for Soochow the following morning Sung knelt for a while at the shrine of his ancestors. It was one thing to kneel with tongue in cheek before the shrine of the Silk Goddess, but quite another to do aught but prostrate himself in simple sincerity before that of his ancestors, among whom he hoped there was an honoured place reserved for him. It seemed to Sung as he knelt in their august presence that there entered into him some of the strength and sureness which had enabled them to smile and hope through the endless toil of lifting their island home above the waters of the lake. When he left them he went aboard his houseboat with a quiet smile on his face and the firm tread of a man who knows what he will do.

ᘒ 5 ᘓ

THE city house of Lok-kai-shing, to which Sung had not previously gone, was clearly the home of a man of substance. It stood back a few yards from the line of a city canal, with a small bay in front where boats could wait without being an obstacle in the way of the countless craft, large and small, which passed all through the day and night.

"I am Sung," he said to a servant who opened a heavy iron-studded door to him. "Tell your master that I am here on most pressing business. I crave his pardon for arriving at this unseemly hour."

"The master will see you," said the servant after a brief delay.

Lok frowned when Sung was announced. He did not care for casual callers. Also, he was much pre-occupied with a new concubine, recently acquired in Hangchow. Had the servant not managed to convey the note of urgency in Sung's message, it is doubtful whether Lok would have received him. In his city home the silk merchant did not relax one iota of his dignity, however informal he might be in his country retreat.

With the minimum of preamble Sung related to Lok all that had transpired since Matsudara had called at the island.

"What has this to do with me?" asked Lok coldly.

"If this Japanese ape will hire others to take my son from me, will he not harm you when he knows that you share my secret? Have you no loved one whose loss would cause you grief?"

"True!" said Lok slowly. "I know these Japanese, better probably than you. They are devoid of honour. They would sell the hair off the corpses of their mothers. Further, there is no end to the money they have."

"I have it in my mind, Lok, that you and I will take some of that money from them."

Lok forgot how unwelcome his caller had been a few minutes before, remembering only his dislike of the Japanese, whose silk industry was already making inroads into China's prosperity.

"I wish to make a certain small confession, Lok," said Sung firmly. "We are men of the same land. We ate the same rice as children. We both enjoy the same honourable traditions, as we hope to lay our bones in this land one day, beside those of our ancestors. . . ."

"What is this talk of confessions?" asked Lok anxiously.

"I confess it with shame, Lok, as I promised my ancestors this morning before I left my home that I would confess, that in my dealings with you over certain matters of which we are both aware, I have not been strictly honourable. I sold you a secret and yet I did not sell you a secret. . . ."

Lok was about to become very angry when he remembered uncomfortably that he, also, had not been entirely without reproach.

"But I have resolved," continued Sung, "that you, Lok, shall suffer no loss by any small deception of mine. I will balance our account to the last cash. You and I together will make the Japanese monkeys pay enough to restore to you all you have expended, and any surplus remaining we will divide equally."

Without further talk, for each of them found the situation very embarrassing, neither having been entirely guiltless, they entered into a most solemn compact.

"It is one thing," Sung said before they parted, "to sharpen one's wits a little and in friendly fashion upon a fellow countryman, but it is quite another to endure the sorrow which, but for the fact that I have friends who tell me many things, this monkey with the gold teeth would have put upon me."

Even as he made the compact, Lok could not help wondering just how Sung had deceived him. Sung was a merry fellow and, doubtless, at some more appropriate time would tell his friend Lok all there was to be told. When the wine jar was low Lok resolved to make certain small confessions of his own. A little time would heal the sting of these things for both of them and the whole incident would become a merry jest. But this matter of the Japanese was in another category and Lok found himself almost as angry as he would have been had his own son been threatened thus.

The memory was still very fresh in China of the humiliating treatment accorded to the aged Li-hung-chang when he went to Japan to make peace after the disastrous—to China—Sino-Japanese War. This aggression against her territorial integrity, and the ever less reasonable claims of all the Foreign Powers, were sowing in China the seeds of a new national feeling. Hitherto no kinship had ever been felt between the Cantonese and, for example, the Pekingese, or between the peoples of Shantung and Szechuan. But out of China's travail was being born a realisation that the old loose-knit feudal system, administered in theory from Peking, could end only in disaster.

Lok watched Sung out of sight round the bend of the canal as the latter went off to keep the rendezvous with Matsudara at the Fifty-three Arch Bridge.

A little after the appointed time there arrived alongside the houseboat a *sampan* flying The Three Bamboos flag at its mast. "You are Sung?" asked the Chinese boatman impolitely. "Then my master will see you at his fine office," the man continued on receiving an affirmative reply.

To cover his rage during the journey to the Fureno office, Sung tried to envisage what his feeling would be if, as Matsudara believed, the Small General were being held as hostage. Sung wanted to play his part convincingly. He wanted to appear before the Japanese in the role of heartbroken father, willing to agree to anything so long as his beloved son be returned to him safely.

Among the crowd of people waiting to see Matsudara were bill-collecting shroffs, minor agents from the villages and other small fry. Studiedly Sung was kept waiting until the last of these had gone.

There was not in Matsudara's eye or bearing a vestige of pity for the broken man who tremblingly entered his office: nothing but cold, malicious triumph.

"The last time we met," said the Japanese coldly, "you told me that my sack of silver dollars was too large for a gift and too small for a bribe. I have remembered. This gift is small enough?" Matsudara tossed contemptuously at Sung's feet a copper cash, so small in value that several would be required to buy a small bowl of inferior rice. "There is no bribe, Sung, do you understand?"

"I understand," quavered Sung, picking up the coin. "But my son, my only son, what of him?"

"Do not mention your son here!" hissed the Japanese. "I know nothing of your son. Let us talk, rather, of your private misfor-

53

tune, whatever that may be—the private misfortune which has made you somewhat less haughty and more reasonable. Let us understand one another, Sung. When I receive certain information from you there will be an end to the sense of loss which appears to trouble you."

"Spare his life, I beg of you, noble gentleman!" Sung's facial contortions served to hide the rage which was consuming him.

"I know of no life—no Chinese life—worth a grain of sand compared with the importance of securing certain information, Sung. I am interested in silk, not lives."

"I am a very humble and ignorant man," mouthed Sung, "and . . ."

"I can see that," replied Matsudara, showing the glittering golden façade of his front teeth. "You will be more humble in a little while if you do not speak. Tomorrow a messenger will bring you a small packet, Sung. Guess what will be inside the packet. The next day there will be another small packet come to you, and another and another, until there is no more left to send you but a larger packet. Do you understand?"

"I will tell you all, noble gentleman. . . ."

"That is better," said Matsudara, lighting a cigarette. "Begin!"

"My honourable father," began Sung brokenly, "made the discovery. It was an accident. Forty years ago there was a great storm on Ta Hu. At that time the family of Sung owned two islands. One you have honoured with your presence. The other—a smaller —was washed away by the storm. It was planted with mulberries. There remained only two rocks with a little soil between them. By a miracle one mulberry tree was saved. My honourable father was very poor. He would go in his *sampan* to pick the leaves of this one tree. After a little while he found that this one tree yielded more than any two others. Accordingly, he gathered the fruit, kept the seeds and planted them. Our few poor mulberries are the children and grandchildren of that first tree."

"If you are lying you will be sorry," said Matsudara. "I will send learned men to test the truth of what you say. If you speak truth we will take a few thousand seedlings and a certain loss will be returned to you. . . ."

"Alas! You cannot take any seedlings. All have been sold to Lok-kai-shing, the great silk merchant. He has many armed men now to guard his property. Sung's island is now Lok's island."

54

"I will talk with this Lok-kai-shing. You may go."

"But my son, what of him?"

"I do not doubt that your son is in a safe place. I wish to learn if you have been lying to me. I will see you a week hence. Go!"

Like a whipped dog Sung left the room.

Smiling complacently, Matsudara wrote a letter to Tokyo, reporting that he had discovered the inwardness of the matter. It now remained for authority to be given him to acquire by purchase the secret he had unearthed. A little thuggery was safe enough, he knew, where an obscure person like Sung was concerned, but in dealing with Lok-kai-shing it would not be safe. A man in Lok's position, President of the Soochow Silk Guild, would have ways of protecting himself. Money and plenty of it would prove the only argument. Happily, there was no lack of money in the Fureno coffers.

Matsudara and Lok-kai-shing had been closeted together for more than an hour at the latter's business premises. In a curtained recess Sung sat, an eager listener, hearing but unseen.

Matsudara was sweating, although the day was not very hot.

"I agree that the price I ask is high," Lok was saying, "but that is because I am not eager to sell. High as the price is, I shall be happier if I do not sell. I am a rich man, you must understand. The buying, selling and manufacture of silk are my business. The growing of silk is my pleasure. It happens by good fortune that in taking my pleasure I have stumbled upon a secret whose ultimate value is beyond calculation. I do not need to tell *you* that!"

"But you must understand," said Matsudara, "that I cannot ask my company to pay such a great sum without investigation of your claims. . . ."

"Then do not ask them," replied Lok indifferently. "And may I remind you for the tenth time since you have paid me the honour of this call, that I make no claims. I have not made any claims. I do not do so now. It is *you* who are making claims by implication. It is *you* who have come here to my place of business to tell *me* that I possess something of great value which you wish to purchase. If it were not so, is it likely that you, the representative here in Soochow of a great company which is not without a reputation for commercial ability, would offer me at least ten

55

times the *apparent* value of my poor silk plantation, the smallest of them all?"

"I came to you frankly and without guile," said Matsudara with reproach in his voice. "That is our Japanese way of doing business. If it ever came to the ears of the illustrious Baron Fureno that I, or any other of his managers, were to deal deceitfully in his name, I think the shame of it would kill him."

"May he live forever!" said Lok piously. "But I would remind you that I have suggested no deceit. I agree that you have come to me frankly and openly to try to buy a certain piece of my property. It is a matter for regret that I do not wish to sell, except at a price which only a fool would refuse. I have named my price. It is too high. I trust nothing has occurred which will cause the illustrious Baron Fureno to die of shame. If it will save you any small embarrassment, I will be most happy to acknowledge in writing that your conduct has been most excellent."

Beads of sweat intermingled on Matsudara's brow, running down and clouding his spectacles. He was teetering on the brink of failure and he knew it. There was no place for failure in the Fureno organisation. Even if Baron Fureno were likely to condone failure, the matter had gone even higher in Japan. Baron Fureno had already conferred with great persons near to the Throne itself. He had been *ordered*, not requested, to obtain for Japan the secret which this obstinate silk merchant refused to sell, except at an absurd price. There was no way of bringing pressure, for the man was too wealthy and powerful.

Matsudara looked at Lok to see whether there were by chance any sign that he would relent his terms, but Lok had risen to his feet and was, with every sign of interest and affection, feeding a pet *minah* bird, which up to this time had taken no part in the conversation.

The silence of the room was rent suddenly by the bird's raucous laughter, followed by an epithet which will not translate politely.

There are many curious traits in the Japanese character, not the least of which is that a Japanese cannot hear laughter without believing it to be directed at himself. Sear a Japanese with hot irons and he will bear the pain with stoicism; ask him in the name of something he holds sacred to jump over a cliff and he will do so unflinchingly; but laugh at him and he falls to pieces, for he has no moral armour.

That it was a senseless bird laughing made no difference to Matsudara, unless perhaps it aggravated the offence. A bird laughs today, a cat tomorrow.

The suave Japanese businessman shed his suavity and became a savage. Lips set in an almost perpetual smile curled back in a snarl, the corners of the mouth turning down like those of a gladiator in his death agony.

The thing was done swiftly. The bird's body lay on the ground, while its neck and head dripped blood all over his hands. Matsudara stared numbly as though he were come out of a trance and did not know what had happened.

Lok's clerks watched him go, his head hunched forward on his shoulders, all the jauntiness gone from him.

"I have seen men walk like that on the execution ground!" said an old man watching him pass.

"I intend to see that he suffers much before he comes to the end," said Lok, who overheard the remark. He had loved the bird very dearly. It had been his friend for years.

Humble pie is the most indigestible dish a Japanese can eat. Even before it reaches the seat of digestion it sticks in his gullet. It is not fitting that the People of the Gods should humble themselves before their inferiors, which term includes the rest of humanity, with particular reference to the Chinese.

Two days passed—two days of acute mental torture—before Matsudara could bring himself to call upon Lok. When he did so he arrived bearing a cage containing many *minah* birds. The cage was of solid silver.

"He will return," said Lok with certainty. "When he does," he instructed the head clerk, "put him in the courtyard where the coolies wait. Tell the coolies that if they jostle the Japanese well there will be a double handful of silver for them."

Lok and Sung were sipping a fragrant tea when a servant announced: "The monkey with the gold teeth has come!"

"I will ring a bell when I am ready to receive him," said Lok.

Three long hours elapsed before Lok rang the silver bell beside him.

The coolies in the yard had earned their silver. Their jostling had been done so well that it might have been mere accident, just

57

the ordinary rudeness of uncouth men. Matsudara had endured it because, as he well knew, all that he held most dear was at stake. All commercial doors in Japan would be closed to a man dismissed from a Fureno company for blundering. The House of The Three Bamboos gave short shrift to blunderers.

Lok and Sung, sitting side by side at a table, leaving Matsudara to stand, heard the Japanese in silence. He grovelled. The cage of *minah* birds was ignored. He had been ill at his last call and but for the fact that the business was so important, he assured his hearers, he would have been in a sickbed. He was now come to renew negotiations for the purchase of the mulberry plantation.

"I have nothing further to do with the matter," said Lok lightly, "for I have appointed my friend Sung to act as my agent. I will be bound by whatever he agrees."

There flashed across Matsudara's face a smile of relief, the first convincing smile of which he had been capable since he had left this same room. He could not deal with the implacable Lok, but with Sung things were otherwise. Unless Sung were prepared never to see his son again, he could be brought to terms.

"Shall we then go to my office," said Matsudara, turning to Sung.

"The matter will be settled here and now—or never!" said Sung.

Matsudara derived much comfort from the fact that he believed Sung's son to be held at his own orders. It made the next few minutes almost bearable.

"The price?" asked the Japanese. "The final price?"

"You have already been told the price by my friend Lok," said Sung quietly. "There is no change in regard to that. But there remains to be settled my commission, since I am now the agent of my good friend Lok. I have decided to fix my commission at twenty-five per cent of the purchase price."

"That is between you and the illustrious Lok," said Matsudara uneasily. "As you are friends I am sure you will agree upon the matter for, being the seller, he pays the commission."

"This commission is payable by the buyer," said Sung gently.

"The price exceeds my authority," said Matsudara. "I must telegraph to Tokyo for further authority."

"For Mex. $10,000 you may have an option for two days. I have another prospective buyer interested. . . ."

58

Matsudara made up his mind. He whipped out on to the table a cheque-book, and began to write.

"Cash!" said Sung laconically.

"You will give me a receipt?"

"Naturally!"

The Japanese wrote there and then an order upon his own compradore for the amount of the option money, sending one of Lok's clerks to obtain the cash. This gave him forty-eight hours of grace. In that forty-eight hours he would see Sung alone and bring pressure to bear upon him through his only son. He looked up at Sung and a horrible thought entered his mind. Sung had not the appearance of a man greatly worried. Was it possible that some slip had been made in the kidnapping of the boy? He preferred not to contemplate the idea.

The clerk was not long gone. When the option money had been paid, Sung handed Matsudara a paper, signed by Lok. In it were the terms of the option. Sung also drafted another short document which, freely translated, read:

I, Kiyoshi Matsudara, manager here in Soo of the Fureno Trading Company of Tokyo, do hereby acknowledge that I, without any solicitation from any person or persons, approached Lok-kai-shing, silk merchant of this city, asking him to put a price upon a certain mulberry plantation belonging to him, situated upon the banks of the Grand Canal. I acknowledge further that the said Lok-kai-shing has never personally or by the mouth of an agent attributed to this plantation any special or peculiar qualities and that if the purchase be completed I buy the said plantation in its present condition without any warranty whatsoever, expressed or implied. I acknowledge further that the purchase price, as set forth in the option bearing this date, is in my good and considered judgment fair and reasonable, representing the true value of the said plantation.

Matsudara signed this in the presence of six witnesses, all independent persons, reading the document aloud to them before he did so.

Two days later, in exchange for the deeds, the full purchase price was paid.

On the Peach Blossom Canal of Soochow, not far from the Fragrant Flowers Bridge, there is a small and very famous eating-house, over whose door might well be hung the sign "For Princes and Rich Men Only." On the evening after the conclusion of the business with Matsudara, Lok entertained here two or three guests, chosen with extreme care from among Lok's fellow members of the Silk Guild. Sung was present as a matter of course, arriving before the others.

"Tell me now, my very good friend," said Lok, "while we are yet alone, what is the secret of the wonderful yield of silk on your small island?"

"Secret! Secret! I know of no secret, my friend," said Sung, with a puzzled air which Lok found most disconcerting.

"Come!" said Lok almost irritably. "We are friends now. We no longer sit up at nights laying traps for each other. There is boundless confidence between us, is there not?"

"Assuredly!" agreed Sung.

"Then tell me the secret before the other guests come, my friend. I confess to a great curiosity."

"Do you recall, Lok, a certain document which was signed in the presence of six witnesses by the monkey with the gold teeth?"

"Of course I remember!"

"That I did not ask you to sign a similar document a long time ago was proof of my confidence in you, Lok. But I would have you remember that it was you who came to me, not I to you. I told you of no secret, nor did I suggest the existence of a secret. You came to me, a stranger. You sought what you sought. I was a reluctant seller. Do you remember, Lok? I was a poor ignorant man, steeped in the traditions of my small island. We agreed to consult the Silk Goddess. Being a brilliant man and a rich merchant, Lok, I have no doubt that you were even more amazed than I that she deigned to reply to my simple questions. I still find it amazing that she knew of your fine houseboat . . . but that is another question, my very good friend. Meanwhile, let us have no foolish talk of secrets between us, for there is none. . . ."

Lok looked narrowly at Sung. He had heard enough. He was not so naïve that he did not know there had been trickery somewhere, but when one has a reputation for great astuteness, it is not a comfortable thoug̶h̶t̶ t̶h̶a̶t̶ o̶n̶e̶ h̶a̶s̶ b̶e̶e̶n̶ duped like a peasant.

nor to realise that one does not know where or how the duping took place.

"You are right, Sung," he said slowly. "There are no secrets between us. But," he added with great emphasis, "I have it in my mind that it was a fortunate day—for me—when the monkey with the gold teeth wished to buy my small plantation."

"Beyond doubt, Lok," replied Sung, "it was a most fortunate day—for us both. I rejoice that you are happy, my very good friend."

"And for the Japanese? Is the day so happy for him?" asked Lok.

"Today is happy, yes! Tomorrow will, I fear, be less happy for him, and the day after that perhaps less happy again. He threatened me through my son, Lok. For that I would laugh while the dog died in agony. In a little while there will be whispers. Then there will be open laughter. This Japanese will not be able to endure the laughter when it is known that he has paid a great fortune for a small piece of land worth a few thousand dollars. He will lose much 'face.' His masters, I am told, are hard men. They will not laugh so heartily when the story reaches their ears. . . . I somehow believe, Lok, that the monkey with the golden teeth will soon be gone from our midst. I am a man slow to anger and with a wide pity, but not wide enough to embrace one who threatens me through my son."

Sung, who had been a rich man by Ta Hu standards, was now a rich man by city standards. That he did not flaunt his wealth was a matter of common prudence, for he had few influential friends who could protect him from the attentions of the tax-gatherers.

Lok, with whom Sung was now established on terms of real friendship, advised the latter to deposit his surplus wealth in one of the great British banks in Shanghai, where being under protection of extra-territorial law, it would be safe from predatory Chinese officialdom.

"In proof that we are now true friends," said Lok, "I will tell you of a matter known only to my most intimate associates. You see me and know me as a Chinese, do you not?"

"What else?"

"Well you may ask, what else? You must understand, Sung, that I am a very rich man. Today I have friends among the great in China, friends who can protect me, but tomorrow—who knows?

61

The official is great only while he remains in office. Afterwards he becomes a man of very ordinary clay. Officials come and officials go, but a silk merchant must continue at his place of business. With these thoughts in mind, therefore, I went some years ago to a rascally foreign lawyer in Shanghai to seek his advice. With his help and by payment of large bribes I became a citizen of the Kingdom of Italy. . . ."

"Where is this Kingdom of Italy?" asked Sung. "I have never heard of it."

"Nor had I until the day I became a citizen of the country," said Lok with a shrug of the shoulders. "I have been told it is on the other side of the world, not far from England. I do not think it is a very great kingdom, because the bribe I paid to the Consul was only five thousand dollars. Some foreign countries, so my lawyer told me, demand a bribe five times as great."

"But I do not understand," interposed Sung, "why a Chinese should demean himself by becoming a citizen of any other land."

"Let us suppose," explained Lok, "that a new Governor of the Province of Kiang-su is appointed. When newly appointed he will be, as all officials, lean and hungry, for he will have paid large bribes to secure the office. He will have an army which clamours to be paid from a treasury which is as empty as a drum. His secretaries will draw up a list of those who will have the honour of filling the treasury. High upon that list will be the name of Lok-kai-shing. A little official from the Governor's Yamen will bring me an invitation to a great feast in honour of the new Governor. He will whisper in my ear a sum of money, and if Lok-kai-shing goes empty-handed to the feast his name goes down upon another list, which is not of invited guests. Soldiers would come and loot my godown of all the precious silks, and when I complained I would be arrested for making false complaints. Greater men than Lok-kai-shing have suffered thus.

"But now, if any official should wish to grow fat at my expense, all I need to do is to put the flag of Italy upon the roof of my house and my place of business, and complain to the Consul of Italy in Shanghai that a subject of Italy is being molested, and the matter is at an end. After the trouble in the North * it is not safe to touch the person or property of a foreign citizen."

A few days later Sung decided that he would go to Shanghai,

* The Boxer Rebellion.

taking the Small General with him. It would do no harm to discuss the matter with Lok's lawyer.

"For five thousand dollars I can make you a citizen of Spain or Italy," said the lawyer. "To be a citizen of Germany will cost a little more. If you wish to become a citizen of Portugal I can find a dozen men to swear that you were born in the Portuguese island of Macao."

"I am told," said Sung, "that it is no bad thing to become a citizen of England or America."

"It is a good thing," agreed the lawyer, "but it is also more expensive and it cannot be arranged here in Shanghai. To become a citizen of England it will be necessary to go to Hongkong or to Singapore. There, through agents of mine, we will find persons who will swear that you were born in Hongkong or Singapore, it matters not which, for they are both English. The Americans make difficulties also. I have agents in Honolulu and San Francisco who could arrange the matter, but the cost is high and there are long delays. My advice to you is to pay the bribe to the Consul of Italy or Spain. My fee will be two thousand dollars—in advance."

"Since my friend Lok-kai-shing is a citizen of Italy," said Sung after a little thought, "it would be more friendly on my part if I became the same."

"I will arrange everything tomorrow," said the lawyer. "Today there are pony races. I have a pony, fresh down from the North, which will win the second race. I must be there to see it."

"I have never seen ponies race," said Sung. "I also will go there, taking my son, the Small General."

Sung's fine houseboat, in which he had come to Shanghai, lay moored in the Soochow Creek a few hundred yards above the Garden Bridge. Leaving the crew of his poor relations on board to guard it, Sung hailed a rickshaw and with the Small General on his knee, told the puller to make for the race-course.

Sung and his son were bewildered and enchanted by the surge of traffic going up the Nanking Road. So many fine carriages, so many strangely garbed foreign men and women! Shop windows filled with foreign merchandise, bearded Sikh policemen!

The lawyer had written down the name of the pony for Sung, but it was necessary to find someone to translate the name into something he could read. Hearing the Soochow dialect being

63

spoken in the crush, Sung ventured to ask a clerkly man how he should back the pony, for Sung was, like all his countrymen, an enthusiastic gambler.

With the help of the Soochow man Sung placed his bet of fifty dollars, had the number and the colours pointed out to him, and settled down to watch the race, which was to be decided between a field of some twenty-seven 'griffins'—that is, China ponies which had not raced before.

"Why do the riders wear coats of bright colours?" asked the Small General.

"To frighten away the devils, of course," replied Sung.

The lawyer's colours were in the lead as the ponies passed the post.

"Trust my good friend Lok to find a good lawyer!" was Sung's complacent comment.

"How do I receive my winnings?" asked Sung of the helpful Soochow man, a question which shook the Small General somewhat as he thought that his father knew everything.

"Give me the ticket and I will collect it for you," said the Soochow man.

When the last race had been run and the crowd had streamed out of the gates, revealing no sign of the Soochow man, Sung sighed deeply. Even the enlightened and honest men of Soochow, it appeared, became dishonest when thrown in contact with the foreign barbarians, who should never have been permitted to live in the Flowery Kingdom. Sung said little, but he was deeply shocked.

A happy thought that same evening, when the Small General was safely asleep on the houseboat, prompted Sung to visit a restaurant which, Lok had told him, was much frequented by Soochow men. The restaurant was, of course, situated in the amusement district, for almost every actor in China hails from Soochow.

Sung selected for himself a quiet table where he could see and not be seen. He had just begun to eat, when he heard, from across the room, the voice of the Soochow man from the race-course.

Now Sung was a charitable man, inclined to think well of his fellows until events made this impossible. It might be, he felt bound to admit, that his acquaintance of the race-course had come to the restaurant expecting to find him and hand over his winnings. In that event justice demanded that he jump to no uncharitable conclusions.

"You are all my guests at this table," Sung shortly afterwards heard the Soochow man call loudly. "I had a stroke of good fortune today."

"You backed many winners at the races?"

"On the contrary, every horse I backed seemed to have lead weights on his feet. Happily, however, I encountered a bumpkin from Soochow who made me a gift of some four hundred dollars, or when I say a gift, you know what I mean."

There was a gust of laughter at the table, for it is considered polite to laugh heartily at the jests of a generous host.

Sung rose from the table and walked across the restaurant, approaching from the rear of the man who was being so generous with his—Sung's—money. To be robbed was bad, but to be called a bumpkin was insufferable. Sung put his hands lightly over the eyes of the thief who, believing that some friend had come to greet him, called "Who is that?"

"A bumpkin from Soochow, who is very angry!" came the disconcerting reply. "Give!"

The wretched man fumbled under his gown for a purse. From it he withdrew a thick roll of bills. A strong hand came down over his shoulder and seized this.

"Some of that is my money!" came an agonised cry.

"Some of that *was* your money!" corrected Sung. "If you have any complaint let us go to the police. I am an ignorant bumpkin, you must understand, a stranger to such matters as ponies which race and thieves who rob men of their own countryside."

The thief made no further protest, for he knew only too well what would happen at the Louza Police Station nearby, where he was well and unfavourably known.

"Doubtless," said the proprietor of the restaurant, coming forward, "you have the money to pay for the sumptuous meal you have ordered? I am sure you have, for you know what happens to smart fellows who try to bilk *me*."

From the thief there came a wail of distress. It was too much.

"I am ashamed," said the proprietor to Sung, "that a distinguished stranger like yourself, coming to my humble establishment for the first time, should encounter such as that one. My name is Wong. I am yours to command."

65

Now Wong, it transpired, came from a small village named Ta-tsien, situated on a narrow peninsula which juts out on to Lake Ta Hu, immediately facing Sung's island. Wong had a fine, firm, well-rounded belly such as speaks eloquently of good living. There flashed between Wong and Sung one of those strange currents between man and man, to form instant friendship and liking. Each felt that here was a man he could trust, one who in sorrow, or over the wine cups, would be a good companion.

Before the evening was over Sung sought the advice of his new friend on a matter very near to his heart.

"My son is of an age when he must acquire learning," explained Sung, "and I am of several minds upon the matter. I am rich and I could give him the best learning in all China, so that he might grow into a Chinese scholar and gentleman. But this short time here in Shanghai tells me that the old way of life is dying and the ways of the barbarians are being grafted on to us, so that the lacquer of China grows very dull. Shall my son, therefore, be taught the ways of the old China or those of the China of tomorrow?"

"Among those who come to eat here," said Wong, "are many foreigners. As among us, there are good and bad. When measured by our standards they are utterly barbaric, but measured by their own standards, which are not so absurd as you might think when you explore below the surface, they have certain qualities. It is their manners, rather than their hearts, which are abominable. But I admit that one needs a strong stomach to suffer their manners. Nevertheless, I am on good terms with several of them, and am greatly impressed by their knowledge of things and ideas which have never penetrated to China. . . ."

"Are you suggesting that my son, the Small General, be educated by the foreigners?" asked Sung aghast. "I realise that at your place of business you must meet men of all types. Doubtless foreign money rings as well as any in your cash box, but there is no need to carry broadmindedness too far. I also meet a few foreigners. They come out for pleasure to Ta Hu in houseboats. I also have observed their manners, which are entirely abominable, but I have observed also that they are fools. They come to me sometimes to buy a few ducks, a small pig, or some eggs. I discourage them by asking three times the proper price. This they pay without question and return for more."

66

"Forgive me, my friend Sung," said Wong courteously, "if I point out to you that it is difficult for you, who have not lived among them, to realise that most of them have much money, earned very easily. It is not uncommon for a foreigner to pay two hundred taels monthly for his house. . . ."

"But I could build a fine house for three months hire at that price," said Sung, aghast.

"Not here in Shanghai," retorted Wong. "What think you I pay in rent for this restaurant?"

"I would say you were mad if you paid more than twenty taels monthly. . . ."

"Then I must be twenty-five times more mad than you believe me, for I pay five hundred taels monthly!"

"The sooner I return to my small island the better, it seems," said Sung, shaken to his foundations.

But when Sung sought his couch that night, aboard his fine houseboat moored in the Soochow Creek, he had made certain high decisions regarding the future of his small son, who lay sleeping so peacefully beside him. Sung had caught glimpses of a new world and of the new way of life which was coming to China. Most of it frightened him, because he was in middle age and set in his habits and thoughts.

"Since there are great changes over the horizon, son," he said softly, so as not to awaken the Small General, "it must be my duty to see that you are equipped to meet them."

❧ 6 ❧

IN the year 1911 of the Christian Era the Flowery Kingdom of China became a Republic. There was much talk of human liberty and dignity, a rash of wild-eyed demagogues and soapbox orators, a little violence and a new Flag. A corrupt and decaying Empire became a corrupt and decaying Republic. Since the power theoretically wielded from the Throne in Peking had for a long while been almost entirely imaginary, the changes were not, in so far as they affected the great mass of the Chinese people, important or far-reaching.

The 'queue,' symbolic of submission to the Manchu Dynasty, was abolished. The young men had their hair cut short, while many of their elders did not. The opium traffic was abolished—on paper, but it flourished just the same, with the difference that, now it was illegal, those who dealt in the drug demanded larger profits.

On Sung's island the effects of the revolution were imperceptible. On the off-chance that trouble might come to Ta Hu, Sung deemed it the path of prudence to unwrap the Italian flag in readiness to hoist it to an improvised masthead. These ten years Sung had been an Italian subject, but as he had never seen an Italian, or heard the language, or troubled to have translated for him the rigmarole on his Italian passport, the effects upon him and his family of this new national status were just about as telling as the transition from subject to citizen had been for the majority of Chinese.

The Small General, a few weeks home from his schooling at the time of the revolution, was most enthusiastic about the Republic, as were most of his contemporaries who had received a smattering of western education. The Small General had learned enough about the Chinese Classics to be able to indulge in polite conversation on the subject. This he had learned in Soochow. From a mission school in Sh———ai h——

tremely badly and to read and write the language even less fluently. He had been taught a smattering of world history, most of which he actively disbelieved; quite a lot of commercial mathematics; and some Christian dogma, which he neither understood nor admired. The chief effect of his schooling had been to undermine his faith in the old ways of life and to give him a profound conviction that western civilisation, ugly and unattractive though it might be, was irresistible.

Sung was sceptical about the Republic and said so.

"We have exchanged officials who once robbed us in the name of the Manchus," he declared, "for officials who now rob us in the name of the Republic. Instead of a few officials who became very ˙ch by their extortions, we now have a greater number of officials who become slightly less rich."

"But we now have Democracy!" protested the Small General. "Surely that is important?"

"Where is this Democracy you prate about?" asked Sung irritably. "Show me some! What does it look like?"

"Democracy is an idea, my father," said the Small General, trying to conceal his impatience.

"An idea!" snorted Sung. "Will it make rice grow where no rice grew before? I am beginning to wish that I had not wasted all this time and money sending you to places where your head has been stuffed with foolish nonsense. Ten years ago, when you were the Small General of the ducks, I had great ideas for you. Now, it seems, after paying others to do so, I shall have to educate you myself. Remember, son, that the world is divided into those who do something well and those who merely talk. You have been seeing too much of the latter, so it is time you re-learned your early lessons."

"What lessons? I had none, my father. . . ."

"You had the best lessons of all, did you but know it, for you learned the first lesson of all: that the soil gives generously to those who give to the soil; that if five thousand ducks try to feed where there is food only for two thousand, three thousand will go hungry, or all will be poorly nourished. It is useless to be rich in silkworms if poor in mulberries, for one mulberry tree can feed a certain number of silkworms and no more."

"Except here on Sung's island, my father, where because of your great wisdom the number is greater than elsewhere. . . ."

"I think we will not discuss that, my son. I am weary of the subject, for every time I see my old friend Lok-kai-shing he asks me how this thing was brought about. Certain Japanese monkeys still show curiosity, for they cannot understand why the mulberry land planted with trees from this island has proved to be no better and no worse than other land."

"Nevertheless, my father, and with great respect, I would dearly love to know the secret."

"You shall know it on the day when you prove to me that you are fitted to be the master of Sung's island. Never forget that everything we have and are is rooted in the soil of this small island. Without it we are nothing. . . ."

"Without my father's great wisdom we are less than nothing."

"Your father's great wisdom also sprang from the soil of this island, for was he not born here? Do not forget also that it will be your task before long to raise our island a little higher above the lake than you found it. I raised it higher than my father, his father and his grandfather put together were able to raise it. . . ."

"Was it not really your good friend Lok who did the work, my father?" interposed the Small General.

"Associating with foreign barbarians has caused you to split hairs over simple matters, son. The sooner your back is bent over the good soil, the sooner will you understand things as they are. The tradition of our line demands that each generation raises the soil of the island higher. The tradition does not say how that is to be accomplished. My honoured ancestors used their sweat and sinews, while when my turn came I used the brains they gave me. In due course it will be for you to choose whether you will delve and toil, dragging mud from the lake bottom like a coolie, or whether you will use your brains to grow long fingernails as a Chinese gentleman should. It is no great matter to me, as I shall not be here to see you, but you may take my word that the latter is the more pleasant way."

"Then, my father," asked the Small General, "is it necessary that, now I am a scholar, I should toil on this land like those clods yonder?" He pointed as he spoke to where four men were hoeing trim rows of cabbages and cauliflowers.

"It *is* necessary," was the uncompromising retort, "for from the soil spring all first laws. Learning without an understanding of first laws is so much wind. Furthermore, no man who has not done his share of hard work is fitted to employ others. I will not have you give an order here to any man until I am certain that you are able to perform that task as well as he. You chatter to me like a magpie about Republics and Democracy, but I have just drawn for you a picture of Democracy, better than your hired windbags could draw."

And because in China a good son does not question his father's authority, or the wisdom of his decisions, the Small General (now grown into a personable young man) seized a hoe and went out into the fields to search for first causes.

There were times, many of them, when toiling with a hoe, pruning mulberry trees, digging in manure, feeding pigs, selecting ducks for the breeding pen or hauling in to shore great masses of lake weed—when the Small General wondered why he had been educated, seeing that all that his education had done for him, seemingly, was to make him unhappy and resentful at menial toil.

"We Sungs are not a princely family," Sung explained to him, "and it is not seemly that we should give ourselves the airs of such. Our roots go down into the rich soil. Heaven in its wisdom decreed that the world of animals, fishes and birds should be divided into many classes. Few things could be more ridiculous than a water buffalo trying to imitate a deer, unless perhaps it were the converse. Men also are divided, though perhaps the dividing lines are not so well defined. It is better to stand high in the class in which we were born than to stand awkwardly at the bottom of the class above."

"But, my father," spluttered the Small General, "under the Republic all men are equal. It is written so. We are no longer mandarins and coolies, but are all fellow citizens."

"We are all equal, eh? Since when have you been able to plough a furrow as straight as Chen? Since when are you as good a judge of silk as my good friend Lok? Since when have you been able to cast a net with the same skill as Li? Do not talk like a fool, son, for this talk of equality is like the chattering of the wind through the bamboos."

"I mean only that we were born equal in the sight of Heaven, for it is upon this foundation our Republic is built. . . ."

Just then there came a fearful uproar from the kitchen quarters, with much screaming, punctuated by thuds. Some years previously Sung's wife, the Small General's mother, had died. After a decent interval, for she had been a good wife, whose shrimp sauce with fish was beyond praise, Sung acquired by purchase two concubines.

One of these came from Soochow, a city renowned for the beauty of its women. She was a dainty, fragile little thing, who for a short while helped Sung forget that he was an ageing man, to such good effect that she presented him with a son.

The other was never given the opportunity to display any amatory prowess she may have possessed, for Sung's interest in her was strictly culinary. She was a plain creature, middle-aged, whose voice had the unfortunate timbre of a hacksaw. She came from Hangchow, whose cuisine is renowned throughout China.

The two women were unable to agree about anything. At first it had been the Soochow beauty's part to queen it over the kitchen drab from Hangchow, but when the brief Indian Summer of Sung's manhood was over, Soochow beauty became of infinitely less importance than the correct ingredients of a sour-sweet sauce from Hangchow.

"This house is not large enough," observed Sung with a frown, "for a peace-loving old man and two viperish women, to say nothing of a son who talks nonsense. If the Young One had not given me a son I would pack her off to Soochow, and if the Old One were not such a good cook it would not distress me never to see her ugly face again. Here am I overloaded with women, incapable of dealing fairly with one. You, on the other hand, who ought to be able to maintain a dozen women in reasonable contentment, have none. The world is quite mad. Does it not occur to you, son, that before you plant me yonder beside my honoured ancestors, I might like to have my best silk gown stained by my grandson? Have you no woman?"

"There is a woman, my father, but it will be two years before she passes her examinations and leaves the university. Then, and with your permission, I will bring her here for your approval. . . ."

"A young man of good standing may seek out harlots to amuse him, but he leaves it to the good sense of his parents to find him a wife. There are certain forms and ceremonies to be observed in these matters and it is not seemly that a Sung should forget them. Furthermore, who and what is this woman that she requires to be a scholar? Whoever heard of a woman at a university? A simpering doll is of no use to a Sung. What you need is a fine strapping wench, country bred, able to go to child-bed in the morning and cook your evening rice for you when you come home from work. I will find you the right kind of wife, and I will make it my business to see that she brings with her a dowry worth having. A young man chooses a wife with his heart, but his father uses a little thought."

"But in the new China, my father . . ."

"There have been a hundred new Chinas, my son, and they are still old China!"

"Nevertheless, my father, I would like to help in the building of the new China."

"When you know enough about the affairs of this small island to be able to tell me that you can perform every man's task as well as or better than he can perform it himself, we will discuss a larger sphere for the genius which your foreign teachers doubtless cultivated behind your unwrinkled brow. That, son, is my idea of equality and justice among men: that no man is fitted to give orders as master until he has learned what it means to carry out those same orders."

These arguments between father and son were frequent, but they were without acrimony. Sung himself did not believe so fervently in the infallibility of the old ways as might have appeared from his speech, but he knew that the new ways were not good merely because they were new. Somewhere between the two lay sanity, and Sung was determined, while his son was still at a malleable age, that he should not go out into the world until he had been able to reach this conclusion for himself.

More than all, Sung abhorred the idea of national politics. There had never been in China a national consciousness. Only among the leisured and educated classes was there a language common to the whole Empire. On and around Ta Hu there were many who could not make themselves understood in Soochow, a city which they were able to see on a clear day. Fewer still had any language link with Hangchow, sixty or so miles to the south of the lake. In Shanghai the men of Ta Hu would have been foreigners as completely as Red Indians, while even Shanghai men found difficulty in understanding the Pootung dialect, spoken less than a mile away on the other side of the Whangpoo River. For tens of centuries China had sprawled from the Himalayas and the Siberian frontiers to the Pacific, or more accurately, the China Sea. In that vast area were teeming millions of people, divided sharply by language and thought, casually called the Chinese race by foreigners who knew nothing of what they said. Fitfully, these scattered provinces paid tribute to Peking, but not if there were any way of avoiding it. Over all there might be said to have been a common bond, in so far as all the provinces and outer territories, with the exception of those in the extreme west which had fallen under the banner of Islam, were under the joint and separate influence of Taoism, Confucianism and Buddhism, all three inextricably mixed in the minds of all but the highly educated.

China was a mere geographical expression, for within her borders were a score of civilisations—of a very high order, but differing more widely, for example, than those of Scandinavia and the Levant.

Meanwhile, for close on a century the foreigner had been looting China shamefully. Parasitical politicians and officials in Peking, without consultation with the people of the provinces vitally concerned, had for long been pawning everything in the Empire of negotiable value. British financiers had been lending money to China—in theory. In exchange they acquired railway, mining and other concessions. The money lent to China was supposed to be used for various high-sounding public purposes, but little of it was ever diverted from the private pockets of those who had sold the concessions. The British and other foreign financiers called these payments loans, but they themselves were never deceived that they were anything but immense bribes. In turn customs, postal and telegraph revenues were pawned to foreigners as security for loans, only a microscopic proportion of which was ever expended upon the ostensible purposes for which they had been made. British financiers were no more or less immoral than their colleagues of other nationalities. They are conspicuous in the story because their plunder of China was on a greater scale than the others, even though their methods were no more vile. Because these British financiers were hand-in-glove with the ruling classes at home—and for no other single reason—they were permitted to use the might of the British Navy as a debt-collecting agency. Again, other foreign powers used the same methods, but on a less conspicuous scale.

China was bled white.

From this grew the first glimmer of national unity, as occidental peoples know the phrase. The far-flung provinces of China, divided by barriers of language, custom and geography, found a measure of unity in their detestation of foreigners, their only truly common bond. To a certain degree a share of this detestation went to the venal politicians in Peking who had sold China to the foreign harpies.

A dawning realisation of these things created China's revolution. The older men of China saw no reason to doubt, so far was the land gone in decay, that the politicians of the new régime would prove as greedy and unscrupulous as their predecessors. That their pessimism was not entirely borne out by events was due in large measure to the fact that little remained for China to pawn.

This was, then, the atmosphere in which the Small General came to manhood, saturated with the grievances of his country, proudly determined to do something to right old wrongs, and fired with a holy zeal to build something new and good upon the old and rotten foundations of the defunct Empire.

Three years after the Chinese Republic came into being there was, it will be remembered, a Great War in Europe, which rocked the whole world but caused little more than a ripple in China, where it came as somewhat pleasing news that the foreign barbarians were killing each other in satisfyingly large numbers. It made very little apparent difference to the Chinese people as a whole that German usurpers were ousted from Tsingtao and Japanese usurpers took their place. It had made very little apparent difference a decade earlier when Russians had been ousted from the filched territory of Southern Manchuria, to be replaced by the same busy and purposeful Japanese. One does not pause to split hairs about the personal characteristics of a thief who breaks into one's home: it is enough that he is a thief and that one thief is very much like another.

It pleased Sung very much more than he admitted that he had a son who had ambitions in a larger field than the small island which had been home and everything to a long line of Sungs. But the father had a shrewdly right appraisal of facts. He knew with a sublime certainty that the difference between life on the island and life in the greater world beyond the lake was one merely of degree. He knew also that no man could achieve a deep and understanding sympathy with the life and problems of China unless he were, like a huge preponderance of its people, near to the rich black silt which gave life to the fertile valleys. Peking had never understood China, because no city-bred parasites and scholars could ever hope to understand four hundred millions of peasant farmers.

Perhaps, Sung mused, beneath his son's callow enthusiasms there lay qualities which would raise the name of Sung high in the land. If it were so, the ageing man knew full well that an understanding of first things would be his best equipment for the struggle.

Chafing impatiently at first, the Small General settled down to the task of fitting himself to take over his heritage. He was able to see for himself the unbreakable chain of causation which lay between the planting of seed and the reaping of a harvest. He learned the inwardness of the Chinese creed that he who neglects the soil is unfaithful to himself; and the glowing pride of a man who sees in summer the fine upstanding crops which the almost forgotten toil of winter made possible.

As a child the Small General had learned the ten rules for breeding silkworms. They had been mere words then: now they were practical wisdom, for they had proved themselves to be the key to success. Sung knew a great happiness when, coming upon the Small General one day unexpectedly, he heard his son teaching the rules to his younger half-brother, Sung's son by his Soochow concubine. Sung listened in silence while his younger son recited the rules which in the course of time he would put into practice.

"When the eggs are on paper they must be cool," the child lisped. "When they are hatched they must be kept warm. When they moult they must be kept hungry. Between their sleeps they must have plenty of food. They must be neither too close together, nor too far apart, but just so." The child illustrated the distance with two stones. "During their sleeps they must lie in darkness and warmth. After they have cast their skins they need cool air and light. For a short time after moulting a little food suffices. When they are full grown they require plenty of food always. The

76

eggs should be laid close together, but never heaped upon each other."

"And now," exclaimed Sung when the recital was done, "I shall go to the shrine of my honoured ancestors and I shall tell them that, thanks to two good sons, their silkworms will be tended well for another generation."

❦ 7 ❧

In the fifth year after the revolution Sung lost all patience with the bickering between the Young One and the Old One. Since it was manifest that there would be no peace while they were under the same roof, and since it is obvious that the utility of the Old One was the greater, the Young One had to go. Sung gave her, therefore, the choice of living by herself in a small house on the opposite side of the island, or returning to Soochow. To the relief of everyone concerned, for she had a strident and unmelodious voice, she elected to return to her native city.

"There, son, is a fine example of the folly of youth," observed Sung as she went. "I chose her for her rare beauty, which faded quickly. For her I neglected the Old One, which proves merely that an old man can behave like a young fool. When the Young One's beauty had gone there was nothing left. On the other hand, I suspect that the Old One never was beautiful. Lift a water buffalo's tail and you would find a face hardly less enchanting. But does that matter to me? Does that make her any the less excellent cook? I do not have to see her. When she comes to discuss the finer points of meals with me, for she is not too proud to learn, she has the good sense to stand out of sight behind me. It is more than two years since I laid eyes on her. Yet it is she who gives me comfort in my old age, when the Young One's beauty is scarcely even a memory. . . ."

At about this time Sung decided that before he died he would like to see his last remaining brother, who had settled at Anking, a busy city on the Yangtsze and the capital of Anhwei Province. In order to observe how his son conducted himself among strangers, he took with him the Small General.

The way led through Soochow and, since Lok-kai-shing would have been mortally offended otherwise, the former Lok houseboat drew up at his summer retreat on the Grand Canal, a little before sunset on the first day.

Sung still took enormous pleasure in his houseboat. Indeed, he never travelled otherwise. Not for nothing have foreigners named Soochow, among several other cities, the Venice of the East.

The boat was some sixty feet in length. Amidships was a bamboo mast and lateen sail, safe to use only with a following wind. The centre saloon and awning-covered after-deck comprised about two-thirds of the entire length. The remaining third was given over to the kitchen and the sleeping quarters of the crew of five, culled from the ranks of Sung's numerous poor cousins, who would provide the motive power for the long journey to Chinkiang. Magnanimously Sung left it to them to choose whether they would toil on the *ulohs,* or toil on the tow-rope from the towpath which is inseparable from Chinese canals. In a corner between what was in effect Sung's private lavatory—he being now insufficiently acrobatic to follow general custom—and the kitchen, the Old One, reclining upon a rough mattress, slept as well she could, which was not very well. Except for going ashore at strange villages to buy provender in unfamiliar dialects, cleaning and preparing vegetables, doing all the cooking for everyone aboard, hauling aboard water and washing the dishes, the Old One had a sinecure ahead of her. The poor cousins in consultation felt that she should take her turn on the tow-rope, being a strongly built woman. But Sung's intervention saved her. He made it clear that he had no objection whatever to the Old One spending three or four hours daily on the tow-rope, always provided that the quality of her cooking did not suffer. Sung was at all times a most reasonable man. These questions had not arisen, however, at the time when the houseboat moored at Lok's summer house, for all the way from Sung's island there had been a fresh following breeze, so that all except the steersman, standing aft with a huge sweep (and of course the Old One), spent a most delightful and leisurely day upon the wide canal which led up from Ta Hu to Soochow.

At Lok's house, to which only Sung and the Small General were invited from the houseboat, there were already several guests assembled. They were all elderly men. The Small General's part, therefore, was to listen. Young men in China, or at least those with any pretensions to good breeding, remain silent in the presence of their elders unless specifically addressed.

The talk that evening—the Great War in Europe was just ended—was chiefly of two subjects. The world price of silver, it

79

will be remembered, had risen out of all reason, so that the silver tael, normally worth in the region of two shillings, was worth approximately three times as much. Imports into China, therefore, were cheap, but disadvantageous exchange rates made exports very difficult. The gathering being entirely mercantile, with the exception of Sung and his son, it is hardly surprising that the exchange position was discussed. The other subject was that hardy perennial, the encroachment of foreigners upon China's sovereign rights which, after a brief lull during the war, was becoming once more a pressing problem.

It might seem that very little emerged from the conversation to which the Small General listened that evening, but to him it was a great deal.

"The time is come," he heard one of his elders remark, "when we Chinese must put our house in order so that we may combat these accursed foreigners . . ." and more in the same strain.

Now to the Small General's ears the remarkable thing was the use of the term "we Chinese." Young men were wont to say this frequently, for the rising generation had begun to think in terms of China as a united nation, even though their thoughts were generations ahead of reality. But elder men were not in the habit of thinking or speaking of their country in this wider sense. They thought regionally, some even with a smaller horizon spoke civically. There were even those who could not or would not see further than the confines of a village. There was animosity frequently for those who lived a mere ten or fifteen miles away, not for any outstandingly bad qualities, but merely because they were "foreigners," which being interpreted meant, those who spoke somewhat differently and had certain peculiar customs of their own.

It thrilled the Small General to the core to hear his country referred to in these terms by his elders, for it meant that China as a great living entity had grown to mean something to the older men, too. It meant that they no longer thought in the narrow terms of village, town, city and province.

The remark just quoted brought from a well-known silk merchant named Chang a somewhat ironical rejoinder. "It is not very polite to your host," he said with a sardonic grin, "to refer to him as an accursed foreigner. Have you forgotten that our worthy host Lok is himself an Italian? Our good friend Sung also is an Italian and, since the nationality of the son is that of his father, we have at least three Italians here present this evening. Then, if I am not mistaken, our worthy friend Kum-soo is a man of Portugal. Six witnesses have sworn that he was born in Macao. Then again there is our worthy friend Li, who unless I am in sad error, carries a British passport up the sleeve of his magnificent gown. Even I—I regret the admission—am a man of France. My mother, so I have been told, gave me life in the French city of Saigon. Who am I to say the contrary, when I know that many good men have sworn this was so?"

The old men assembled round Lok's hospitable table looked at each other searchingly. The result of this mutual scrutiny was slow in coming. One old man, so old that he needed help, rose to his feet. He was Chun who, like the others, was a silk merchant.

"It seems," said Chun in a quavering voice, "that I am the only one present who may talk about the accursed foreigners. I am an old man, going very soon to join my honoured ancestors, the oldest among you. I am entitled, therefore, to be very frank. Great age has few privileges, but this is one. I am what I was born—and what I will die—a man of China. To me Soochow is the greatest city of all China, but I believe that China is greater than Soochow. You, my friends, all of you, have sold your birthright. You carry the umbrella of a foreign nationality which is more evil than the rain from which you think it protects you. I have said nothing in the past of what I think, because I believe it to be a poor thing to criticise others unless one has perfection oneself. I am far from perfect. I am what I was born, but while I enjoy the princely hospitality of my Italian friend Lok I cannot hear without protest references to 'accursed foreigners.' To submit silently to that would be to become as ill-mannered as the foreign barbarians themselves."

Chun sat down amid a cold silence. He had touched his hearers on the raw.

The Small General, who had heard all this, was deeply and bitterly ashamed. He had not until this evening known that he was, by virtue of his father's defection, an Italian subject.

"I am no Italian!" said the Small General, greatly daring.

"You are not permitted, even thus indirectly," said Sung coldly, "to rebuke your father."

gence of opinion between father and son might easily have ended in open rupture. Not so in China, where the accumulated weight of four thousand or more years of youth's submission to age pressed hardly upon the consciousness of young and old alike. Even Chun, whose opinions were precisely those of the Small General, looked up in open horror at hearing them echoed by a youth in the presence of his father. The utter rightness of the young man's declaration was in Chun's eyes of infinitely less importance than the impiety of its declaration.

Then, as though their junior no longer existed:

"Example must come from the top," observed Lok quietly. "Why should not relatively humble merchants seek protection where they please, when the great ones do the same? Even Sun,* whose tongue is a great patriot, shelters behind the foreigners in the French Concession in Shanghai."

It is a matter of record that on at least one occasion the much revered Chinese patriot, Sun Yat-sen, took refuge aboard a British warship which enjoyed extra-territorial rights, when his political activities ashore had made China too hot to hold him with any degree of comfort. But the same Sun Yat-sen apparently saw nothing inconsistent between sheltering behind foreign extra-territorial privileges at one moment and inveighing against those same privileges bitterly when he no longer required the comfort and security they had given him.

In turn war-lords, absconding officials, political and military governors, and scores of others in all walks of life who had offended against Chinese law, did not hesitate to take refuge in the foreign concessions of Shanghai, Hankow, Tientsin and elsewhere. Once within the sanctuary of these international settlements, the fugitives, all of whom arrived heavy with loot, found not the smallest difficulty in bribing venal foreign consuls to give them extra-territorial status.

The consuls of Spain and Italy were the worst offenders in this respect; and one may only guess at the number of persons of pure Chinese blood, who had never left China, who spoke no word of any tongue but Chinese, and who had no business or other interests outside China, who became at various times subjects of the appropriately entitled "Most Catholic Majesty" Alfonso XIII of Spain, or the diminutive Victor Emmanuel of Italy. The consuls who represented these monarchs, although miserably paid, retired from their service in China with large fortunes.

To the vast majority of the Chinese people sufficiently well informed to be aware of these matters, the position became subject for cynical laughter. But there were a few earnest patriots, honest men, who dreamed and planned for a day when these abuses would be put to an end. These in turn caught the ears and captured the imaginations of the rising generation. Among these was the Small General who, truth to tell, had but a smattering of education, Chinese or foreign, and certainly insufficient knowledge of human history and progress to view these happenings clearly and put them in their proper perspective. All he knew, with a burning conviction higher than reason, was that the people of China—his people—were playing an unworthy part in the affairs of a changing world, servants instead of masters in their own house, hiding behind the skirts of foreigners instead of evicting them.

Along the length of the Grand Canal, from Soochow as far as Chinkiang, where the great flood of the Yangtsze River breaks the canal into its two main sections, the Small General saw with horror the extent of foreign penetration. At every major village and town along the route were the agencies or depôts of the great British and American oil companies, on which the lamps of China depended. Rival brands of British and American cigarettes, advertised by means of gaudy posters stuck upon ancient walls and monuments, were flaunted everywhere. Never a village so small that it did not boast the agency of an American sewing machine. Missionaries everywhere, battering vainly at the walls of a civilisation that was old when Europe was engulfed in black savagery, and Red Indian hunters roamed the plains of America, undisturbed by any premonition of a civilisation which one day would spell extermination.

Steam tugs hauled barge trains loaded with foreign goods. Thousands of Chinese coolies waited patiently and humbly to serve foreign masters. Telegraph lines, pawned to foreigners, ran beside the ancient waterway whose traffic was growing less because of the craze for speed which gave the railways an advantage. The railways, too, were in pawn to foreigners.

At the various customs and *likin* * stations the lordly administrative jobs were held by foreigners, agents for the parasitic

* Stations akin to the French *octroi*.

83

bankers of the world who had made their infamous bargains with the great ones in Peking, and who cared less than nothing for the great Empire, now Republic, which was bleeding to death under their extortions. The bankers wanted the pound of flesh stated in their bond, nor was the quality of mercy allowed to stand between them and their prey.

To the Small General it seemed the last straw that the people of China might not even travel in their own land immune from search and detention by foreigners.

At Chinkiang it was insufferably hot. Here Sung and his son had to wait for two days, before completing their journey by one of the great foreign-owned river steamers which plied from Shanghai as far as Ichang, and some even through the famed Yangtsze Gorges to Chungking.

Sung and the Small General watched awhile on their first afternoon while white-clad foreigners played tennis in the blazing heat, their faces red with exertion as though suffering from apoplexy. Even dogs lay panting in the shade, near the limit of their endurance.

"If I ever doubted that foreigners were mad," observed Sung, "now I have no doubts. Are they compelled by some strange religious custom to suffer thus?"

"They play this game for their pleasure, my father," said the Small General. "I have seen them many times at Shanghai. . . ."

"The dutiful son does not mock his aged father," reproved Sung sternly. "Tell me without mockery why they do this insane thing!"

"It is the truth, my father, that they do this for their pleasure."

"If you believe that, son," said Sung with a gesture almost of pity, "you are more gullible than I hoped in a son of mine. They have plenty of money, these foreigners. For a few cents they could hire coolies to beat the ball for them, if it amuses them. Are they so mean that they will not pay the sum, or is it that they are entirely lacking in dignity and decency?"

The four men who had been playing left the court, wiping the sweat from their faces. Two other men and two women then came out to play. The women played an acrobatic and somewhat revealing game, exhibiting to those who cared to see large sections of beefy thigh. Both women were of the heavy-breasted type, so disgusting in Chinese eyes.

84

"If the one with the yellow hair is not careful," remarked Sung coarsely, "her breasts will either stun her with a blow on the chin, or lame her as they strike her knees. That I should live to see such a shameless sight! The men are as bad, for they condone the affair by their presence and approval."

"But I assure you, my father," protested the Small General, "that they do this thing for their pleasure. . . ."

"Nonsense!" said Sung. "How could any men take pleasure from leaping about in this heat in company with fair-haired harlots whose breasts would not disgrace a water-buffalo cow? Let us go from here before I vomit on the ground and put us both to shame!"

"Sir!" remarked a well-dressed Chinese who had overheard the discussion between father and son. "Forgive me that I intrude myself, but I feel it right to tell you that, incredible as it may seem, these foreigners are leaping about for their pleasure. I have it from their own lips. Furthermore, the women are no harlots. They are the wives of *taipans* highly respected in the foreign community."

"Then they are mad—mad and shameless!" said Sung with finality.

"That is as may be," said the other, "but since you mention shamelessness this is nothing beside the disgusting conduct that will take place this evening. In yonder building tonight they will dance. From a spot I will show you there is a clear view through the open windows. I will tell you nothing of what goes on there, for were I to do so you would not believe me. See for yourself!"

When he had indicated to them the coign of vantage the stranger bowed politely and went on his way.

Sung and the Small General, after an excellent meal served on the after-deck of the houseboat, where a river breeze made the evening bearable, gave their food time to digest and then, at the older man's suggestion, went to see the foreigners disporting themselves at the dance.

A small orchestra of indigent Russians provided the music. The pianist had learned to play in a Muscovite mansion which, but for the accident of the Russian Revolution, he would have inherited. The first violin had once been addressed as "Excellency!" The second violin had played in his infancy with a rattle made of pure gold in a cradle of carved ivory. The harpist, a woman, was not a Russian. Born in Vienna, she had gone to Russia to teach music to a princeling who was related to the Romanoffs.

Seen through European eyes, the dance was a model of decorum, attended strictly by the most highly respectable and worthy people, who would have been horrified if they had been so unfortunate as to hear Sung's ringside comments. These were many and pointed. The gist of them all was that there was no class of persons in all China so degraded, so lost to shame, that they conducted their amours to music and in the full view of all who might care to look through the window.

When Sung retired to his virtuous couch that night he thanked his ancestral gods that he would not live to see the end of the western depravity which was sweeping through China.

Sung-li, the brother of Sung of Sung's island, though the younger of the two, had aged more completely than his brother. These many years he had owned in Anking a small but prosperous establishment making fine embroidery. Anking cross-stitch work has always been known as the most delicate needlework done in all China. Its best specimens found their way to Peking where they gladdened the eyes of the Imperial Family.

The deplorable modern tendency to depart from old and tried ways, Sung-li declaimed, had brought him to ruin. Merely because the nameless and inconsequential girls who performed these miracles with the needle were apt to go blind through close application to their work, stupid sentimentalists, prompted by interfering foreign missionaries, had killed a highly lucrative industry.

One of these girls, who had almost lost her sight in Sung-li's service, waited upon Sung and the Small General upon their arrival in Anking. For three years she had laboured incessantly upon one piece of work, a peacock, whose rainbow magnificence had been beyond praise. So delicate was the work that even a close inspection failed to reveal to any but the most discerning eye that this colour symphony was the product of the needle rather than the brush.

"The last three months of the work were most anxious," Sung-li told his brother and nephew. "There was doubt whether her eyes would last long enough to complete it. See here"—Sung-li pointed to the topmost extremity of the peacock's outspread tail—"there are a few false stitches, but few eyes would detect them. The girl did her best, so I did not scold her. Happily, enough of her sight remains for her to see a bright light. She knows her position in the house in daytime by peering towards the windows, and after nightfall there are bright hanging lanterns. They are too bright, I confess, for good taste, but with their aid she does her work well enough. . . ."

"How are you called, girl?" asked Sung benevolently.

"They call me Peahen," was the quiet reply. "It is done in mockery, I think, but I am well content with the name, for the peahen is the mother of the peacock, than which nothing is more beautiful."

Peahen was in literal truth a part of the vast human flotsam of the Yangtsze Valley. In a year of famine higher up the river the unwanted girl babies had been sold as slaves—or as many as could find buyers. Others, including Peahen, had been committed to the swirling might of the river in a roughly improvised floating cradle, made of a wooden box lashed to a few bamboos. The river in spate had washed Peahen up on to a sandspit, whence she had been rescued by a fisherman who, knowing that he might secure a dollar for his trouble, had sold the girl to Sung-li.

Put to work at the age of seven, Peahen had shown great aptitude with the needle. She would have been a very profitable investment, Sung-li told his brother, if her eyes had not failed at the age of fifteen. Now at sixteen, being a man charitably inclined, he allowed her to earn her rice as a maid-servant.

Peahen had a certain serene beauty which struck the Small General forcibly while his elders were talking of her, and in her presence, in terms of her investment value.

"Are you not sad that you cannot see?" he asked her the first time he saw her alone.

"I do not think I am sad," was the even sadder reply.

It dawned upon the Small General that sadness can only be seen against a background of happiness.

Peahen had not often heard kindly and sympathetic remarks, which is not to say that she had ever been brutally treated. It was rather that all the treatment meted out to her ever since she could remember had been cold and impersonal. She had never been permitted to regard herself as a sentient individual. She had always been just a *thing* which plied a needle skilfully. So, for those few casually spoken words, Peahen gave to the Small General a dog-like devotion. When he entered the room her face was illumined by a gentle smile. When he left it the smile was replaced by a look of expectancy, which faded to resignation if his return were long delayed.

"I give the girl to you as a gift," Sung-li told his nephew, noting the latter's interest and sympathy. "It is time you were married. She would soon make a useful servant about the house, sparing your wife's beauty a little longer from the ravages of toil. Take her, boy, and welcome."

So Peahen came down-river with Sung and the Small General, to rejoin the houseboat, which lay at Chinkiang awaiting them. Amid the terrifying activities of a Yangtsze River steamer, on which she travelled, of course, as a deck passenger, the girl knew something which approached the state generally known as happiness. She would, she had been told, serve for the future a being with a kind voice. And, since orders given kindly are so much more palatable than those given harshly, Peahen was happy, even to the extent—greatly daring—of wondering whether the owner of the voice were handsome.

There had been a time when visual beauty had been the mainspring of Peahen's life, for great works of art cannot be created by those who have not a genuine love for beauty. Now that visual beauty was but a memory, the girl found a satisfying substitute with her ears—satisfying to the degree that it helped to kill the dull and inarticulate ache for beauty which was a part of her being.

"It is well for her," observed Sung succinctly, "that she will not have to gaze upon the Old One's face as she helps in the kitchen."

On his return to his island home, Sung, who had enjoyed the trip to Anking with great zest, fell ill of his dietary indiscretions. He had never troubled with doctors in his life, but now, remembering much talk in Soochow of the wonders performed by a Chinese physician, inscribed a letter detailing his symptoms, asking for speedy relief. Three days later there arrived a box of the famous Pills of Ten Thousand Indispositions, probably no more harmful than most of the patent medicines marketed elsewhere in the world but which, even in the eyes of their most ardent admirers, must have seemed a little wide in their application.

Sung's condition rapidly worsened, greatly to the Small General's alarm. There were no proper doctors on Ta Hu and although the older man would have been content with a village quack, his son thought otherwise. His small contact with Europeans had persuaded him that, whatever might be their other shortcomings, the system of medicine practised in the West was far ahead of that practised in the East.

Taking matters into his own hands and without consulting Sung, the Small General made his father comfortable in the houseboat and set out forthwith for Soochow. At a mission hospital which shall be nameless, because there is no sectarian axe to grind, a young American doctor after a brief examination diagnosed with certainty an acute condition of the liver demanding immediate operation. Sung was by this time in a state bordering upon coma.

"Your father, I am afraid," said the young doctor, "has the Ten Thousand and First Indisposition. It is very fortunate for him that you brought him here."

The young American, whose Christianity was of the practical order, then began what he afterwards described as "the biggest excavation job of my life." Sung's belly had by this time reached truly noble proportions.

For two weeks the Small General haunted the corridors of the hospital until, after many days of acute anxiety, the American doctor announced that Sung was out of danger, but would have to remain another month to recuperate.

"How can I repay you?" asked Sung with more sincerity than the rather trite words may imply.

"Easily," said the doctor. "I will tell you how. The next time you see any human being suffering pain or sorrow, try your utmost to ease the pain and end the sorrow. You will then be—even if you do not admit it yourself—a Christian. It is the first step. Afterwards go on doing the same all your life and, when the reckoning comes I do not think it will be held against you that you did not observe all the outward forms."

The doctor laughed at the bewildered expression on the Small General's face. He understood it. Real altruism is rare enough anywhere, but it would seem that i̅n̅c̅e̅r̅i̅t̅y̅ v̅a̅r̅i̅e̅s̅ w̅i̅t̅h̅ t̅h̅e̅ the civilisation in which it grows. In China, where civilisation is very old and human motive has been laid bare for a long while, altruism is not quickly recognised for what it is.

To question such a plain and unequivocal statement is not polite—anywhere, so the Small General went away wonderingly.

That same evening, as he was eating the meal cooked for him on the houseboat by the Old One, served to him by Peahen, it occurred to the Small General that here, beside him, was a way of taking the young doctor at his face value. Peahen, who had learned to grope her way about the houseboat with the help of an extra bright hanging lamp, was feeling for dishes which the Old One had put upon a serving table between the kitchen and the saloon, when an idea struck the Small General.

Even though only a woman, he mused, this Peahen is surely a human being. She is, furthermore, a good and willing young woman. Through her I will find out whether the foreign doctor speaks truth when he says he does not love the chink of silver dollars.

It would be unkind, he felt, to say anything to Peahen in case the foreign doctor could do nothing. But in the morning, when he went to see his father, he would broach the matter.

The young doctor was at his father's bedside when he reached the hospital the next day.

"Your respected father has made a wonderful recovery," said the young American in stilted Soochow dialect.

The Small General, who believed he spoke English better than the doctor spoke his own tongue, did not reveal the fact, for he did not want to be tactless.

Sung, who had been about to say something, fell asleep before he could say it.

"Touching the matter of payment for your kind offices," said the Small General, "there is a young woman outside, a servant of our family, whose eyes see but dimly. I think she would be very happy if she were made to see. Is it possible, think you, that you could give her sight?"

"How can I say?" asked the doctor. "I have not seen her. Bring her to my surgery and I will do whatever is possible."

The Small General could hardly repress a smile at the novelty of the arrangement. Who ever heard of a man who had done a piece of work being paid for it by being given more work to do, also for nothing?

The following morning the Old One, who had grown to love Peahen as a mother loves a daughter, dressed the girl in her best for the visit to the foreign doctor. Her best was no finery, but it was clean and neat.

"Why do I go to the foreign doctor?" she asked the Small General.

"Because he is a very skilled man. Has he not healed my respected father who was dying?"

"But I am not ill!" protested the girl.

"Nevertheless, it is a fine thing to see a foreign doctor," said the Small General, ending the discussion. He did not want to raise false hopes in the girl's heart.

Before the morning was over three foreign doctors had peered into Peahen's eyes with strange-looking instruments, consulted together in a corner, and had then begun the examination all over again. Through it all the girl remained patiently quiet.

"She has been a sew-sew girl?" asked one of the doctors.

The Small General nodded.

"We think we can restore her sight," said the doctor who had operated upon Sung, taking the Small General apart into a private room. "But before we do so there are certain instruments which must be bought. We are not a rich hospital. Is it possible that you can pay for these?"

The doctor knew nothing whatsoever of the means of the Sung family, for neither father nor son dressed with any ostentation.

"And the cost?" asked the Small General.

"Between two and three hundred dollars, probably nearer three hundred," was the reply.

"Do you think I am an idiot?" asked the Small General in shocked surprise. "For three hundred dollars I could go into the famine area and buy a hundred girls, any one of whom would make a better servant than this girl. In Honan, they tell me, girl children may be bought for as little as fifty cents."

"And then," one of the doctors muttered under his breath, "there are those who say that China has undergone a change of heart since the Revolution."

"Yesterday," said the young American doctor, "when I told

you that your respected father was on the road to complete recovery, do you remember what you said?"

"Of course I remember," replied the Small General.

"You asked me, did you not, how you could repay me?"

"I did!"

"I told you how, did I not?"

"You did," replied the Small General, a suspicion of indignation in his voice. "And because of what you said I have brought this girl. I confess I thought it a strange way of repaying you. But the idea was yours. I will take the girl away . . ."

"Yesterday you were prepared to pay money, were you not, or you would not have asked me?" said the doctor.

"Yesterday I would have given you anything you asked, if it had lain within my power."

"Then why not today?"

"I have paid you for the healing of my father by bringing you the girl, have I not? Then what would be the sense of paying you three hundred dollars to heal the girl's eyes? I should not be able to hold up my head for shame. It would be said of me that I valued a servant girl's eyes at a greater price than my honoured father's life. How could any dutiful son bear such shame?"

"But you are still prepared to pay for the healing of your father?" persisted the young American.

"Most assuredly," replied the Small General. "If you have repented your bargain I am, nevertheless, most grateful. Put a price upon the healing of my father and, if we have it, you shall be paid. There may be a day or so of delay if the price be too great, but no more. That I promise and we Sungs do not break our promises."

"Very well," said the doctor with a smile. "The price of healing your father is three hundred dollars. Can you pay it?"

"I did not come here to be insulted," said the Small General very haughtily. "I trust also that I have been courteous, for it has been my only thought. If the price for healing the servant girl was three hundred dollars, the price for healing my father must be greater. My father is Sung, of Sung's island."

"Very well," said the young American doctor patiently, "now that I understand these matters, the price of healing your father shall be raised to one thousand dollars. Is that agreed?"

"It is agreed. Once more I would say that I am most grateful.

Now I will go to find the thousand dollars and will take the servant girl with me."

"No, do not take her," said the doctor gently. "We will keep her here and will restore her sight if we can."

"But what do you want with her? The price of the healing of my father will be paid within the hour. I brought the girl to you because I thought yesterday that to bring her would please you. Now you say you want her. Before I leave I would wish it to be understood that when the price of my father's healing is paid, as it will be within the hour, I have no further obligation towards you. Or, if I have any further obligation, I would like it to be stated now. What is more, I will pay no three hundred dollars for the healing of the girl's eyes."

"It will not be necessary—now," smiled the young doctor, "for with the thousand dollars you are going to pay we shall be able to buy the instruments to heal the girl's eyes, and, we hope, the eyes of many other poor people. With the remaining seven hundred dollars we shall buy nourishing foods for many hundreds who come to us for help. . . ."

The Small General bowed profoundly and made his departure.

"Let me out of this mad house!" he said fiercely to the porter at the main door of the hospital. "How thankful I am that I have no business dealings with these foreigners, for they make a bargain one minute and break it the next."

The Small General had no money of his own so he went to his father's old friend Lok-kai-shing, who at once sent a messenger to the bank for the sum required. This was brought in shining new silver dollars. These Lok's cashiers sorted into rouleaux, wrapping each rouleau in richly embroidered silk. These in turn were put into a silk-lined box. With this box, slung from a bamboo pole between two coolies, the Small General made his way back to the hospital.

"Here is the price of my father's healing!" he said with dignity. "I make you a free will gift of the servant girl also."

"That you cannot do," said the doctor, no longer smiling. "She, like you and me, belongs to God. If, when we have healed her, which by God's mercy I hope we shall, she wishes to remain here, we will keep her. But the choice is hers."

"As you please!" remarked the Small General with indifference, bowing to all three doctors and making a dignified exit.

93

This last was not easy for, coming unexpectedly upon a set of quite new standards of conduct, he was feeling bewildered and, inexplicably, cheap. These foreigners did strange things which seemed absurd, but there was no gainsaying the truth that they had saved his father's life. And yet, what a fuss about an almost worthless slave girl!

Feeling that he could now do so with decency, since his father was on the highroad to recovery, the Small General spent a night with one of the famous Soochow beauties, whose soft and clinging arms were skilled in the arts of coaxing foolish sums of money from the old and rich merchants who vied for her favours.

8

WHEN Sung returned from hospital to his island home a great change had been wrought in him. The magnificent belly, generally conceded to have been the finest on all Ta Hu, had gone. Where it had been there now flapped, empty and useless, an apron of wrinkled flesh as the only reminder of the distended paunch which for years had hidden its owner's feet from his eyes.

Of the once jovial and fleshy face was left only the memory. Sung now presented to the world a refined, almost ascetic face. It was now possible to see the bone formation of his head. He would perhaps have been recognised by one who knew him in youth, but certainly never by his friends of middle and late life.

But, despite the ravages of age and illness, Sung was happy. He had watched his son, the Small General, at first discontentedly, later with resignation and at last with pride and joy, fit himself to take over the small island kingdom which dead and gone generations of Sungs had sweated to dig from the lake bottom. If he were to die without warning, Sung reflected happily, his son was already a fit and proper successor. There was further cause for happiness in the reflection that a daughter of his old friend Lok would be the mother of the Small General's children.

In a cane chair, lashed to two bamboo poles, and carried by poor relations, Sung made his first tour of inspection of the island since his return. Although disposed to be critical, he could find no fault with his son's stewardship.

For several years there had been no mention of the girl student in Shanghai, with whom the Small General had once dreamed dreams of building a new China. Sung shuddered as he thought of what life would be like with a scholar for wife.

But during the prolonged absence of Sung and his son, strange things had occurred on the island, reminiscent of the days when unheralded visitors had arrived in quest of Sung's secret, with the difference that those earlier visitors had come openly.

95

It is a very human failing to be gullible. The dupes of spiritualists, for example, when confronted with indisputable proof that they have been duped, more often than not prefer to remain dupes. Probably in some devious fashion vanity is involved, for very few humans care to admit that they have been deceived.

Among such as these was Matsudara, ex-manager in Soochow of the Fureno Trading Company's interests.

When it became apparent to the shrewd brains controlling the House of The Three Bamboos in Tokyo that, despite their shrewdness, they had been duped by either Lok-kai-shing, Sung or Matsudara in the matter of the purchase of Lok-kai-shing's small mulberry plantation, they cut their losses, which were heavy, and remained silent.

They deemed, rightly, that Matsudara had been tricked, rather than that he had betrayed his employers. Since the Furenos did not care to allow too many people the privilege of laughing at them in their discomfiture, it was decided that, instead of dismissing Matsudara in summary fashion, the latter should be translated to some other sphere of activity under the Fureno banner. Matsudara was thereupon sent as book-keeper to one of the Fureno salmon canneries in Saghalin. There, if he showed a disposition to chatter, it would be easy to silence him.

Now the said Matsudara was not so naïve as not to know that he had been duped. That he was forced to admit—to himself. But he still believed, several years after the event, that the secret for which he had paid out large sums of his employers' money did in fact exist, even though he had so signally failed to secure it.

During the years of colourless exile in Saghalin these thoughts haunted Matsudara's waking and sleeping hours. Far away to the south on a small island in Lake Ta Hu, he was convinced, reposed a secret process, or processes, which would revolutionise the silk industry of the world.

For more than fifty years the silk industry as a whole had been threatened by extinction as, even in the most socially-backward countries, the cost of living and the level of wages had been rising steadily.

In a world which paid as much regard to the dignity and decency of living conditions among the toiling masses as it did to the apparently more important fact that a privileged few should be able to clothe themselves in smooth, sleek, silken garments, there would be no silk industry permitted to exist. *It is not possible to produce raw silk under conditions which give to the worker anything remotely like fair living and working conditions.* To buy a silken garment in this age is to become an active ally and accomplice of slave-owners.

Every single process in the production of raw silk is a hand process. No machine has been devised to shorten the weary tasks performed by underpaid labour. An increase in wages, which the western peoples would call microscopic, would in all probability raise the cost of raw silk to the point where world consumers would find it too costly. The silk industry would thereupon die, as those who know it best hope it will die.

Matsudara, who was fully aware of these things, was obsessed by the belief that on Sung's island there had been evolved some means of producing three silk cocoons with the same area of land, the same number of mulberry trees and the same number of underpaid workers which elsewhere, so long experience had shown, produced only two silk cocoons. Such a discovery would give the silk industry of Japan another century of life, perhaps, against the rising tide of wages and living costs. Japan relied upon the silk industry to finance her war-like plans which, even in the early nineteen-twenties, were looming over the horizon.

If he, Matsudara, were the man to bring this priceless secret to Japan, what rewards might he not expect at the hands of a grateful Emperor and people? The vision dazzled him to the exclusion of all else.

By this time the House of The Three Bamboos had forgotten Matsudara. Time had destroyed his capacity to harm them by making them look ridiculous. So, when Matsudara's resignation was offered on grounds of ill-health, the event did not cause a ripple within the organisation. He left Saghalin on the next Fureno steamer to call there for a cargo of canned salmon.

That, insofar as the House of The Three Bamboos was concerned, was the end of Matsudara. Fureno tools had to be sharp if they wished to avoid the rubbish heap.

Matsudara had learned only one thing from his visits to Sung's island and his subsequent conversations with some of Sung's poor relations, who were the chief labour force of the island: he had learned that these poor relations bore very little love for Sung, of whom they were very envious.

97

Without this item of information, since Matsudara was an Asiatic, he would have used the time-honoured method of bribery, Asia's traditional short-cut to the heart of almost any problem. Between the Levantine countries and the Pacific one does not ask "Will he accept a bribe?" but "How large a bribe will he demand?"

In Hangchow, where he was unknown, Matsudara rented a comfortable houseboat and set out for Lake Ta Hu in the guise of an artist bent on pleasure. He was, in fact, a water-colourist of no mean attainments, so his behaviour lent verisimilitude to his professed purpose.

For over a week he lurked in the vicinity of Sung's island before he encountered one of Sung's nephews, a surly youth who had previously accepted small bribes from him for quite useless pieces of information, as events had turned out. This Sung-wah, as Matsudara remembered, had spoken very spitefully of his employer and uncle.

Sung-wah was out cormorant-fishing for pleasure and the table, when he was hailed from the houseboat. Having a good catch, and believing that here was some foreigner who would pay a good price for fish, he came aboard with his basket. Matsudara, under pretext of examining the fish, drew Sung-wah aft out of earshot of the houseboat crew.

"Your respected uncle, Sung, is well?" asked the Japanese.

"He is in a Soochow hospital where, I hope, they will cut out his heart!" was the reply.

"You bear no great love for him, it seems."

"Why should I bear love for an uncle who, although very rich, treats his blood relations like common coolies?"

"Indeed, why should you?" agreed Matsudara soothingly.

It was agreed between these two that, three days hence, when almost everyone on the island would be away at a wedding feast nearby, Matsudara should come to Sung's island, there to see everything he wished to see. In a few hours, he believed, provided there were no interruptions, he could fathom the secret which had baffled him earlier.

Matsudara was very thorough. After inspecting every process and finding nothing unusual, he packed into a small valise a few of the silkworms and some fresh mulberry leaves. From six different spots in the island he took soil samples, together with samples of the manure which lay in heaps ready to be applied to the mulberry trees. These he would have analysed. There was logic in this, for unless Sung had evolved some entirely new species of silkworm, which could subsist upon a smaller bulk of food than any other known, the secret must lie in some means of making a mulberry tree produce more fresh leaves in a given time than any other tree had ever been known to produce.

After taking many photographs, both outside and in the silkworm rearing houses, Matsudara paid Sung-wah the agreed bribe and left the island, arranging to meet him two miles away the following evening.

At this second meeting Matsudara elicited the information that while there undoubtedly was some secret which enabled Sung to have prospered so mightily, it was Sung-wah's belief that only his uncle possessed the secret.

News had just been received that Sung was about to return home. It seemed probable to Matsudara that, fearing his secret would die with him, Sung had communicated it to his eldest son, or that if he had not done so, he would surely do so in the very near future. Giving Sung-wah an address in Hangchow which would find him, Matsudara left the vicinity of the island, promising Sung's treacherous nephew a large sum of money for further information.

Red Tiger, king of the Ta Hu pirates, was now an old man who seldom left his comfortable mountain retreat on the west side of the lake. When he did so it was merely to visit old friends. He still controlled all piratical operations, but took no active part in them beyond keeping in his own hands all the channels of information which enabled the very hazardous profession of pirate to remain relatively safe. Good staff work is as important to a pirate as it is to a general in the field.

Red Tiger sat pleasurably in the evening sunshine smoking a few pipes of opium prepared for him by his oldest granddaughter. Opium, he found, sharpened his wits when used moderately.

In one hand was a small slip of paper inscribed with a few Chinese characters. He read it for the third and fourth times:

"The monkey with the gold teeth once more concerns himself with Sung's island. Sung-wah eats his bribes."

The missive came, as Red Tiger knew by a device in one corner, from a reputedly blind beggar who sat beside the Bubbling Gold water-gate in Hangchow, observing all who passed.

Word had already reached Red Tiger that his old friend Sung was now recovered and was on his way home. Very little happened on and around Ta Hu which did not come to Red Tiger's sharp ears.

It was the hour of sunset when Red Tiger's fast sailing *sampan* sighted Sung's island after an exhilarating sail across the width of the lake. At various points en route apparently casual fishermen rose to their feet and with pre-arranged signals from their small craft told Red Tiger that he might proceed in safety. One man waved his arms, another hauled up a lateen sail to half its height, while a third released three cormorants simultaneously. To obviate confusion and the chance of treachery, each watcher had a different signal. It was by the exercise of this methodical care that Red Tiger had always eluded the authorities over the years. When some two years previously the commander of a power-propelled launch, armed with a quick-firing gun and called by the press a gunboat, had opened fire upon a perfectly innocent fishing-boat, drowning all hands, Red Tiger by his silence had helped the commander to establish his quite fictitious claim that the pirate leader had been killed.

"The search for a dead pirate is less careful than the search for a live one!" had been Red Tiger's sage refusal to allow his followers to contradict the news of his death, until even the gallant commander of the gunboat began to believe that by some amazing stroke of fortune his lying report had turned out to be true. The people of the islands and the lakeside, of course, knew the truth, but whether from fear, or loyalty, their mouths were tightly buttoned. One day the boastful gunboat commander would be made to pay for his impudence, but there was no hurry.

So, there being no watch, Red Tiger made his way in peace and safety to Sung's island to felicitate his old friend on his recovery and, less pleasantly, to warn him of certain matters.

It was unfortunate for Sung-wah that he should encounter Red Tiger face-to-face as the latter stepped ashore for, as the pirate said to Sung a few minutes later: "A man who will betray his own family will not hesitate to betray me. There is, let it not be for-

100

gotten, a price of five thousand dollars on my head, and I have no fancy to sell my head in order to make him a rich man."

When Red Tiger had told his story Sung nodded sadly.

"Bring your cousin here," he ordered the Small General. "We owe it to him to hear what he has to say, for he is a Sung."

Sung-wah's bearing spoke more eloquently than words when, wide-eyed with fear, he was dragged into the presence of Sung and Red Tiger. The wretched man looked round the circle of accusing faces, seeing only the cold glint of anger. He did not waste words by denying his guilt, but hung his head ashamedly as Red Tiger taxed him with his perfidy.

"Where is the monkey with the gold teeth?" asked Sung.

"He is in Hangchow, awaiting word from me. . . ."

"You were to write to him, or go to him?"

"I was to write."

"Then write you shall," interposed Red Tiger. "I would have speech with this man of Japan, for I have not forgotten that he offered me a bribe to steal the son of my friend Sung."

When paper, ink and brush had been found, Red Tiger dictated a cryptic note which read: "That which was hidden is uncovered. Come the fourth night after the full moon."

"What of me?" asked Sung-wah fearfully when he had written the note.

Red Tiger looked expectantly at Sung, waiting for him to draw his hand across his throat. The pirate did not waste words. When the expected sign did not come he knew that Sung would not have the blood of a member of his family upon his hands.

"I have a safe place for him," said Red Tiger. "I will take him with me this night. When it is no longer important that he be held, I will see that he is put aboard a ship going to a far place."

During his sojourn in Hangchow Matsudara, who was a stranger to the city, lodged in a European-style hotel on the West Lake, where he deemed it unlikely that he would encounter anyone he knew. By chance there was staying at the same hotel a Danish official of the Chinese Maritime Customs, recently transferred from Soochow, where he had known Matsudara by sight.

On the following day, by an unlucky chance for Matsudara, this Dane was called upon in the course of his duties to inspect a consignment of Japanese goods landed at Ningpo by a Fureno ship and forwarded by rail under Customs seal to Hangchow.

During the idle conversation which took place while the crates of goods were being opened for inspection, the Dane remarked to one of the Fureno employees present that he had seen Matsudara the previous evening, and asked whether this meant that he had come to take charge of the Hangchow office.

The remark was promptly forgotten—by the Dane who, the inspection completed and the duty paid, went on his way. Before nightfall, however, Matsudara's presence in Hangchow was known to the manager of the Fureno Trading Company and by him the news was passed on to the Japanese Consul, with whom he dined that evening. Because of what had gone before, for Matsudara's disgrace was known to all Fureno employees, it was deemed wise to pass on to Tokyo the fact of his presence. The news was telegraphed, with the result that by the following afternoon the Japanese Consul in Hangchow had been ordered to set a careful watch upon Matsudara, to report the names of those with whom he was in contact and to ascertain discreetly why he was in the city. This was done at the simple request of the Fureno organisation in Tokyo and as a matter of routine.

If Matsudara in the course of the next few days did not report himself officially at the Japanese Consulate, in conformity with standing orders to all Japanese subjects in foreign countries, he would be liable to heavy penalties. To have even a thought, or intention, without declaring it to the proper authority is a serious crime.

At this point there was no suspicion whatever attaching to Matsudara and the action taken was pure routine on the part of the smooth-working Japanese organisation in China.

At the end of a week Matsudara had spoken to nobody except the hotel servants and had received no letters, nor had he reported to the Consulate. His name was transferred from a white to a pink card-index, which meant in effect that he was now an object of suspicion.

On the ninth day one of the Japanese secret police reported to the Consulate with news.

"I saw the man in conversation with the *laodah* of a house-boat," he reported. "When he had left I bribed the *laodah* to tell me what he had said. I learned that he has hired the houseboat for two weeks and that he will go to Lake Ta Hu to paint pictures."

For a bribe of fifty dollars the *laodah* of the houseboat agreed to include an unknown Chinese in his crew. The Chinese was in the employ of the Japanese secret police.

Matsudara's activities on Lake Ta Hu have already been described in some detail, but three days after his return to Hangchow, they were being read in very much greater detail, by none other than Baron Fureno himself in the House of The Three Bamboos in Tokyo, the nerve centre of the whole Fureno commercial empire.

From that hour Matsudara could not sigh in his sleep without the fact being noted. The Fureno organisation, which had once written him off as a fool, now believed that he had used Fureno money to buy for himself an immensely valuable secret. Outside Japan every resource of the Japanese diplomatic and consular services was, and had been for many years, at the disposal of the multifarious Fureno ramifications. A request from the House of The Three Bamboos, however politely phrased, was an order.

Suspicion did not become certainty in the minds of those who arranged for Matsudara to be kept under close surveillance until a cryptic letter, addressed to him at his hotel, was intercepted and a photostatic copy made before it was delivered.

They gave him time to arrange for the hire of the same houseboat, thus providing a link in the chain of evidence against him. Then they pounced, as a cat pounces upon a mouse.

Under the extra-territorial jurisdiction, the Japanese consular authorities were answerable to nobody, except their own government, in their treatment of a Japanese subject. The Chinese authorities were as powerless in the matter as they were completely uninterested. A Japanese subject was reported to them as having disappeared from his hotel. They informed the Japanese Consul, who took note of what they said, and appeared to forget the incident.

In a back room of the Japanese Consulate Matsudara was given a foretaste of what was to come. At first they beat him, renewing the beatings every hour. Then they did unmentionable things to him, things calculated to break a man's moral resistance, to sap every spark of courage from him. When they had finished with him there was not one least nook or cranny in his soul, one tiny inconsequential memory back to childhood, which he was not ready to reveal when they should begin to question him. The short span of life which was left to Matsudara was just a mist of searing pain.

They were very thorough and they knew their work, these men of the secret police. When they questioned a man, after proper preparation for questioning, he did not lie, for he could not; he did not withhold anything, for to withhold something signifies possession of a will and an individuality. By the time two of the great ones of the Fureno organisation arrived in Hangchow from Tokyo, in order to be present at the questioning, Matsudara had forgotten that he ever was a man. He was just a vehicle for pain.

"That which was hidden is uncovered," quoted one of the questioners in the polite and formal tones of an examiner. "Tell me what is this something which was hidden and is now uncovered?"

"It is the means by which a certain Chinese named Sung is able to produce more silk than his neighbours," replied Matsudara in a completely toneless voice, almost as though he were an automaton.

"The same Sung who lives on an island in Ta Hu who, with the aid of Lok the silk merchant, brought you to great folly some years ago?"

"The same."

"Who wrote this letter?"

"Sung-wah, a nephew of the same Sung, who hates his uncle."

"What is the secret?"

"I do not know."

The last question was not repeated, for they knew that it was the bare truth. Matsudara would never tell another lie.

"You were planning to go to Ta Hu to see this Sung-wah?"

"I was."

"Where and when would you have met him?"

"A little before midnight on the evening of the fourth night after the full moon. I would have waited about two miles to the north of the island and he would have come to me."

"Do you believe that this Sung-wah has filched the secret from his uncle?"

"I believe it."

"You believe, then, that there *is* a secret to filch?"

"I believe it. I have always believed it."

Matsudara had ceased to be useful, for he had told all he knew.

Silk had brought Matsudara to his undoing. It was as though fine strands of silk were woven through the pattern of his destiny, for it was a silken noose which, upon a curt signal from the questioners, strangled him. In the same room was a zinc-lined case. They thrust his still limp body into it. They fastened the case carefully. The Japanese Consul withdrew from his pocket a label, already prepared, which one of those present affixed to the chest. When the consular seal had been attached the chest, marked "Consular Papers—Urgent", was sent by the next train to Shanghai. Thence, by a Fureno ship, it went to Tokyo, where a clerk, having noted a secret annotation on the label, knew what to do with it.

Not a few such cases returned every year from China, filled with the broken remains of men—and women—who had been foolish enough to suppose that Japan, on conquest bent, permitted her sons and daughters to behave, or speak, or even think, in unorthodox fashion.

Sometimes those who went to Japan in zinc-lined boxes were not Japanese. They were just careless or unfortunate persons who knew too much.

The houseboat approached the Bubbling Gold water-gate at Hangchow in the easy fashion of its kind, waiting its turn with all manner of craft leaving Hangchow on their several errands. Most were returning to the country empty, having brought their loads of fresh vegetables in the morning. A few were on pleasure bent. Some, deep-laden and unwieldy, carried a turgid cargo of sewage, causing strong stomachs to turn over as they passed. Only the country people taking the sewage back to their farms seemed indifferent to the vile stenches. A few even appeared to like it, but their apparent liking was in reality a recognition of the truth that the crowded cities must pay their tribute to the soil if they want its fruits.

It was the same houseboat which had taken Matsudara to Ta Hu, but this time it was taking a different route. After some bargaining, the passengers had arranged to take their own crew. Once clear of the city, it had been arranged for a small motorboat to meet them, so that the tedious journey could be shortened.

A strange arrangement when, to all appearances, the party was on pleasure bound. But then, as the watchers from the banks well knew, the Japanese had strange tastes.

The blind beggar by the Bubbling Gold water-gate, whose keen eyes beneath half-closed lids missed nothing, watched them pass: six smiling Japanese gentlemen taking a holiday on the water, nodding pleasurably as the portable gramophone on the deck played to them a tinkling record of *samisen* music from Tokyo. One of the party was pouring from a frost-encrusted bottle the golden "Asahi" beer, perhaps to remind them of home.

The blind beggar shuffled away from his customary seat, disappearing into the crowd. He might have been seen a few minutes later in the back premises of a rice dealer, writing a note which was destined to reach Ta Hu before the party of pleasure-seeking Japanese.

"Six monkeys," the message ran, "but not gold teeth are coming."

They were, indeed, a strange company for a pleasure cruise on Lake Ta Hu, but no stranger than the cargo they carried below deck. Four of the party were just ordinary gunmen of the Japanese secret police, hard-faced ruthless killers, disciplined until there was left to them no individuality, no passion and no fear. In all circumstances they would carry out orders, or die trying to do so.

More interesting, perhaps because more intelligent, were the other two Japanese. Probably no two men living at the time had a wider or more profound knowledge of the scientific aspects of silk production. Their interest in and knowledge of silk ended at the point where the gossamer strands were wound off the cocoons. The older of the two men was Professor Shidehara, a benign-looking scholarly man in his sixties, who three days previously had been routed from his bed in the early hours of the morning and into a special train, sent for him to take him to the *Yamashiro Maru*, held at Nagasaki for his arrival. In Shanghai the Consul-General's car had taken him to the Hangchow train, where a private compartment had been reserved.

The younger man, Professor Suzuki, perhaps forty years of age, wore the same air of scholarly aloofness, heightened by a slight stoop and gold-rimmed pince-nez.

The main saloon of the boat was filled with specimen cases and all manner of scientific equipment, which the two savants were anxious to use. They were sceptical of what they had heard, naturally enough. The possibility that three silk cocoons could be produced where two had been produced before seemed to them very remote. Either one of them, upon evolving a way to produce twenty cocoons where nineteen had been produced before, could have asked his Emperor for almost any honour within his gift.

Silk was Japan's life blood. Her position in the world's markets amounted almost to a monopoly, the nearest Japan was ever likely to approach a monopoly of any commodity in general demand. Those who wanted Japan's silk had to pay Japan's price. Women who demanded that their legs be encased in sheer silk stockings; men who insisted upon pure silk ties, pure silk linings to their suits (and their numbers were growing beyond calculation)—were all contributing their quota to the grandiose schemes Japan was planning under their noses. With the help of silk Japan would conquer the world. Let her silk industry die and Japan would die too.

Small wonder, therefore, that the hearts of these two great scientists beat faster as they contemplated the possibilities implicit in the discoveries said to have been made by a little Chinese farmer on a lonely island in Ta Hu. If a few lives had to be taken it would be a pity, but each of these kindly-looking and scholarly men was agreed that even ten thousand lives, if it were necessary, should not be permitted to stand between them and this discovery—if it were a discovery. Their coldly logical and scientific minds refused to accept the hypothesis which had brought them on this long and hurried journey, until they had had the opportunity to sift the evidential wheat from the tares. Nevertheless, and this they would admit from their knowledge of their fellow men, it was unlikely that such a one as Baron Fureno himself would have set in motion the forces which were responsible for their presence on the houseboat, unless he had some solid ground for believing that a Chinese peasant had stumbled upon a discovery, which had eluded diligent investigators over more than four thousand years, culminating in Professors Shidehara and Suzuki themselves.

The fussy motor-boat, emitting clouds of blue smoke, towed the houseboat to where a canal debouched on to Lake Ta Hu, in about half the time which rowers, sweating on the *ulohs*, would have taken. At the last camel-back bridge before the lake was reached a beggar, revealing bleeding stumps where legs had been, whined for alms.

"I have in my case a phial and a needle which would put an end to his cries," observed Professor Shidehara regretfully. "It is a pity that it cannot be used."

"All China cries out for our civilising influence," said Professor Suzuki almost piously. "Happily, it will not be long now."

"I cannot help thinking," said Professor Shidehara, a faraway look in his eyes, "how unlikely it is that a people so degraded as are these Chinese, have made any discovery regarding silk which has escaped us, the Superior People. We will, of course, make our investigations, but even before we begin them, I am oppressed by doubts. Some years ago, when this matter was first mooted, I read such evidence as there was on the subject, but there was nothing with the smallest appeal to a scientific mind. . . ."

As soon as the lake shore had receded a little way and there was no chance of being overlooked, the four hard-faced gunmen brought on deck a handsome leather suitcase. From it they extracted the parts of a machine-gun, which they began to assemble. This done, they fell to cleaning their pistols, which were already unreasonably clean.

"Do the noble gentlemen understand the use of pistols?" asked the leader of the four gunmen, bowing profoundly to the professors.

"We do not," replied Professor Shidehara. "They are for you to use. We will use our own tools."

The gunman bowed. A silence fell over the boat except for the chugging of the motor-boat which was towing the party across Ta Hu at some four knots.

Ta Hu is a lovely stretch of water, between forty and fifty miles across at its greatest length and width. It is very shallow. Sudden windstorms can lash it to fury, almost without warning, making shallow-draught vessels, the only type which can ply its waters, dangerous and unmanageable.

It is small wonder that since before the dawn of history men have paid obeisance to the Elements. So many high human ventures have gone astray because of storms, that with most it has become instinctive to scan the horizon, even to those who are not weather-wise and cannot interpret the signs rightly.

The Japanese, strangers all to Ta Hu, looked around the sunset sky and saw, for their vision was limited, a perfect evening for their task. The Chinese *laodah,* now in the employ of the Japanese secret police, had been born on the shores of Ta Hu. He looked across to the West and what he saw did not comfort him. The sky was too clear. The colours lit by the sinking sun were too bright, too transparent. It amazed the weather-wise *laodah* that the others could not read danger from its very innocence.

Except for the hills to the West, the houseboat was now out of sight of land. In a little while the lights on the large island of Tung Dung should become visible. The *laodah* hoped it would be possible to run under the lee of the island before the storm broke.

"A great storm is coming," he told the professors.

"Do not talk like a fearful child," said Shidehara, smiling his superior smile.

"It is a judgment on me for selling myself to these Japanese apes!" muttered the *laodah* between his teeth, resolving firmly at the same time that if a chance presented itself, he would not be among the missing that night.

9

ON SUNG'S island the fourth day after the full moon dawned just like any other day. A fairy mist hung over the lake, softening all outlines and giving the promise, when it should lift, of another burning summer's day.

The Small General, from long habit, was an early riser. He stood smiling with contentment on the foreshore as a lad, his cousin, marshalled the older ducks, led now by another drake, and prepared to open the pen where thousands of piping ducklings clamoured for release, longing to be out on some nearby mudbank where a kind providence placed so many succulent morsels to delight small ducklings.

Signalling to the new general of the ducklings to get into his *sampan* and row clear of the shore, the Small General opened the pen himself, watching the old familiar stampede as he had known it years before when as an almost naked small boy it had been his daily task.

The ducklings were young for the long swim ahead, but there was no choice, for the mudbanks in the immediate vicinity of the island had been stripped bare of everything edible. Incredible as it may sound, the chief cause of mortality among ducklings is drowning. Before they grow their full waterproof plumage their down is small protection against water. When it becomes sodden its wearer becomes chilled. A chilled duckling is very nearly a dead duckling.

The Small General watched the flock out of sight into the mist and then he turned back to the land which he had learned to love so well. The mulberries looked so trim and neat, every tree pruned in accordance with an old custom which enabled it to produce as much leaf and as little wood as possible. Except between the interstices of ancient stone paving, the Small General believed, there was not a weed of any kind growing on the small island.

Beyond the mulberries were two rows of huge white Savoy cabbages, sleek and shining in the morning dew, their hearts as hard as wood, so tightly had they grown. These would have to be cut in the cool of the evening, to be shipped during the hours of darkness to the market in Soochow which, in the greedy fashion of cities, engulfed all that the countryside could grow. They were the pride of the Small General's eyes, those great Savoys. They would be the first on the market. The seed bed had been sheltered from the cold winds of Spring by means of a thick layer of rice straw laid on its surface and a fence of bamboo on the windward side. Now they would command a great price. A week hence there would be a *sampan*-load of fine cauliflowers, ahead of their season by the same means.

The Small General, now close to the soil which his ancestors had so laboriously created, laughed at his own youthful follies of a few years previously, when Sung's island had seemed too small a world for him. As always, his father had been right. There was a deep contentment in this peaceful spot, which he never could have found in the tawdry life of Shanghai or the other great cities. The Small General knelt on the moist warm earth and, thrusting his arm down to elbow depth in the deeply-worked tilth, looked instinctively in the direction of the ancestral grave mounds, while inarticulate thanks tried vainly to find expression.

At that moment, with no less ferocity of determination than he had once known to quit the humdrum daily round of the island, the Small General resolved firmly that here he would, as his forbears had done, make his life and, when it was come to the end, take his place yonder among those others.

But it is events, not high resolutions, which shape human destiny. Events were, even then, converging upon the island and its people, events which would make human resolves look almost as foolish as they generally are.

The Old One had no sooner thrust into the Small General's hand a bowl of hot tea, than from the lake, still shrouded in mist, there came a hail. Taking a wooden mallet, he beat a low-toned gong, whose notes were like those of an organ. The sound would give the newcomer his bearings. Ten minutes later, the mast of the *sampan* lowered, and the craft itself hidden among rushes, Red Tiger strode towards the house at the head of a dozen men.

"Word has come to me that you will have visitors today," said

Red Tiger. "My men and I will help to give them a suitable welcome. Your honoured father is awake?"

"He sleeps late since he has returned from the hospital," replied the Small General. "But he will be happy to see you, his old friend."

"Perhaps not so happy when he hears my news," retorted Red Tiger with a grunt, but without further explanation. His news was first of all for the ears of Sung.

"The Old One shall prepare food!" said the Small General, knowing better than to ask questions. At the best of times Red Tiger was a taciturn man and it was obvious by the size of his escort that something of moment was afoot. It was also obvious that that something concerned Sung's island primarily, for Red Tiger was too good a friend to involve others in his piratical ventures. With these deductions the Small General had to be content.

Red Tiger waited outside the house until the mist had lifted.

"See yonder fishing-boat," he said, pointing to where a small craft lay about two miles off-shore. "Post a watcher with sharp eyes. Tell the watcher when he sees the sail hoisted to the mast-head, lowered and then hoisted again, to call me. I go now to eat. I will sleep until I am called, or until your honoured father awakes."

Red Tiger's escort, all younger men than himself, evidently were not in such need of sleep, for they sat around under the shade of a few peach trees, chatting in low tones and taking no notice of others. Each man was armed with an ancient muzzle-loading gun. Twice, as the Small General passed them, he noticed that, from a sack which they had brought ashore with them, they were wrapping in paper cylinders enough brass scrap and filings to fit the muzzles of their ancient weapons. The paper wrappings were, evidently, to make loading a more rapid process.

There was in the house a cheap hammer gun of Belgian manufacture which the Small General used after the rice harvest, when the snipe were heavy on the wing. The few cartridges remaining were filled with small bird shot. The Small General removed this, placing in its stead jagged pieces of lead cut from a section of piping. These missiles at a range up to thirty yards would disembowel a water buffalo.

Sung's island was ready for what the day might bring.

An hour before sunset a watcher in the fork of a tree reported that the agreed signal had been given by the fishing-boat lying off shore. At about the same time Red Tiger, his nostrils distended, said: "There will be big wind soon."

Sung puffed contentedly at his opium pipe, inhaling great gulps of the acrid smoke with relish.

"I think, my good friend," he said easily to Red Tiger, "that you exaggerate the possible dangers. I know this Japanese. I outwitted him once and, I have no doubt, I can do so again."

"I dare say," replied Red Tiger with a quiet smile of amusement, "that if I had just smoked my seventh pipe this evening, I might also fall into your error. Because I did not wish unduly to alarm you, I have not mentioned certain matters. I will mention them now. Firstly, Sung-wah's letter to Matsudara was intercepted by the Japanese secret police, who seized him immediately. It is they, and not Matsudara, who will keep this evening's appointment. They bring with them two men of scholarly appearance. Below decks are many cases. These were too well guarded for my men to look at them. I know much of the other men. They would kill as lightly as they eat a bowl of rice. They are come determined to wrest from you the secret of your island. It has brought you much wealth, this secret, but tonight it brings trouble."

"We are prepared to meet trouble with trouble," said the Small General, patting his Belgian gas-pipe. "Before it grows dark, Red Tiger, what are your orders for me and my men? We are all ready to do your bidding."

"It begins to look as though the wind will solve our problem for us," said the pirate. "According to the signal, which was passed by a chain of my boats right across the lake, the Japanese are in the very middle of the lake now. The wind will bear down upon them within the hour. It will find them not less than an hour from the nearest land. I will take my men now and go to meet them. When we meet the Japanese they will be glad of our help. . . ."

"Why help them?" asked Sung. "Surely it is simpler to let them drown?"

"It will not serve us to let them drown, old friend. If they drown more will come, and more, and more. The two scholarly men are very important. . . ."

"And the others? The killers?" asked Sung.

"We will have them tell us all they know and then . . ."

Red Tiger drew his forefinger across his throat.

"And what of us here?" asked the Small General.

"If we are able to bring them here they will come unsuspectingly. From the moment when they set foot ashore, remain in concealment and keep them covered with your gun. We want no shooting, remember, unless there is no other course. The storm will have passed and sound carries far across the lake at night."

With its heavy lee-boards, Red Tiger's fast sailing *sampan* stood as good a chance as any craft on the lake that night and better than most. The unwieldy houseboat and the trumpery motor-boat towing it, stood almost no chance at all. In the shallow waters of the lake they would bump themselves to pieces in five minutes when the storm came.

Red Tiger's boat soon disappeared into the gathering darkness, and the Small General occupied himself by giving orders to all the men on the island, of whom there were some twenty. Each man had his station and his orders. Three only, in addition to the Small General, had firearms. The others equipped themselves with long bamboo poles, at the end of which they lashed sharp knives. They knew almost nothing of what was afoot except that danger threatened.

Barely half an hour after Red Tiger had left the island the wind came down from the mountain on the West side of the lake. It was one of the worst storms in living memory. At one moment the calm of evening brooded over the lake, while a few seconds later, with the suddenness of a stage effect, the water boiled and ten thousand devils seemed to be screaming through the air. Great waves beat vainly against the stone holding walls of the island, which shook noticeably, so that the Old One ran screaming from the kitchen.

In forty minutes the wind had dropped to a gentle breeze and the water of the lake was resuming its customary placid appearance.

Nobody said so, because to utter the words might be unlucky, but it was believed by almost all on the island that Red Tiger and his men would never be seen again.

"He will be here within two hours," said Sung with confidence, cutting across the thoughts of those around him. "He may die in one of many ways, perhaps even at the place of execution, but he will never drown, for he is a man born with a caul. Such as he are never taken by the water."

A little before midnight, when even Sung's airy optimism was beginning to wear thin, there came a loud hail from across the water.

"It is he, Red Tiger!" whispered Sung. "Go to your places!"

There followed the sound of creaking *ulohs,* which came closer.

"Show a light!" called Red Tiger.

Leaving his gun in the shadow, the Small General ran down to the jetty and hung there a lantern.

"We need food and shelter for the night," called Red Tiger. "We have no money, but we are nearly exhausted. We have with us the crew of a houseboat. They were at the point of drowning. Their boat and *almost* everything in it was lost. . . ."

"That means," whispered the Small General, "that the Japanese still have their arms."

A score of men, indistinguishable in the lantern light, stepped ashore, their clothes sodden with water.

"You will give us food and shelter?" asked Red Tiger. "We will call down the blessings of the gods for your kindness, for we are exhausted."

"I must ask my honoured father," replied the Small General, playing for time to think. "He has never yet refused shelter to storm-bound travellers, but I must, nevertheless, ask."

"As a dutiful son should," said Red Tiger piously. "We will wait, my men on this side"—he indicated the side of the pathway with a sweep of the hand—"and the strangers we took from the water on the other."

The only man rescued from the houseboat who spoke the dialect of Ta Hu and its surroundings was the Chinese *laodah,* who so bitterly regretted having sold himself to the Japanese. Despite all the casual talk, his quick ear had detected a note of urgency in the exchange. It seemed more than probable to him that the wild-looking crew which had rescued his party had not only done so by design, but were pirates into the bargain. He also knew that, their feet once again on dry land, the Japanese would soon become their assertive selves again. Lead would be flying before many minutes. There was little time to think. Meanwhile, he preferred darkness to the pool of light around the lantern, which made him a very good target.

Quick as the *laodah* was in fading from the scene, one of the Japanese gunmen was quicker. His interpretation of the *laodah's* move was the right one. If he were allowed to get away the man would talk, with incalculable consequences.

At this point none of the Japanese was aware that the island was the one to which they had originally intended to come. Sung-wah's failure to keep the rendezvous could easily mean that he had perished in the storm.

As the *laodah* moved quickly out of the circle of lantern light a shot rang out, followed by a groan and the horrible gurgle of a man shot through the lung.

The other Japanese did not have time to draw their weapons before a rush of men, with all the advantage of darkness, over-powered them. The Japanese who killed the *laodah,* however, had his weapon in his hand and before he was overpowered he had fired three more shots.

When the six snarling Japanese had been trussed like chickens, Red Tiger dismissed his men, while the Small General told his to go back to their homes, and then hurried into the house to acquaint his father with the outcome of the affair.

The Small General's cry brought all the dispersed men running towards the house. There, slumped across a low table, lay Sung, while a pool of blood spoke only too eloquently of what had happened.

Red Tiger, who had had much experience of wounds, ripped off Sung's gown, revealing a bullet wound in the abdomen.

They carried Sung to his bed, where Red Tiger staunched the flow of blood.

"It is useless to do more," said the pirate sadly, "for he is come to the end of the road. If he awakens he will suffer great pain. It is always so with belly wounds. Tell one of the women to prepare opium pills."

A little before dawn Sung stirred, opening his eyes slowly to see the anxious faces of his sons, Red Tiger and the Old One around him. He had no memory after the moment when the bullet struck him.

"Why do you look at me thus?" he asked in a weak voice. "Ah!

116

I now remember. The Japanese monkeys came. Where are they now? What has happened?"

"We have them all securely, my father, but there was a short fight and a chance bullet entered the window and struck you. They shall pay for the night's work with the torments of hell. That I swear to you, my father."

"The bullet, where did it strike me?" asked Sung.

Red Tiger pointed to the spot in silence.

"A few months ago," said Sung with a wry smile, "it was such a fine belly that no bullet could have missed it, but it is strange that now, when it is shrunk to nothing . . . well, it has been a good belly and has always served me well. It is the end?"

"It is the end," said Red Tiger sadly.

"A few hours remain to me?"

Red Tiger nodded and, as though to gather strength, Sung closed his eyes and fell into a deep sleep.

"Watch our father and call me if he stirs!" the Small General said to his younger brother, a delicate and somewhat effeminate boy, who was growing into the image of his mother, the Young One. Because of this amazing likeness and, doubtless in part because she had hated the boy's mother, the Old One had nicknamed him Rose Petal. The name was so apt that it had stuck, as slightly malicious names will cling to those on whom they are pinned.

The pirate and the Small General went off to make sure that their prisoners were safe.

"It is a pity that one of us here does not speak their tongue," said Red Tiger, "for before we send them to the Pit there are certain questions I would like to ask them."

"Many Japanese speak Mandarin,* I am told," said the Small General.

"Try them!" said the pirate. "I have made my plans. I would like to get to the heart of certain matters concerning the Japanese. The two men who look like scholars do not matter. They will know nothing. But the others are, unless I am in sad error, of the secret police."

In cold tones the Small General addressed the prisoners in Mandarin Chinese. A look of understanding came into the eyes

* The language of the upper classes throughout China.

of one of the Japanese, who was barely conscious from the beating he had received a few hours earlier.

"Untie him," Red Tiger ordered his men. "Give him a little food and drink. Later we will question him."

In the middle morning Rose Petal called to say that Sung was awake and demanding tea. With Red Tiger's consent the Old One brought tea.

"An old man in a *sampan* has come," announced one of the pirates just as the tea was served. "He demands to see Sung. We have told him nothing."

"What is he like, this old man?" asked Sung with interest. "Has he by chance a beard like an aged billy goat?"

"He has," replied the pirate.

"Has he certain large baskets in the *sampan*?" asked Sung.

"There are many baskets."

"Then have men carry up the baskets," said Sung, "and tell the old man I will see him. When he comes I would be alone with the old man and my older son. There is much to be said and little time to say it. Forgive me, old friend," said Sung to Red Tiger, "but there are certain matters which my son must know."

When the Small General returned to the room with the old man who looked so much like a billy goat, Sung was laughing. For a moment it seemed as though a miracle would occur and that he would recover.

"Have the baskets put safely in the house until night falls," said Sung, "but have one of them brought here to my bedside."

Bewildered, the Small General did as he was bidden.

"You find me in sorry state," said Sung to the newcomer, "for had you come a few hours later I should already have joined my respected ancestors. Open the basket, old friend, and show my son what is in it."

With trembling hands the old man opened the lid of a bottle-necked basket, full to the brim with silk cocoons.

"These," said Sung, chuckling, "come from the shores of Zung Hu, a small lake not far from Soochow, to the South and East of the city. They are of fine quality, as you see. They come from the mulberries of my good friend Kwong, who stands before you. He owns just half the number of mulberry trees which stand on this island."

118

"I do not understand, my father, why he should bring his cocoons here. We are not silk merchants. We have no filature. . . ."

"Patience, son, patience! For many years now I have bought all Kwong's cocoons. I have paid him always double the price he could secure from my old friend Lok."

"Why did you not tell me this before, my father? Who carried the baskets from the boat? Who . . . ?"

"Questions, questions!" chuckled Sung. "When you grow a little older, my son, you will understand that the fewer persons who share a secret, the longer it remains a secret. My old friend Kwong and I have kept tight mouths these many years so that not even my beloved son knew the secret of Sung's island, which has made us passing rich. You have been a good son for you have concealed the curiosity which must have consumed you. In a little while you will be Sung of Sung's island. It is fitting, therefore, that you should enter the secret of how our small island has become famous. Where we grow two cocoons, Kwong grows one cocoon. Kwong has always brought his cocoons here by night, but doubtless last night's storm delayed him. It is very simple, is it not, my son?"

The Small General threw back his head and burst into peals of laughter.

"How can a good son laugh at his father's deathbed?" asked Red Tiger angrily, hearing the unseemly sound from many yards distant.

"But I would have you understand," said Sung virtuously, "that I told no lies. In the days when Lok's agent came here to buy my cocoons he did not ask me whether all the cocoons he brought were produced on this small island. It is possible that if he had asked I should have remained silent with indignation. But he did not ask . . ."

Once more the Small General's laughter rang out, causing frowns of disapproval from those who heard.

"I have brought you cocoons for the last time," said Kwong warningly. "I am grown too old. In a little while I, too, have an appointment with my ancestors."

"It is as well," said Sung. "The small secret has served its purpose. But I would much like, with your permission, Kwong, to have my son share the secret with my honoured and astute old

119

friend Lok, for he always loved a merry jest. Is it permitted, Kwong?"

"It is permitted," chuckled Kwong. "The jest has been a good one. It is as I told you many years ago. There are always those who try to explain simple things in wonderful fashion, while a few wise men look through and beyond marvels for simple causes."

"When I have joined my honourable ancestors, son, go you to Lok and for a two-fold purpose. It is my command that your marriage with his daughter goes forward speedily. It is Lok's wish also. I am to blame that I did not overcome your reluctance long ere this. When the matter of the marriage is settled, and not before, choose your moment well. Lok will appreciate the jest better when he is full of wine, for it is in such moments that we look charitably upon many things. . . ."

Sung chuckled happily as he thought of all that had passed between him and Lok over the matter of the secret of the island's silk production.

". . . And now, son, it is time to call the others, for I would take leave of them. There are devils tearing at my vitals. If I am to die with a smile on my face, as a man should die, see that the Old One brings me some opium pills . . . quickly."

"Shame on you that you laugh with your father dying beside you!" said Red Tiger as he entered the room.

"The fault is mine, old friend," said Sung contritely. "We have shared a merry jest, my son and I. You heard his laughter because he has not a bullet in his belly. Mine I must muffle, that is all. He has been a good son. . . . What is that noise I hear?"

"It is good music for you," said Red Tiger more happily, seeing that he had misjudged the Small General. "Hark! My men are pulling the toenails off the Japanese who shot you. In a little while I will file his teeth down to the gums . . ."

From outside there came a crescendo of shrieks. Sung cocked an ear pleasurably to listen.

"They must not leave here alive," Sung warned Red Tiger. "Not one of them. Let it be thought that they perished in last night's storm. But do not let them die too easily . . . they swarm like locusts in the rich cities of our land . . . like locusts they will soon eat us up if we are not careful. I do not like them . . . the yellow-haired barbarians are bad enough, but the men of Japan will force a reckoning before many years are gone. . . ."

Sung's pain eased soon after he had swallowed the opium and for a short while he lost consciousness.

"We have made a compact, your son and I," said Red Tiger when Sung's eyes opened.

"He has been a loyal friend—always!" gasped Sung to the Small General. "He will be a loyal friend to you. . . ."

All the Sungs on the island were waiting to pay their last respects to the dying man. As there was little time the Small General admitted them. They filed past the bed with downcast heads. Sung had been a just man, as they knew justice.

From the Old One, crouching on the floor beside the bed she had never shared, came deep sobs and a cry which would not be stifled.

"Hush, woman!" said Sung. "One master dies and another takes his place. It was always thus. Look after my son well. See that he eats well and grows a fine belly like mine. You have been a good woman to me, even if your shrimp sauce was not all it might have been. . . ."

The dying man's breathing became harder.

"Do not forget, son! Only when he is full of wine will he enjoy the jest. At other times Lok carries his head too high . . . it was a good jest . . . it will be remembered of Sung that three silkworms grew fat where there was only food for two . . . first Lok and then the Japanese . . . three silkworms. . . ."

Outside there was the sharp cry of a cormorant, harsh and discordant. It was Sung's own bird, which knew before those assembled in the room that its master's soul had fled.

PART TWO

WITH a broad smile on his face and his hands clasped across an
ample belly, Fung-li stood at the door of his shop and watched
while his son took down the shutters. Soochow was almost hidden
by sheets of driving rain. A glance at the leaden skies confirmed
Fung-li's hope and belief that the rain would continue throughout the day. He found the thought comforting, fully as comforting as the realisation of his own virtue and prudence, and almost
as comforting as the knowledge that, before the day was over, his
virtue and prudence would be rewarded by a till full of shining
silver dollars.

Across the street, on the canal beyond, Fung-li could just see
the awning of a barge coming in from the country with produce
for the market. On the awning was pasted a bold legend:

Only Traitors
buy
Japanese Goods

In contrast there was, across the front of Fung-li's shop, in proof
that the proprietor was a great patriot, a banner which read:

All Goods Sold Here
were
MADE IN CHINA

Furthermore, the statement was true. Fung-li had, of course,
a very large stock of Japanese goods of many kinds. But having
received a private warning the previous evening of what the day
was likely to bring, these had all been packed carefully and sent
away to a go-down owned by his brother-in-law. It was also true
that on the shelves in the shop were thousands of yards of cotton-
piece goods, made in Shanghai by an ostensibly Chinese-owned
mill, whose proprietors were in fact (though this was not gen-

erally known) the Fureno Trading Company of Japan. What gladdened the heart of Fung-li most on this fine wet morning was that, to the best of his knowledge and belief, his was the only considerable stock in Soochow of Chinese-made umbrellas.

Now it is a human foible all the world over that people postpone the buying of an umbrella until the rain has actually begun to fall, just as most delay repentance until the doctor has shrugged his shoulders.

By noon Fung-li had sold every umbrella on the premises, over five hundred of them. On each of them he had made, of course, a slightly higher profit than on the competitive Japanese umbrella. But this, he felt, was not so much extra profit as the inevitable reward of virtue.

Donning a waterproof cape, made in Osaka, to protect his fine silk gown, up the sleeve of which he put a package of cigarettes made by an Anglo-American concern in Shanghai, Fung-li set off under the last of the Chinese-made umbrellas to a near-by eating-house. Here it would be very pleasant to eat a well-chosen meal and listen to the woes of his competitors who had not been so virtuous—or far-sighted, just as one cares to think of the matter.

On every building, on shutters, on glass windows, on the hats of coolies, on canal craft of every kind, were the glaring strips of paper warning everyone not to buy Japanese goods. Several of his competitors, Fung-li noted, trying very hard not to look pleased as he passed, had ignored the warnings. Their premises had been wrecked. The gutters outside their shops were filled with merchandise which the passing crowds trod delightedly into the mud. At the offices and showrooms of the Fureno Trading Company, above which flew the Japanese flag defiantly, business had come to a standstill. Even had any Chinese merchants dared to visit the premises there were excellent reasons for them to change their minds. Around all the entrances crowded some two hundred of the most verminous and disease-ridden beggars in the city, some of them revealing great flaking patches of pinky-white skin due to skin leprosy. But here was no violence. The Japanese staff, to and fro on their several errands, were compelled to push their way through the stinking throng, touching garments heavily encrusted with lice, pushing aside raw and suppurating stumps of arms, braving the infections from open ulcers, pink eyes. But there was no violence of any kind.

126

Fung-li, shuddering, was very thankful that he had listened to his friend, the emissary of the Beggars' Guild, who had warned him in time.

Charity ranks high among the virtues in China. The profession of beggar, therefore, is an honourable one. It follows logically that if charity be a virtue—and who would dare deny this?—the beggar, the object of charity, shares in the virtue for the reason that he provides an ever-present opportunity to display charity. In every city in China the Beggars' Guild is highly organised, performing a valuable public service. All business premises and private residences are assessed on a most reasonable scale for an annual payment which secures immunity from the unwelcome attentions of beggars. Wise men pay the amount at which they are assessed, or they take the consequences of failing to do so. There are, of course, those who occasionally resist. But scenes such as that witnessed outside the offices of the Fureno Trading Company usually demonstrate that resistance to the modest demands of the Guild is very foolish. Shoppers in search of bargains will not soil their clean clothes, or risk disease, by contact with verminous beggars.

In Fung-li's favourite eating-place the talk was all of the Japanese boycott.

"This time it will succeed," said one man, "for it is being organised by the Brotherhood! The Brotherhood does not fail."

"It is the same in all cities and villages beside the Grand Canal, from the Yangtsze River down to Hangchow," said another. "Before long it will be carried north of the Yangtsze as far as Peking itself."

"I thank Heaven that I have no Japanese goods in my shop," said a virtuous voice.

"And I!" "And I!" came a chorus.

"I sold over five hundred umbrellas this morning," observed Fung-li with an irritating complacency. "They were made in China, of course," he added.

"Of course!" agreed his hearers, biting their lips with vexation.

"But when will you be able to buy more?" asked one merchant. "That is the question. I have been told that I cannot have one for at least six months. The factory has so many orders that it will not accept more."

The same thought had occurred to Fung-li, but he did not voice it.

"They are executing the five pirates very soon, perhaps to-morrow," said a newcomer loudly, killing umbrellas as a subject of conversation. "But it is being freely said that the Brotherhood will not allow them to be executed."

"Even the Brotherhood cannot perform miracles," said Fung-li.

"If I were a merchant," said a man who was eating alone at a small table, "I do not think I would be so bold as to cast doubts publicly upon the ability of the Brotherhood to do what it wishes to do!"

It was Fung-li's turn to bite his lip and to wish that he had kept his mouth shut. When he opened his purse to pay for his meal he had a rude shock. Before leaving his shop he had taken a banknote from the till. The banknote was still in his purse, but pinned to one corner was a small slip of paper which read: "The Brother-hood sees all and hears all."

How had the piece of paper been pinned there? Fung-li paid his reckoning hurriedly and departed for his shop, for he had remembered that at the back of his desk was a large pile of in-voices for Japanese goods bought during the preceding few months. He stood beside the small iron stove until the last sheet had been utterly consumed. Not content with this, he pulverised the burned paper until it was beyond all possible recognition.

In another part of the city of Soochow, close to the execution ground, which is overlooked by the Great Pagoda, five men lay groaning in their agony.

The law of China says that no man condemned to death for a crime may be executed unless and until he has confessed his guilt. The origin and purpose of this law, it would seem, was merciful and just, but in practice it is neither merciful nor just, for the law does not specify the means which may be used to extort a confession from a condemned man. The innocent and guilty alike, when they are come to the end of their endurance, confess avidly, hoping for the flashing blade which will bring an end to their sufferings.

For seven weeks, ever since they had been condemned, these five men had lain in pools of their own excrement, shackled like wild beasts. Adequate food was provided for them, for it would be unseemly if they were to cheat the executioner's sword by dying from starvation. Their gaoler knew, from long experience, that these men were approaching the point when their iron determination would break, when they would cry out for witnesses to listen to their confessions, so that the magistrates would send their orders to the executioner, whose sword would bring the relief for which they hoped so fervently.

The gaoler spat contemptuously at these five men. They were, from every point of view, unsatisfactory prisoners. They had no relatives, or if they had, they would not involve them by naming them. It was customary in cases such as this for condemned men to name certain relatives who might be prepared to come forward with an offering of money, to be divided between gaoler and executioner.

"Have you no friends?" asked the gaoler, his greedy eyes glinting. "Give me their names. Nothing will happen to them. Nobody shall reproach them, or question them. If they will give me as little as three dollars for each of you, I will arrange matters so that the honourable executioner shall not bungle the affair. One clean stroke of the sword! Is that not worth whispering to me the names of your friends? The executioner tells me that unless he is given the price of a few cups of wine to steady his hand the sword may slip. It might need two blows, three even, before his work is done. But for three dollars he will greet you with a steady hand. Think well before you refuse again . . . tomorrow I will come to you for the names of your friends. . . ."

But many tomorrows came and went. Still the condemned men maintained their obstinate silence, for hope was not yet extinguished in their hearts.

They were Red Tiger's men, these five. Red Tiger never forsook his own, nor did he ever break his pledged word. He had sworn to them, risking his liberty to come near them at the trial, that come what may, he would save them from the fate mapped out for them by the magistrates.

The bitterness of their imprisonment was even more bitter because each of the five knew that, but for a traitor, he would not be where he was. They had set out in the ordinary course of their work to loot and scuttle a barge owned by the Japanese, transporting a load of piece goods and other merchandise from Soochow to the villages on Lake Ta Hu. The spot chosen for the attack had been the last camel-back bridge over a small tributary stream which ran from the Grand Canal to the lake. Here the intention had been to drop from the top of the bridge on to the deck of the barge, overpower the crew and scuttle the barge with its Japanese cargo in deep water.

The plan had been interrupted by the unfortunate fact that the barge, instead of containing Japanese goods, had contained well-armed Chinese soldiers. That there had been a traitor was obvious and that Red Tiger would find him was sure, but in the meanwhile, there was a living death to endure.

"You have changed your minds, my honoured guests?" asked the gaoler tauntingly. "Or would you prefer that on The Day the executioner should bring a blunt sword with which to hack your heads slowly from your miserable bodies? Only three dollars! It is a small fee to save you from so much! . . ."

"When the Brotherhood gets us away from here," said one of the condemned men in a flash of defiance, "it will be our pleasure to cut out your liver."

"The Brotherhood! The Brotherhood! You make me laugh. You may be able to frighten foolish shopkeepers with your talk of the Brotherhood, but I do not notice that the magistrates walk in fear of them. But since you will not listen to reason, and offer insults in return for good advice, the price tomorrow will be five dollars, instead of three."

In the *Yamen* the magistrates awaited a deputation of the city's leading merchants and bankers. They shuffled uncomfortably in their seats as they thought of the coming interview. It is notoriously a most embarrassing thing to have to refuse requests made by men whose bribes one has eaten. Yet, as each of the magistrates knew, the requests would have to be refused, for the alternative would mean open defiance of what was called the Government of China. The matter had gone beyond the Provincial Governor.

The magistrates listened in silence to the deputation, whose spokesman was none other than Lok-kai-shing, now a very old man and highly respected.

"If the honourable magistrates do not grant our request and give these men their freedom," said Lok soberly, "we fear that there will be a great civic uprising and much destruction of property."

"We have our orders from above," said the spokesman of the magistrates uncomfortably, "and on no account will the men be reprieved. The Japanese have brought great pressure to bear. They say that, unless the boycott is ended at once, they are prepared to bring troops into Soochow and other cities along the length of the Grand Canal to protect their interests. Do you wish to see Soochow occupied by Japanese troops? Under their treaty rights they can do this. . . ."

"Since our persons and our properties, it would seem, are to be endangered either by the indignant citizens of Soochow, or by the soldiers of a foreign army," said Lok slowly and with dignity, "we, as men who love and respect our country, would prefer to defy the Japanese and let them do their worst."

"Nevertheless," said the spokesman of the magistrates, "the five pirates must die."

"We deny that they are pirates," said Lok hotly. "They are patriots!"

"They may be patriots," was the firm reply, "but they were caught in piracy. The penalty for piracy is death."

"If those men are executed," continued Lok, "it is not only they who will die. The sword of the executioner will cut down the very flower of our honour, for there is no honour left in a land where it has become a crime to be a patriot."

Seeing that no useful purpose was to be gained by further talk, Lok bowed profoundly to the magistrates and with the rest of the deputation left the *Yamen*.

The time was a little before the New Year, when in China all who like to hold their heads high pay their debts to the uttermost cent. That same night it was intimated to the magistrates that unless certain large sums owing by them privately were paid before the New Year, the names of the debtors and the amounts of the debts would be published broadcast.

Four of the five magistrates left Soochow within a few hours of learning what would be the result of refusing to accede to the request of the deputation. The fifth, Chang by name, who was an upright man and owed no debts, sat up late wrestling with his conscience.

Chang was one of those rare men who are able to take a god-like view of the world and human problems. He was by inclination a patriot, too, which complicated matters still further for

131

him. In Chang's conception the five pirates, whether they were patriots or not, deserved to die. To condone piracy was unthinkable. If the problem had begun and ended with the disposal of five pirates he would without hesitation have taken steps to ensure that they confessed speedily, in order to conform to the letter of the law, and would have handed them over to the public executioner without further ado. As he wrestled with himself, Chang tried to forget that the men were pirates, remembering only that they were patriots. Now anything, however small and humble its origin, which could light in Chinese hearts the fire of patriotism was, in Chang's conception, worthy of patient examination and earnest thought. The problem which he had set himself was to determine to his own satisfaction whether the five patriots—they were no longer pirates—would better serve the cause of patriotism by dying or living. There was the chance, of course, that they were not patriots. In this event their deaths would not be martyrdom for a high cause, but merely the act of expiation by common criminals. Either way, Chang was much relieved to find, he did not have to study the welfare of the five individuals concerned. He was a humane man. If they were in fact patriots, he argued, and by dying they could serve the highest interests of their country, they could offer no logical objection to dying as martyrs. If, on the other hand, they were not patriots at all, but merely criminals, their lives were already forfeit. So, by the application of reason, Chang decided that it was not worth while troubling to make up his mind whether the men were pirates or patriots.

Now, as is well known to everyone who has read any history at all, there is a certain type of man so insignificant as to be unable to make by the manner in which he lives the smallest impression upon the outcome of contemporary events, but who is enabled, by factors entirely outside his own control, to make a profound impression by the manner in which he dies. In such a category, Chang mused, were the five piratical patriots or patriotic pirates. Was it better to restore public faith in the machinery of law and justice by pardoning the five men, or was it in the nation's best interest to allow them to die martyrs' deaths and by so doing inflame public passion so that even the supine Central Government would be forced to take action?

Over his fifth pipe of opium, at which point his brain was

always at its keenest, Chang decided that the question was one beyond his power to answer. Other factors intruded themselves, chief among which was this Brotherhood of the Grand Canal, which seemed to be upon everyone's lips. If, as Chang hoped, the Brotherhood consisted of earnest men pledged to restore China's greatness and to oust the accursed foreigners who strutted through the land like conquerors, it was for them to decide.

The ninth or tenth pipe of opium usually made Chang (or so he believed) psychic. On this particular evening it was the eleventh pipe which led him to the conclusion that only one man of his acquaintance would be likely to know how he could establish contact with the guiding brains of the Brotherhood of the Grand Canal, and that man was Lok-kai-shing.

Chang had a great disinclination for exposing himself to cold night air at any time, but particularly after a few pipes. He realised, however, that Lok, who was an older man than himself, even if socially inferior, could not be expected to turn out of his comfortable home.

Chang's arrival at Lok's house and the message of apology for the intrusion, given to the servant who opened the door, burst in upon a scene of simple domesticity. Lok's favourite concubine, a pretty little thing of about sixteen summers, whose virginity was sadly in no danger from her lord and master, sat with him upon a comfortable settee. They were playing the game which in China amuses the young and brings back tender memories to the old, the ancient game of stone-paper-scissors. In the intervals of the game, which Lok invariably won, his playmate filled his opium pipe for him.

On the other side of the room in bored silence sat the Small General, now Lok's son-in-law. Beside him sat Lok's daughter, a dumpy and not very bright girl of about nineteen years of age, who giggled with or without provocation.

On hearing the name of magistrate Chang announced, the Small General rose to leave the room.

"No, stay!" said Lok. "It is better that two should hear what he has to say. I do not know whether he comes as magistrate or as friend. However, he is a most virtuous man in many ways. Three times, I recall, I have tried to bribe him in certain matters, but I have never been sure whether he refused the bribes because of his integrity, or because they were not large enough."

Further speculation upon the point was cut short by the arrival of Chang himself. The women withdrew hurriedly.

"My poor house is honoured by the presence of the illustrious Chang," said Lok, acknowledging his visitor's bow.

"Apologies are due for the late hour of my call," said Chang, "but there are times when courtesy must give way to necessity. This is such a time. I am come to seek advice upon a certain matter from that wise and respected man who is my host."

"It is inconceivable to me," said Lok urbanely, "that there could be any single matter, except perhaps the vagaries of the silk market, upon which I could presume to offer advice to the illustrious Chang, but such small wisdom as I may possess is unreservedly at his service."

"I feel that the matter is one for the ear of Lok alone," said Chang, looking at the Small General.

"To my son-in-law, who is also the son of my valued and lamented friend Sung, I confide everything," said Lok politely but firmly, making it abundantly clear that the Small General would remain.

"Touching the matter of the five men—the five pirates or patriots—who lie under sentence of death, I have a great and consuming curiosity," began Chang. "When this morning I saw my wise and respected friend Lok acting as spokesman to a deputation on their behalf, I argued with some logic, you will agree, that a man of such infinite wisdom and high integrity would not have appealed on behalf of these men unless he were in possession of some information which I, as a magistrate, lack. The indictment calls them pirates. You, doubtless with the best of reasons, call them patriots."

"I am a silk merchant," replied Lok. "I am also, I trust, a patriot."

"I, too, have faced the possibility that men can be pirates and patriots at one and the same time," said Chang. "Thus far, I know that they are pirates. I seek evidence that they are patriots. How shall I find that evidence?"

"It is said," observed Lok, picking his words very carefully, "that a certain organisation called, I believe, the Brotherhood of the Grand Canal, has evidence that these men are patriots. I cannot be sure of what I say, naturally . . ."

"Naturally!" agreed Chang. "Then the problem would seem

to be to find a way into the heart of the Brotherhood, of which there is so much talk in these times. But how?"

"Indeed, how?" echoed Lok. "Alas! I am too old to spend my time gossiping. I hear very little of what goes on outside my home and my place of business. But perhaps my son-in-law, who is still young enough to enjoy himself, has heard some whisper, some chance piece of gossip?"

Lok looked expectantly at the Small General, who was thinking fast.

"It is said that if any man wishes to meet those who are at the head of the Brotherhood," said the Small General, "he must go, one hour before midnight, to the Shrine of his Ancestors. There, upon their honour and upon his, he must swear that, come what may, he will divulge nothing of what he has seen and heard. This may be mere idle gossip. I cannot guarantee its truth, naturally."

"Naturally!" agreed Chang thoughtfully. "One hour before midnight, you said? Then I have just time to take such an oath tonight if I hurry. The Shrine of my Honourable Ancestors is situated in the garden of my house. Happily, the gate which leads on to the towpath beside the canal is always open."

"Doubtless, being a magistrate, you have no fear of thieves," said Lok.

"It is not that I am a magistrate which causes thieves to shun my house. It is, rather, that I am a poor man," replied Chang gently, but there was mild rebuke in his voice.

"A magistrate for more than twenty years," said Lok wonderingly when Chang had gone, "and yet I believe him when he says he is a poor man. Now hurry, my son, or he will reach the Shrine of his Ancestors before you. It was a happy thought of yours. Stand in the shadows and hear him take the oath. To him it will be sacred."

Everyone in Soochow knew Magistrate Chang's little house, which stood on the western side of the city, fronting on to a narrow creek within two hundred yards of the Grand Canal itself. The Small General's two rowers overtook Chang's *sampan*, which was not being rowed quickly, in time for a place of concealment to be found out of sight, but within earshot, of the Chang mausoleum, outside which was the family's ancestral shrine.

In a little while Chang entered the garden, prostrating himself upon the cold wet ground before the shrine of the ancestors whose honour he had tried sincerely to keep unsullied. On the same spot he had once sworn that he would never accept a bribe.

The Small General, listening from his place of concealment, heard Chang take the solemn oath in a firm clear voice, and as he listened knew that it would not be broken.

"And you, young man," asked Chang, as he and the Small General were being rowed back into the centre of the city, "are you a piratical patriot, or a patriotic pirate?" Having coined the phrase, Chang found that he liked it.

"I am not a pirate," the younger man replied, "but I would turn pirate tomorrow if I believed that it would help China to free herself from the shameful shackles of foreign bondage."

"Then it is not only against the Japanese that your Brotherhood wages war? All foreigners come under the ban of its displeasure, eh?"

"The Brotherhood will speak for itself," said the Small General as courteously as it is possible for a young man to speak when offering a mild rebuke to an elder and a social superior. "I am speaking for myself. As I see these things the foreigners, all of them, have wrought nothing but evil in our land. But the capacity for harm of the red-haired barbarians is almost ended. Having endured them for so long, it may be good policy to endure them for a little longer. It may be that they, because they are jealous of the Japanese, will help us drive the monkey-men out of our land. The sun of the Japanese is rising in Asia, as their flag depicts. The sun of the western barbarians is setting."

"You make me wish I were young again," said Chang thoughtfully, "for I think you have drawn a true picture of the troubles which beset our land. If we drive out the red-haired barbarians we shall be at the mercy of the Japanese, whereas if we keep alive their greed they will help us, because it is in their best interests to do so. The red-haired barbarians are concerned only to steal our wealth, as they have been stealing it for more than a century. The Japanese want our wealth also, but they strive to steal our souls, as in the past they stole our arts, our philosophies and our language. Nevertheless, it is not by piracies that we shall achieve anything. There are better ways of opening an egg than by smashing it with a hammer."

The *sampan* drew in to a flight of steps above which there hung a Golden Duck, the sign of a very famous eating-house.

"Follow me," said the Small General, leading the way up the steps and into a doorway. To the right were the public rooms. Straight ahead down a narrow passage was a door which led into a private dining-room. Here the Small General stood aside for Chang to enter. There was a brief delay while a trap-door, concealed by a heavy carpet, was being opened. Taking an oil lantern from a shelf, the Small General again led the way down a flight of wet stone steps and along a subterranean passage some three hundred yards in length. Water dripped from the roof, forming into puddles on the rough stone floor.

Soochow is equipped with an entirely superfluous system of sewers, built parallel to the main canals, which have always been used as sewers just as they have also been used for domestic water supply. More than a century before this the map of the sewers was lost and, since they had never been used, nor were likely to be used, nobody troubled about the matter.

There was a well-paid official, of course, whose duty was to make periodical inspections of the sewers, and when he died others were in succession appointed to the sinecure. The time-honoured system of carrying out the duties of sewer inspector was to employ, at his own expense, two coolies. One of these, who was very clean, was sent down a manhole at one end of a sewer. The inspecting party then walked to the far end of the sewer where, after a short delay, up came a very dirty coolie. The presumption, quite without warrant, was that in traversing the length of the sewer the clean coolie had become dirty, proving that the duties of the sewer inspector had been duly carried out.

Just how and when the map of Soochow's sewers, missing from the city's archives, had fallen into the hands of Red Tiger's grandfather, is beyond the scope of this story. But it goes a long way towards explaining how the pirate's father and grandfather, both of whom had followed the same profession, had been able to enter and leave the city at will, despite the utmost vigilance of the authorities. Beneath the city there existed a complex system of underground sewers and passageways, some of them below canal level. Legend credited them with being part of a defence system dating back to a remote age, but to the citizens of Soochow almost nothing more was known about them than that they were believed to exist.

Magistrate Chang found himself in very mixed company that night, for men from all walks of life had joined the ranks of the Brotherhood of the Grand Canal. The Brotherhood was for patriots, whether they were bankers, merchants, beggars or toiling coolies.

On Chang's right hand sat Red Tiger, presumed dead for more than a decade. On his left was the venerable President of the Beggars' Guild. Opposite sat the no less venerable President of the Thieves' Guild. There were in addition railway and telegraph workers; *laodahs* of canal barges and stevedores; postal officials and house servants in the employ of foreigners. Almost every industry and occupation in Soochow was represented. In addition there were representatives from Chinkiang, Shanghai, Wusih, Hangchow, and from even further up the Yangtsze Valley.

There was a short silence when the Small General led Chang into the chamber.

"Let him take the oath!" growled a voice as Chang prepared to seat himself.

"What oath is this?" asked Chang.

"The oath of allegiance to the Brotherhood," was the reply.

"How can I take an oath of allegiance to the Brotherhood," asked Chang softly, "when I know nothing of its purposes and methods? Even if I were to swear such an oath it would be valueless. I have already sworn that I will reveal nothing of what I see and hear tonight. More than that I cannot and will not do, for I will not swear allegiance blindly to any man or any group of men until I know something about them."

"Those are the words of an honest man," said Red Tiger.

Chang bowed his acknowledgment. He was completely at his ease, for he was a Chinese gentleman, than which no more perfectly poised human being exists.

"I seek guidance," he said at length, "in the matter of five men, condemned pirates, who lie under sentence of death."

"They are my men," said Red Tiger. "They must be released."

"Forgive me if I do not find the argument conclusive," said Chang. "Your loyalty to your men is to be applauded, but that is a matter which concerns you and them. I am thinking of a higher loyalty, that of our native land. It may be that the best interests of China will be served by releasing them. On the other hand, it may be that they can best serve China by dying. Permit me to point out that the final decision, whether they live or die, lies with me, for my four colleagues have departed from the city."

"If you did not come here to help us, why did you come?" asked Red Tiger angrily, irritated by the other's well-polished phrases.

"I thought I had made it clear that I seek guidance. All I know at present is that these five men were justly convicted of an act of piracy, for which the penalty is death. I suspected, but did not know, that these men were members of this Brotherhood, whose name is bandied everywhere. Where, pray tell me, could I expect to find better guidance if my guess turns out to be the right one, as I suspect it has?"

"If those men die," said Red Tiger, "I shall die with them."

"I would deplore the event," observed Chang, "but I would not allow it to influence my judgment. Let me make myself clear. It is my opinion that greater issues are at stake than the life or death of five pirates—call them what you like. I am concerned whether China lives or dies. I hope most earnestly that I am in the presence of men who are likewise concerned. What are the lives of five men when famine, flood and pestilence take more than five millions of our people every year? I am amazed that grown men should waste time upon such a matter!"

"You will not leave this chamber alive until you have sworn to release the men," growled a voice.

"Then I suggest, my friend, that you kill me now, for you will get from me no such oath, now or ever. I came here for guidance. The decision is still mine. Threats will not influence me. I am already in the evening of life. I have no son to comfort me in old age. What have I to fear in death? Again I ask you: give me some guidance. If those men die your Brotherhood will lose much 'face,' so much so that it will probably be swept away by laughter. That might be a very bad thing—for China. Or it might be good. I do not know. Instead of wasting your time and mine with threats, tell me what are your aims and how you propose to achieve them. If they are worthy I would like to join you. If they are not, you may go to perdition. . . ."

Amid deathly silence Chang sat down, waiting attentively with folded arms for someone to speak.

"I think that the Honourable Chang has reason behind what he says," said the Small General, realising as he spoke the risks he ran. "Mere loyalty to our friends is a very small and selfish thing if our loyalty to them is to harm China. If those five men did what they did for China, and I believe that this is so, is it not also true that they will have done it in vain, if we permit them to live to the harm of China? I say that we need a plan, need to know where we are going. Those five comrades are and must be a part of our plan, whether they live or die. China freed from foreign shackles is our goal. The lives of those five men and all of us here are but an incident on the way. Let us debate the matter."

"He may be young, but he talks sense!" observed a greybeard.

"I prefer plain, simple talk," said another. "There is no place among us for scholars who wrap up everything in smooth phrases."

"It seems we have a communist among us," remarked Chang.

"And why not?" was the aggressive reply.

"I am no communist!" snorted a portly banker. "I am a patriot."

"We are all patriots, are we not?" asked Chang. "But I suspect that we have here patriots of the left wing, patriots of the centre and patriots of the right wing—three separate and distinct ways to patriotism! Perhaps it ill becomes me, remembering that I am not even a member of your Brotherhood, but I cannot help observing that our patriotism will be more practical if we all approach it by the same road."

"That is right!" shouted Red Tiger, thumping the table. "The learned magistrate is right. I am no orator to spin words. I am a man of action. But the learned magistrate, for all his fine phrases, has hit upon our weakness. If he will become one of us I will relinquish my high position among you. Let us put it to the vote."

So it was that Magistrate Chang, who sought out the Brotherhood for guidance, remained to give it guidance.

2

ALTHOUGH at first Magistrate Chang refused to accept the office of President of the Brotherhood, which was thrust on him, he consented to sit on the governing council in a strictly advisory capacity. It was, nevertheless, significant that his advice when given was taken with the same celerity as though given in the form of a command.

"Since we are conspirators," he observed sagely, "it is highly important that we do not behave like conspirators. Let us, therefore, not meet in damp cold underground vaults. A time may come when we shall be glad of them as a refuge. . . ."

For the future meetings were held at various places in the city, in private houses and in the private dining-room of the "Golden Duck," whose proprietor was a member of the Brotherhood.

"Violence," remarked Chang on another occasion, "is the last refuge of the mental bankrupt. Violence is the weapon of the strong, for violence begets violence. China is weak."

And his new-found comrades of the Brotherhood, most of whom had believed in violence passionately, wonderingly agreed with him, for they found he was right. For the most part they were simple men, glad to have another to do their thinking for them.

But always they pressed him about the fate of the five men.

"I am come to the conclusion," he said at last, "that it will be better if the five pirates live."

"The five patriots!" shouted Red Tiger angrily.

"We know that they are pirates," Chang retorted gently, "but we do not know whether they are patriots. Let that be as it may. I am impelled now to think of the words of a western barbarian, a man of France, I believe. He was not altogether without wisdom when he said that no seed sown in the earth brings forth a quicker harvest than the blood of martyrs. Let us, therefore, find martyrs!"

"I do not understand," said Red Tiger, a puzzled look on his face.

"It is agreed, is it not," said Chang smoothly, "that as a magistrate I am of more value to the Brotherhood than as a private person?"

"Of course!" came a chorus of agreement.

"How long, think you, would I remain a magistrate if I were to sign an order for the release of the five—patriots. A day? An hour? Then you will also agree that on a not far distant day the sword of the executioner must descend five times. The question then remains to be decided: on whose necks shall the sword fall?"

"Ah!" grunted Red Tiger. "I will soon find five men for you. Nothing is more easy. I will find you a score if you wish. . . ."

"Innocent men?"

"Innocent or guilty, what does it matter? I am concerned that my five men regain their freedom."

"To eat steel might be a happy release for many," said Chang, "but I feel, nevertheless, that to hand over to the executioner five innocent men would be unworthy of our high aims. You know, do you not, that your five men were betrayed?"

"We have always believed it," said Red Tiger, "otherwise how could the soldiers have been warned?"

"It may interest you to know, then, that not only were your men betrayed, but that it is my duty tomorrow to hand the reward to the informer. . . ."

"His name?" snarled Red Tiger.

"I do not know," said Chang. "The reward was given by the Japanese business house of Fureno. It was handed to the magistrates to be given to whomsoever should give information leading to the arrest of members of the Brotherhood. The man, or men, will be identified by possession of a torn piece of paper, of which I have the other half. Tomorrow there will be many who will come to see me at the *Yamen*. One of these, perhaps more, will be the informer. One man will leave my presence with white powder on his gown. That man will go immediately to the Kut-ching bank, on which I shall draw an order to pay him without question the sum of one thousand dollars. Nothing must happen near the *Yamen*. Nothing must happen until he has been paid the reward. That is understood?"

"And afterwards?" asked the Small General.

"Let whatever is done be done quietly. Take him to a safe place, for there are certain questions which might with profit be put to him."

Magistrate Chang looked out from a window in the *Yamen* on to the courtyard beneath, where a throng of lawyers, petitioners and others full of their own affairs, awaited his convenience. Years of contact with people such as these had not improved his faith in human nature. To serve their own selfish interests, he knew, there was hardly one of those waiting who would hesitate to perjure himself, or otherwise defeat the ends of justice. He knew also that many of them were discussing with friends, lawyers and witnesses whether to offer a bribe to the magistrate and, if so, how much. It was strange, Chang reflected, that although his refusal to accept bribes was almost notorious, so many litigants simply interpreted this as meaning that he would not accept small bribes. So, over the years, while the offering of bribes had become rather less frequent, the size of the bribes had grown steadily larger. To many otherwise normal people the idea of a magistrate administering justice blindfold, without fear or favour, seemed to be too absurd to entertain. Men came before him with, as it turned out, valid cases which, judged on the facts alone, ensured them a favourable verdict. When their bribes were refused, as they always were, they would turn away hopelessly to await judgment against them. Chang would laugh inwardly at the bewilderment on their faces when, after hearing both sides, he awarded judgment in favour of those whose bribes he had refused. Some of them would call upon him a few days later to thank him for his verdict. As they were leaving they would drop a newspaper on his desk with apparent carelessness. Underneath it would be a tight wad of bank notes. On his desk Chang had a pair of small brass tongs such as are used to feed a charcoal brazier. With one hand he would lift the newspaper, while with the tongs he would hand back to the donor the wad of notes, a gesture which clearly revealed, even to the most obtuse, the distaste he felt for the money and the manner of offering it.

In his early days as a magistrate Chang used to punish those who offered bribes, but he had long ceased doing this. The custom was so deeply ingrained into Chinese life that he found himself blaming the system rather than those who perpetuated what seemed very right and normal.

As he looked out of the window that morning, he found himself wondering how many of those below, although he had refused bribes in the past from several of them, really believed that justice would be theirs as a right and without payment. Not very many, he realised sadly.

That, and other things, was what was wrong with China. In their reverence for old things and old customs the people of China had become wrong-headed. If only they could be made to realise that only good ideas, customs and conceptions were worthy of survival if they were old, and worthy of adoption if they were new! Instead of which the people gave their reverence to the old customs solely on the ground of their antiquity, quite regardless of their essential goodness or badness. Men earned the approval of their fellows by glib quotations from the wisdom of Confucius, the inner grace of which had in large part been lost behind the stilted pedantry of those who had recorded him for posterity. If The Sage himself were to be reincarnated, Chang believed, and were to repeat his profound utterances under another name and in more modern language, better suited to the time, China would not give him a hearing. The reincarnation of Confucius would have to wait another twenty-five centuries before antiquity gave his wisdom the ring of authority so dear to China.

It was easy to see why the thrusting foreigner had found it so simple to bleed China, whose people were so busy looking to the past for guidance that they could not find the time to examine the dangers and perplexities of the present, which threatened the very existence of their country and its ancient institutions which they professed to love so much.

Chang did not altogether approve of this Brotherhood of the Grand Canal, its members and its methods. A turn of the wheel one way could make it a potent instrument for harm, while a turn the other way could as easily light a fire in Chinese hearts whose fierce heat might cleanse and purify China.

There had been a time when Chang had believed that example alone was a great enough force to achieve reform, but he had latterly come to the belief that, no matter for how long a dog con-

144

templated a bird, he would not learn to fly. His fellow magistrates had known for years that he did not accept bribes, but the knowledge seemed in no way to have lessened the alacrity with which they seized every bribe offered.

Chang sighed deeply as he contemplated the wide gulf which lay between the Ideal Man and the great mass of humanity, its silly fears, diminutive stature and endless greed.

One of those waiting yonder in the yard, he mused, was the informer, the lowest of all things which had learned to walk erect. This was one of the very few subjects on which men of every race, creed and social rank were agreed. The traitorous informer, whether the cause he betrayed were worthy or not, was outside the pale of human consideration. Even those who hired informers were not, illogical as it might seem, so low in the moral scale.

Magistrate Chang sat down wearily at his desk, ringing a bell to tell the *Yamen* servants that he was ready to receive petitioners. Even in this simple matter, as he well knew, there was no honesty. These who proffered a fee were ushered in first, while those who did not, waited until the end and were very likely sent away to come another day. The informer, Chang guessed, would be anxious to have done with things, to collect his reward and be on his way. He would be sure to fee the servants well.

The first petitioner complained that during the widening of a canal a few miles out of the city there had been an encroachment on the graves of his ancestors, as a result of which the skeleton of his grandfather had been exposed to the mockery of all who passed along the canal, causing him great shame.

"It is a lie," said an official who had been charged with the survey for the widened canal. "The graves of this man's ancestors lie a full fifty paces from the canal. The skeleton which was exposed he bought for three hundred cash from a Ningpo man, who found it on the sea-shore. I have the man here now. . . ."

The past, mused Chang, always the past!

The fifth petitioner, a soberly dressed man of clerkly mien, entered the room furtively, looking over his shoulder to make sure he was not being observed. The pupils of his eyes were contracted, a sure sign of fear. Before the man pulled from his sleeve a torn piece of paper Chang knew that he was the informer.

With a pair of tongs Chang took the torn sheet, comparing the tear with the other half, which reposed in a drawer. Before handing over the bank order-to-pay he looked up into the informer's face, which wore a haunted, hunted look.

"You have already paid far more than a thousand dollars in suffering, have you not?" Chang asked gently. "The rice bought with such money has but a poor flavour."

"I will take my money and go," said the man. "I have earned it."

"Indeed, you have earned it. The Kut-ching bank will give you one thousand dollars in exchange for this. No questions will be asked you. Now go!"

Without a word the informer seized the bank order, which he tucked into his sleeve. As he turned his back Chang squeezed a rubber ball he held concealed in his right hand, so that a great white patch of powder appeared on the man's gown, which was of a dark blue fabric.

"He is not one of us," whispered Red Tiger when the informer emerged from the *Yamen*. "Go on ahead and tell those waiting at the bank not to seize him there, but to follow where he goes. We shall then learn who is the informer."

The Small General ran on ahead to issue the instructions.

Beads of sweat stood out on the informer's brow as he handed the slip of paper to a clerk in the Kut-ching bank. He had not known at the time he laid the information that he would feel as he did. His teeth chattered and his knees felt weak under him. There was nothing to fear, he told himself. Everything had gone according to plan. See! The clerk was already counting out one thousand dollars. Four hundred of them would go to pay old debts, and with the rest he would be able to buy a share of his uncle's business, which was in Chinkiang, far away from Soochow and any fear of recognition.

With the thousand dollars safely tucked up his sleeve the informer left the bank to keep a rendezvous in an eating-house on the other side of the city. From time to time he looked over his shoulder, glancing quickly at the faces of those behind him. After some ten minutes of fast walking, dodging down little-frequented turnings where followers would become conspicuous, the realisation dawned on him that he *was* being followed. He was an active man and, provided his knees did not collapse under him, he believed he could shake off pursuit. An opportunity came sooner than he expected. As he was approaching a camel-back bridge over one of the canals the prow of a motor-propelled barge was just entering the arch. Leaping on to the parapet of the bridge, he dropped lightly on to the deck of the barge some ten feet below.

Quick as he had been, the Small General was quicker, landing on the after-end of the barge a bare two seconds later, twisting his ankle slightly as he did so. The foothold he secured was precarious, on the curved top of a deck-house over the living-quarters of the barge crew. Pursuer and pursued each seized the first weapon which came to hand. The Small General seized a hatchet, which had been left lying by a man who had been using it a few moments earlier. The informer, noting with satisfaction that his pursuer had hurt himself, grabbed one end of a heavy pole. His rush caught the Small General off his guard, precipitating him overboard into the filthy water of the canal, but not before the hatchet sank into the left hand of the informer.

The barge, travelling at a fast walking pace, disappeared round a bend in the canal as the Small General, deeply mortified at his failure, made his way to the canal bank. As he swam towards a flight of stone steps there bobbed to the surface a cleanly severed finger.

The President of the Beggars' Guild, only after considerable pressure, consented to entrust his messages to the telegraph. He had eyes and ears everywhere.

"I can send a message more quickly in all directions than a barge can travel," he snorted, "even though it be driven through the water by a stinking foreign engine. A mouse will not escape through the net I will spread . . . but telegraphs! Furthermore, I do not believe that the message runs along the wire. . . ."

"Nevertheless, it is so," observed the Small General patiently. "A message can be sent a thousand *li* in less than a minute."

"But a barge cannot travel a thousand *li* in one night. . . ."

"The barge cannot, but who knows where the man will have left the barge?"

"Very well," said the aged President of the Beggars' Guild, "give me the sense of your message and I will write pieces of paper for the telegraphs."

"The barge was black in colour," said the Small General. "It carried a cargo of Soochow pottery. It was travelling in the direction of the Great Fork, where it might have turned east to Shanghai, or south to Hangchow. The *laodah* will have lost a hatchet—this is it in my hand—it fell into the water with me. The man I seek is a clerk. He has one thousand dollars in his possession, but he has lost the first finger of his left hand. See! I have it here . . . !"

The Small General unrolled a wisp of rag to exhibit the finger.

A few minutes later telegrams flashed over the wires in all possible directions, warning sharp-eyed and -eared beggars to watch for and report on a barge whose *laodah* would be bewailing the loss of a hatchet, and whose passenger, whether he bewailed the fact or not, would have lost the index finger of his left hand.

A little after sundown there came a report from Kwenchan that the barge had passed through, an hour before the telegram had been received. Its destination was, therefore, Shanghai. A man had been seen to step ashore at Kwenchan. The net was closing.

Magistrate Chang had reported that the informer spoke with the accents of Shanghai. The chances were, therefore, that after stepping ashore at Kwenchan, the man had gone on to Shanghai by train. The railway time-table revealed that, if he had done so, he would already have arrived at his destination.

It was winter time, when cold winds from the north induced the vast majority of Chinese abroad in the streets of Shanghai to walk about with their hands up their sleeves, which much facilitated concealment by the informer of the fact that he had lost a finger. Since he was unlikely to betray himself out of doors and since the beggars of Shanghai had very little opportunity of watching for him anywhere else, other means had to be employed.

Word went out from the Brotherhood's headquarters in Shanghai to maintain a watch in eating-houses, in hotels and outside the premises of doctors.

A fugitive, whether from justice or injustice, on arriving in the great cosmopolitan city of Shanghai, would be far more likely to hide himself away in the International Settlement, or the French Concession, than in the Chinese city. There is no place in all China where there is less curiosity about the comings and goings of individuals, whether Chinese or foreigners.

In Soochow the meetings of the Brotherhood would be fraught with embarrassment until the informer had been traced. To both

148

Red Tiger and the Small General the man was a stranger. He must, therefore, have secured his information from some member of the Brotherhood in Soochow. Nobody outside Soochow knew of the projected raid upon the Japanese barge. Someone at the very heart of the Brotherhood, therefore, must be a traitor. There could be no peace of mind until he were found.

It was some few moments before the young American doctor at the mission hospital, the same who had attended Sung in his illness, recognised the Small General.

"I have come to you because of your great skill and knowledge," said the Small General. This was not strictly true, for he had come because foreign doctors were notoriously close-mouthed.

"You appear to be in the best of health," said the doctor, peering over the top of his spectacles, "and not at all in need of my great skill and knowledge. Nevertheless, I am flattered. What can I do for you?"

"Supposing," said the Small General, "that one wished to preserve a severed finger, what would be the best way of doing so?"

Now doctors the world over dislike hypothetical questions, probably because of the unpleasant implication in them that those submitting the hypotheses lack complete confidence. But whatever the reasons, the young doctor was no exception to the rule.

"There are several methods," was the cryptic reply, "and none of them which is not foolish, as far as I am aware. Of what use is a severed finger?"

"Very little use," the Small General agreed, "but it is well known that some persons have strange whims. If it were my finger, I assure you, I would not trouble to preserve it."

"There is a finger, then?"

"Yes, there is a finger. It so happens that it is the finger of a friend who has gone on a journey. He left in a great hurry and, before he left, he expressed a wish that it should be preserved for him. A foolish whim, I know, but one cannot ignore the wishes of an absent friend. It seems that many years ago he travelled in a ship to India. There he went to a very holy place and, with the first finger of his left hand, he was privileged to touch a most holy tomb. Naturally, he wishes to keep the finger. . . ."

"Naturally," agreed the doctor. "Where is the finger?"

It is a pity, reflected the Small General, unrolling a piece of rag containing the finger, that these foreigners are so blunt and impolite. He laid the finger on the table.

"I will preserve the finger for you," said the doctor with a smile, taking down a small jar from a shelf.

"You are most kind! When my friend returns I will call for the finger."

"When your friend returns," corrected the doctor, "let him come for the finger. If it is his I will give it to him."

"That brings me to another question," said the Small General. "If my friend comes to claim his finger—he may, of course, be too embarrassed to do so—you would be able with absolute certainty to state that it was his?"

"With absolute certainty!" replied the doctor.

"I am glad," observed the Small General, with an entirely fictitious air of relief, "for it would be most unfortunate if the wrong person were to claim the finger, would it not?"

"It would, but it would also be most unlikely, I feel. I am busy now, so when your friend returns he may come here to claim his property. I trust that he has not been touching any more—holy places."

Since it penetrated the Small General's consciousness that the doctor was amusing himself at his expense, he left hurriedly, noting the position of the cupboard where the jar containing the finger was locked up. It would be a very simple matter to send a thief to fetch it when needed. There were thieves in the Guild who could steal the bed from under a sleeping man without awakening him.

In a way which he could not analyse, the hospital irritated the Small General profoundly. It was so absurdly clean, for one thing, and for another it smelled always of powerful drugs. But it went deeper than that. Everyone was so busy there, doing apparently useless and stupid things. He stepped in the ante-room to the doctor's office, where a neatly dressed Chinese nurse in hospital white was fiddling about with a lot of shining instruments. In point of fact she was sterilising them preparatory to an operation.

"Why do you do that?" the Small General asked her.

"To make sure that they are clean," was the reply.

"Any fool can see that they are already so clean that they cannot be made any cleaner," he said contemptuously. "If you do not wish to tell me what you are doing you need not do so, but please do not tell me foolish tales like that. It is not polite."

He stalked haughtily across the room to where swing doors led out on to a passage, but halted at the threshold on hearing the sound of a sob. Curiosity, coloured a trifle perhaps by the fact that the girl was so very good-looking, made him turn, which he did just in time to see her wiping a tear from her eye with the corner of her apron.

The girl, with downcast eyes, continued with her task of arranging the tray of instruments to her satisfaction, her deft fingers working with an amazing precision like (although the Small General did not recognise the likeness) the fingers of a skilled surgeon. He looked at her narrowly, realising as he did so that her face was familiar.

"I remember!" he said. "You are Peahen!"

"I am Peahen," she replied, her face illumined by a very lovely smile of pleasure that he had remembered her.

"Are you not afraid of cutting yourself on those knives?" he asked, remembering that she was almost blind. "With my two good eyes I would not care to handle them so quickly."

Peahen did not reply. For answer she drew herself to her full height and, smiling proudly, walked across the room to him.

"The daughter of Lok-kai-shing does not brush your gown carefully," she said lightly, picking a minute piece of cotton thread off his sleeve. The thread was black and the gown was dark green.

"How long has your sight been restored to you?" he asked wonderingly.

"God gave me my sight three years ago . . ."

"*Who* gave it to you? You mean the foreign doctor . . . ?"

"God gave me my sight, using the hands of the foreign doctor. . . ."

"Do not talk like a fool, woman! One moment you say that God gave you your sight and the next that the foreign doctor gave it to you. Which do you mean? Talk plainly, woman, and do not forget that you were only a servant . . ."

"As I told you, God gave me my sight. . . ."

"I understand now," said the Small General scornfully, "you have allowed the missionaries to fill your head with nonsense.

Since God, whoever he may be, gave you your sight, perhaps he will also give you good manners, for you need them badly enough."

But despite his curt treatment of her, the Small General carried away from the hospital a picture of her which obtruded itself across his line of vision at the most disconcerting times and places. If she had not talked such nonsense he would have been kinder to her, for he remembered that, as an almost blind girl, groping in the half light in which she lived, she had been a very attentive servant.

⋐ 3 ⋑

ALMOST every large-scale activity of Chinese life has a Guild, which exercises a rigid control over members, the conditions of their work and the ethical standards considered desirable. Some of these latter are very high, while some are not so high.

In every town and city in China the hotel workers are banded together in close-knit organisations and, for purposes of mutual aid, these town and city organisations are closely linked with each other. When a transient guest departs from an hotel it is customary for his room-servant to make certain cryptic marks on his baggage. The ordinary person would neither notice nor understand these marks; but no matter where the traveller went in China, and even beyond, to such places as Malaya, where Chinese servants predominate, within five minutes of his arrival in an hotel, or aboard a steamship, a thumbnail biography would be in the possession of the staff.

Mostly these cryptic marks deal with money matters. The guest tips well, or does not tip at all. He is bad-tempered in the mornings. He consorts with peculiar people. He is a person of great refinement, or the converse. There is neither beginning nor end to the remarks which hotel servants thus inscribe for the benefit of their fellows elsewhere.

Now it so happened that in the large Yip Lee Hotel in Shanghai, situated on one of the intersections of the Nanking Road, one of the house-boys was not only most observant, but a very conscientious member of his guild. One of the guests in the hotel, a man named Ling, occupied a room on the top floor which was serviced by the aforesaid boy. The guest, Ling, stayed at the hotel for one week, at the end of which he departed for an unstated destination. For baggage he had one brand-new fibre suitcase.

The evening that Ling arrived in the hotel he asked the boy whether he could give him the name of a reliable doctor in the vicinity. The boy immediately recommended a certain Dr. King,

153

with whom he had a standing arrangement which yielded him ten per cent of all fees collected from patients thus introduced. The arrangement is common practice in China—and not only in China. Ling complained that he had hurt his ribs.

This everyday incident would have passed entirely without notice but for the chance that the hotel boy lay awake that night with a severe earache and, at the first opportunity the following morning, visited Dr. King.

"I hope you were able to cure the ribs of the patient I sent to you last night," remarked the boy casually.

"You sent me no patient with an affliction of the ribs," the doctor retorted.

"That is very strange," said the boy, "because I sent you a guest named Ling who, after his return to the hotel, reported to me that you had given him great relief."

"It is true that you sent me a patient named Ling," said the doctor, consulting his book, "but if there were anything wrong with his ribs he did not tell me so. I treated him for a severed finger which, he told me, had been crushed in a machine. I wondered why he should tell me such a foolish lie, for a child could see that the finger had been severed by a very sharp instrument, which cannot have been too clean."

The doctor and the boy from the hotel shrugged their shoulders. As they both knew very well, many persons disliked discussing their ailments with strangers and, for their own good reasons, lied about them.

Most people feel a certain resentment against those who tell wanton and gratuitous lies. Perhaps it is that they are somewhat insulting. Furthermore, with the certain knowledge that a man has told one lie, however unimportant, there is a tendency to suspect his every utterance and to weave about his head somewhat fantastic theories.

However this may be, when Ling left the Yip Lee Hotel for an unstated destination, his new fibre suitcase bore certain cryptic markings under the grip of the handle: "Tips well—never shows left hand—goes out only at night—great fear."

It stood to reason that the President of the Soochow Hotel-Workers' Guild was a member of the Brotherhood of the Grand Canal, for such an association was mutually helpful. The President, therefore, received the Small General with the utmost cordiality.

"I seek a man," the Small General explained. "He lives in great fear. Of that I am sure. I do not know his name. He is, I would judge, a clerk, a man of about thirty years of age, of a most respectable appearance. He had lost the first finger of his left hand—very recently. I know only that he reached Shanghai some five days ago. He may have friends there, for it is said that he speaks with the accents of Shanghai. But he also knows Soochow well, for, when he was told in connection with a certain matter to go to the Kut-ching bank, he walked there without hesitation. For a little time, I think, he will avoid friends and places where he is known. He knows, furthermore, that those who seek him are aware that he has lost his finger."

"It is not much," observed the President, "but I think it will be enough. The matter is very urgent?"

"It is of the utmost urgency!"

"In affairs such as this," said the President, "I have always found that the offering of a reward expedites matters. With a reward to spur them, the diligent become more diligent."

"One hundred dollars is enough?"

"Two hundred would be better. . . ."

"So be it! Two hundred is the reward."

Within two hours of the Small General's departure from the premises of the Soochow Hotel-Workers' Guild, the President had written an identical letter to the affiliated Guilds in every town and city in the Yangtsze Valley as far up-river as Ichang, as well as to ports as far south as Amoy and as far north as Chefoo and Tientsin. The letter was short, but to the point:

> We desire news of a clerkly person, aged about 30, name unknown, who glances fearfully over his shoulder. He was in Shanghai five days ago. The first finger of his left hand is missing, but he will conceal the fact with great care. For this news we will pay twenty-five dollars and the cost of a telegram.

It had been the President's intention to offer ten dollars, but he increased the reward to twenty-five since the Brotherhood had impressed upon him the urgency of the matter.

If the man who called himself Ling, instead of telling the hotel-boy a direct and provable lie, had contented himself with asking for the name of a reliable doctor, without offering any reason therefor, the chances are that he would still be enjoying a modicum of prosperity as his uncle's partner in the Chinkiang business. With ordinary care he would not have had the smallest difficulty in concealing the fact that a finger was missing. There was nothing otherwise at all conspicuous about him. His description was identical with that of a million other clerical workers in the Yangtsze Valley and, without that foolish lie about the non-existent rib trouble, he could have merged into the background of his chosen life as inconspicuously as a blade of grass among ten million others.

But the man who called himself Ling lied and, by one of the slender chances which govern human destiny, lied to a hotel-boy with earache, who discovered the lie and, because of it, noted certain little peculiarities which he would not otherwise have noted.

The man who called himself Ling wished to attend to certain matters of business in Hankow, which lies many hundreds of miles up the Yangtsze River. To go thither he bought a ticket by a British river steamer, the *Kut Wo,* travelling up-river in surprising luxury, sharing a cabin with a Chinese merchant. On his previous trips to Hankow he had always travelled as a deck passenger for a microscopic fare, well suited to his slender means. As a deck passenger, of course, there would have been no attentive cabin servant to do his bidding and, equally certainly, nobody to read the small inscription under the leather grip of his new suitcase.

The cabin steward in the *Kut Wo,* seeing a shining new fibre suitcase belonging to the younger of the two passengers who shared cabin number 43, turned down the handle, read the inscription and noted with satisfaction that its owner was generous with tips. The other occupant of the cabin he knew well, so he did not trouble to scrutinise his baggage.

In conversation with his cabin mate, the man who called himself Ling told another lie, which the cabin steward chanced to hear. When asked in the most casual possible fashion where he had stayed in Shanghai, a question which travellers may address to one another without any impertinence, the man who called himself Ling gave the name of an obscure hostelry in the Chapei district.

Why, the steward asked himself, should a man who had stayed at the excellent Yip Lee Hotel on the Nanking Road trouble to tell a fellow traveller that he had stayed at an unsavoury inn in Chapei?

When the new fibre suitcase left the *Kut Wo* at Hankow another inscription was neatly added to that already under the grip. It described the owner of the case as "a great liar". This, of course, was read and noted by the room-servant of the Kiukiang Hotel who, in the natural order of things, paid more attention to this quiet and well-mannered guest than would otherwise have been possible in the overcrowded condition of the establishment.

Two days after the arrival of the great liar who called himself Ling, who had been seen through the keyhole of his room to be applying medicaments to the stump of his finger, the room-servant had a free evening, during which he took the opportunity to visit the premises of his Guild, where his dues were slightly in arrears. From habit he read the notices pinned to the board, among them that which had been circulated by the President of the Soochow Hotel-Workers' Guild. Knowing from experience that if he mentioned the matter to a Guild official he would be compelled to disgorge a great part of the reward of twenty-five dollars, the hotel boy paid his dues to date and wrote a letter to Soochow stating that he had under observation the man they wanted, who was at the Kiukiang Hotel. He refrained from sending a telegram because the notice did not specifically state that, even if an error were made, the cost would be refunded.

Two days after this, which was two whole days before the Guild in Soochow received the letter, Ling paid his bill and departed from the hotel, announcing that he was going by that night's up-river steamer to Ichang. His room-boy followed him to the steamship office, determined not to lose the reward money, and listened to the argument which took place there. Ling, it appeared, had a return ticket which would take him as far as Shanghai, which was in the opposite direction to Ichang. He wanted to travel as far as Chinkiang and, being of a careful disposition, demanded the return in cash of the difference, which was not given to him. Now Chinkiang is the last important down-river port of call before Shanghai, situated, as will be remembered, at the point where the Grand Canal debouches into the Yangtsze. Realising that his letter would not yet have been delivered and, having already lost fifteen of the twenty-five dollars reward at the gambling tables, the hotel boy decided that he would risk a telegram. This explains why, when the man named Ling stepped off the steamer at Chinkiang he was, for all practical purposes, already dead.

The Small General recognised him instantly, pointing him out to members of the Brotherhood who were charged with the duty of watching his every move, until such time as he had revealed to the watchers the identity of the traitor or traitors within the Brotherhood itself, who provided information which enabled him to lay advance information with the authorities about the projected raid upon the Japanese cargo. To make matters doubly sure, among the watchers were brothers and other near relatives of the five men who still lay under sentence of death in Soochow.

The correct name of the man who called himself Ling, it was learned within a few hours of his arrival in Chinkiang, was Samling, he being the nephew of Sam-wei-yu, a small but highly respected merchant of the city. A few hours later still it was possible to establish with the irreducible minimum of doubt that Sam-ling's two brothers, members of the Brotherhood, living in Soochow, were the actual traitors who had supplied the information. These two, it was now remembered, had suggested the precise spot for the attack on the barge.

Sam-ling's two brothers were confirmed gamblers. On the evening after Sam-ling stepped ashore at Chinkiang these two went to a house of ill-fame in Soochow where, on an upper floor, a variant of the game of poker was played for high stakes. Here they were so fortunate that, long after midnight, they rose from the table heavy winners, so heavy, indeed, that they were quite unjustly suspected of having given fortune certain artificial aids.

It is a strange commentary on human nature that these two brothers, who had not hesitated to break a most solemn oath, or betray five comrades to the executioner, would have scorned to cheat at any gambling game. Neither, for example, would have known a happy moment while gambling losses remained unpaid, just as neither would have hesitated to steal in order to pay the losses.

The Brotherhood's long arm reached out and seized these two brothers as they left the gambling den. Quilted sacks, expertly thrown over their heads, stifled their cries for help. The Brotherhood seized these two first for a twofold reason. Firstly, they had forsworn their oath, and secondly, if their brother had been seized before them in Chinkiang, some warning might have reached them.

"As a private person," Chang remarked in his most judicial manner, "I fully agree with your opinion that these three men are in fact blood brothers. But, as a magistrate, I tell you that you have failed to establish this as a fact. One of the three is guilty of being an informer. I can testify that he is the man who came to me at the *Yamen* to claim the reward. You can testify that he is the man who cashed the order at the bank. You can also testify that you *believe* he is the man whose finger you severed with a hatchet. . . ."

"I did sever his finger with a hatchet," said the Small General indignantly. "You have only to look at his left hand to satisfy yourself that this is so."

"That would tell me merely that he has lost a finger," corrected Chang. "The man himself states that it was severed in Shanghai when his hand was caught in the spokes of a rickshaw wheel. As a private person, I think he is a liar. As a magistrate, I tell you that, in the absence of proof, his statement is as valid as yours."

"Happily, I have proof," said the Small General triumphantly, "for at the mission hospital there is a glass jar in which lies the severed finger. The doctor told me that he could identify the owner of the finger with absolute certainty when he came to claim it. If one doctor can do this, so can another. I will send a thief to steal the finger. We have now a doctor who is a member of the Brotherhood. He will tell us that the finger is that of the informer."

"Excellent!" said Chang. "But before you leave there is another matter. You and others assert that, according to information which was given to you in Chinkiang, these three men, the informer and the other two, are blood brothers. They state that they are not. They state that they are strangers to each other. So far no person has come forward to state from personal knowledge of all three that they are in fact blood brothers. They may be speaking the truth. What then?"

"With great respect, illustrious Chang," said the Small General, "I say that you go too far in giving these men the benefit of such negligible doubts, if they are doubts."

"The three of them are traitorous dogs," roared Red Tiger, "and I say they should die—slowly."

"Listen, my impetuous friends," said Chang commandingly. "I would like to ask you a question. Let us suppose that you have just bought a fine new broom with which to sweep out your house. Would you, tell me, before beginning to sweep dip the broom in filth?"

"Of course not," roared Red Tiger. "I am not an imbecile. But what has this matter of sweeping houses to do with these traitors?"

"Only this," replied Chang softly and with great earnestness. "We are men who have taken upon ourselves the task of trying to cleanse our native land. We wish to evict foreigners who flout our laws and customs. We wish to root out the dishonest officials who have pawned our land to foreign bankers. Above all we wish to create a state of life in China in which there is justice—for all; where rich and poor, weak and powerful, can come before the courts safe in the certainty that their pleas will be judged on their merits and that bribes will not tip the scales of justice. I am right, am I not, in stating these and other things as our aims?"

"Aye!" came a chorus of assent.

"Then how can we hope to achieve these aims if we begin the task of sweeping away filth and corruption with a filthy broom? These two brothers whom we suspect of treason are human beings. The third whom, with the merest shadow of doubt, we believe to be the informer, is also a human being. These three are a small part of the toiling millions who are China. As we demand justice for ourselves, I demand justice for these three. If the Brotherhood is, as we say, a tool dedicated to high purposes, let us not dim its shining splendour by unworthy uses. I am a newcomer to your midst, but there is no place here for me unless we are agreed that as we demand justice, so we will give justice."

There was a deadly silence as Chang resumed his seat. Those who heard him were, for the most part, rough ignorant men, but the simple force and logic of what he had said could not be denied.

What a very irritating habit it was of the American doctor, the Small General reflected, this habit of peering across the tops of his spectacles. It was disconcerting, too.

"My friend has returned from his journey and he would like his finger. . . ."

"Tell him to come here and claim it, then, and I will give it to him," replied the American doctor, and there was that in his face which suggested that to prolong the conversation would prove fruitless.

Peahen was in the ante-room as the Small General emerged from this profitless interview.

"You are very beautiful this morning," he remarked easily, "and I see that your gown is still white and clean."

"I have a clean white gown every day," said Peahen proudly. "In a hospital there must be nothing dirty."

"I always thought foreigners were mad, but now I know it," he remarked, stung by a certain condescension in the girl's manner. It also occurred to him to wonder how it was that when he was in daily contact with her he had failed to notice her truly striking beauty. Perhaps those unknown parents who in time of famine had cast their daughter upon the sweeping flood of the Yangtsze had been people of noble birth, for Peahen had none of the marks of a peasant. The theory was most improbable, as the Small General well knew, for famines did not touch people of noble birth. They either escaped, or they had secret hoards of food. It was, nevertheless, pleasant to weave the little romance about Peahen's head.

Another thought occurred to the Small General: one not so pleasing. This American doctor was young, unmarried and passably good-looking, in a barbarian manner, and so might appeal to empty-headed Chinese girls. Peahen behaved as though she were infatuated with him.

"There is a small thing you may do for me," said the Small General after an awkward pause, putting aside fanciful thoughts and remembering that he had an errand.

"It would make me very happy to help you," replied Peahen with a very sweet smile, "for I have not forgotten that it was through you I was brought here and had my sight restored to me. I am very grateful."

"You have many gratitudes these days," was the caustic retort.

"First you are grateful to God, then to the American doctor and now—to me. I am honoured to find myself in such company."

"I have only one gratitude," said Peahen serenely, "but it is divided into many parts."

"The biggest part, doubtless, being for the American doctor? In fact, your gratitude to him is so great that you share his bed with him, is it not so?"

The Small General bit his lip. What a fool he was to have injected this note into the conversation at this time!

"There was mention of a small service I might render you, to prove my gratitude," said Peahen coolly, ignoring the outburst. "Please tell me of it."

"A short time ago I left here a severed finger, belonging to a friend. I was guarding it for him. A few minutes ago I asked the American doctor for it and he would not give it to me. Please steal it for me to-day. I wish merely to show it to my friend and then, if the American doctor wishes, he may keep it. . . ."

"I did not offer to become a thief for you," said Peahen with quiet anger. "I am trusted here."

"You would not be a thief," said the Small General. "If anyone is a thief it is the American doctor, for he detains that which does not belong to him."

"I will not do this thing for you!"

"Then, as I suspected, you are an ungrateful bitch!"

The President of the Thieves' Guild was a tall, distinguished man of the old school, whose courtly manners and loftly diction singled him out from the common herd. He was, strange though it may seem, one of the chief pillars of law and order. Bearing the surname of Kung, he claimed descent from the Great Sage himself.*

In Soochow and for many miles around thieves did not prosper, or perhaps it would be more correct to state that free-lance thieves did not prosper. For more than twenty years under Kung's iron rule, all the thieves, and other undesirables who were potential thieves, had been gathered under the wing of the Thieves' Guild.

Now it is axiomatic that if thieves are debarred from stealing, they are still under the common human necessity to eat. The Thieves' Guild provided the thieves with food, shelter and a

* The correct name of the Great Sage was Kung-fu-tze, Latinised to Confucius.

modicum of the lesser luxuries, depriving them at once of the excuse that they stole to eat, a plea often made by thieves.

In Western lands, which take such pride in their institutions, nobody prevents theft from occurring. The police try to prevent it. Insurance companies will, in return for an annual premium, reimburse a policy holder for the value of goods stolen, taking into account only intrinsic values. A locket containing a dead lover's hair, for example, may be worth only a few shillings. The hair itself, in the eyes of the insurance company would be worth nothing, and it is upon that basis that the policy holder would be reimbursed.

China faced these facts and difficulties centuries ago and, what is more to the point, overcame them.

Naturally, since the Thieves' Guild charged itself with the cost of feeding indigent and inactive thieves, it had to have a revenue. From what source could it draw its revenues more justly than from the chief beneficiaries of its activities, the householders of Soochow? All private residences and business premises were, therefore, assessed by the Thieves' Guild for a premium payable annually, very much smaller and more effective than that charged for burglary insurance in Western countries. The assessments, furthermore, were subject to appeal and arbitration, for it was no part of the Thieves' Guild's plan to act harshly or unreasonably— toward either householders or thieves. Upon reflection it will be seen that such an arrangement would only work in an atmosphere of sweet reasonableness, with which the venerable and courtly Kung surrounded all his transactions.

Once a householder had paid his annual assessment it became a matter of honour that the Guild should immunise those premises against thieving, and this was done with a scrupulous regard for the sanctity of contract.

One does not care to contemplate what would have happened to one of the thieves sheltering under the wings of his Guild, if he were so foolhardy and base as to steal from premises marked with the sign which proved that the owner had paid his assessment. Drastic things would befall the offender who so broke faith and, what is more important, caused the Guild to break faith. For upon its good faith rested the Guild's revenue and the not inconsiderable perquisites of the venerable Kung.

It need hardly be added that, on the occasion of the looting of a barge of Japanese cargo, for which the five patriotic pirates were condemned to death, the incident occurred beyond the jurisdiction of the Soochow Thieves' Guild. The venerable Kung and his organisation were an integral part of the Brotherhood, which could not have committed so gross a breach of etiquette as to have embarrassed the Guild in Soochow itself.

It is recorded that a very distinguished British personage once visited Soochow, wearing a heavy cable watch-chain and a massive gold-hunter watch. He wore these, like his dignity, with great prominence. To a competent pickpocket the watch and chain were almost an affront. One of the lesser brethren, however, saw this mass of bullion and decided to annex it. The personage was a foreigner and stealing from him could hardly offend the Guild. In the crush outside the premises of the Silk Guild a pin was delicately pressed into the foreigner's buttocks, and in the excitement which followed his howl of pain, the massive gold watch and chain were removed, together with a well-filled wallet.

"Look what I have here!" said the thief a few minutes later, entering the premises of the Thieves' Guild.

"Where did you get it?" asked Kung.

"A large foreigner wore it across his belly. I took it from him by the Silk Guild. . . ."

"You should not have done that," chided Kung, "for the man is the guest of our city. Certain high officials will lose much 'face' if the theft is discovered. Give them to me."

There happened to be present at the time an expert pickpocket, whose fingers were so light that he had crowned his professional career by stealing a woman's ear-rings while talking to her.

"These must be returned at once!" said Kung severely. "Please arrange this."

The crest-fallen thief and the expert left together, the former pointing out the distinguished stranger and the pockets from which the articles had been removed. Now on one end of the chain was a bunch of gewgaws, so that it had been necessary to snip out the buttonhole before removing the entire chain. When the expert approached to restore the articles the stranger was on a platform at a meeting, hemmed in by a crowd of notabilities.

It was very simple to restore the wallet to the inside breast pocket of the jacket. This was done first, even though it bulged with money. The next move proved that even experts can make mistakes. Like most westerners, the stranger habitually wore his watch on the right-hand side of his waistcoat and the gewgaws on the left. The expert replaced them in reverse order. The most difficult task had yet to be done: the cut buttonhole, through which the chain had been threaded, had to be repaired. The task had barely been completed when the foreigner reached down to consult his watch, only to find in his hands the odds and ends attached to the opposite end of the chain. The inexplicable incident provided him with a topic of conversation until his train had arrived in Shanghai.

Most important of all, however, was the fact that the Thieves' Guild, with proper civic pride, had prevented a breach of hospitality being committed in Soochow. It was entirely unimportant that the expert, vastly impressed by the bulging wallet and the weight of the watch and chain, took the same train to Shanghai and in the press at Shanghai North station, removed both for the second time that day and, before nightfall, was back in Soochow with them. At that time there was a certain coolness between the Thieves' Guilds of Soochow and Shanghai or the incident would have been a breach of etiquette.

"Is it not the Small General Sung that I see before me?" asked Kung rising to greet his caller. "I cannot think of any more welcome guest. Tell me, is there some small service I can render you?"

"There is, illustrious Kung!" replied the Small General. "In a heavy iron safe at the mission hospital, or so I have been told, there reposes a small glass jar. In it is a finger. The abominable foreigner who holds the keys refuses to give me the jar, even though it was given to him for safe keeping. For certain reasons which we need not discuss, the owner of the finger cannot call for it himself. I require it tonight. I have, of course, a plan of the rooms."

"It is fortunate," remarked Kung, "that the hospital is assessed for no dues. Otherwise, and with immeasurable regret, I would have had to refuse you. It is also fortunate that we have here at this time a brother who, you may remember, opened a safe at a foreign bank in Shanghai not long ago. If that which you seek is in the safe it will be in your hands tonight. He will welcome this break in his enforced seclusion and inactivity. His fingers, he tells me, are growing stiff from disuse. . . ."

Kung stalked off majestically to discuss matters with the safe-breaker concerned.

"It is an old safe," the latter reported to Kung that night. "I opened it without difficulty. There was nothing in it except a little money and some small bottles, none of which contained a finger."

In a room far underground, below the city of Soochow, Sam-ling was shackled to ring-bolts in the wall. His eyes rounded with horror as he saw certain preparations being made. Beside him was a wooden chopping block such as used by butchers. On the other side of the room Red Tiger was putting a keen edge on a heavy cleaver, while on a charcoal brazier there bubbled a pot of boiling pitch.

"It is as well that Chang does not know of this," whispered the Small General. "I do not think he would approve."

Red Tiger's reply was unprintable.

"This will set at rest all doubts," said the Small General.

"Doubts!" snorted Red Tiger. "Who has doubts? The man is a traitor. You know and I know and Chang knows that. But, as you say, we do not want to offend Chang. Now let us get this business done. Hold his arm on the block!"

Sam-ling screamed. All this for a miserable thousand dollars. But it was too late to be sorry.

In Red Tiger's expert hands the cleaver cut cleanly through Sam-ling's left wrist. The hand wriggled a little after it had fallen on the floor. It required much strength to plunge the stump of Sam-ling's wrist into the boiling pitch, but it had to be done, or he would have bled to death, which would have been a pity.

"He does not wish to see you," whispered Peahen. "Go away! It is useless for you to wait."

"Nevertheless, I shall wait," said the Small General, folding his arms and looking very important. He found it very difficult to deal with a woman who gave herself airs and who was, seemingly, vested with a certain authority. The fact that she had long ago been his servant did not make it any the easier to endure.

When he had arrived at the hospital the Small General had felt that his story was completely water-tight, but after an hour of waiting there were certain flaws which became apparent.

"I am a little weary of seeing you here," said the American doctor when he finally arrived from the wards. "What do you want?"

"I am here upon a most important matter," said the Small General. "I shall not trouble you again."

"What is it?"

"You refused to let me have the finger I entrusted to your care, did you not?"

"I still refuse. Let your friend come here to claim it."

"He cannot. Two days ago he went away on a journey to deal with certain matters concerning land, I believe. He has been captured by bandits."

"Tell him that when he is released he may come and claim his finger."

"I do not now ask you to give me the finger," persisted the Small General. "It is upon another matter I come to you. There is some question as to his identity. The bandits demand a ransom of one thousand dollars. I, with certain other friends of his, are prepared to find this large sum provided that we are certain that it is my friend who is in the hands of the bandits."

"I don't see what I can do in the matter," said the American doctor. "I have never seen your friend, so how could I help? I doubt even"—here he peered irritatingly over the tops of his spectacles—"whether you have a friend, or if you have, whether he has been seized by bandits, or even if this happens to be true, that you would pay one thousand dollars ransom money. In all other respects, however, I am sure you are telling the truth. Now I am busy."

This was the triumphant moment for which the Small General had been waiting. He would show this big-mouthed foreigner a few things—one, to be precise.

"I overlook your impoliteness to me," he said haughtily, "but I have proof of what I say. Here"—he unwrapped a parcel—"is the left hand of my friend, which the bandits sent with the threat that they would kill him if the money were not forthcoming."

"I still do not understand how this concerns me. . . ."

"It is very simple. You assured me that if you saw the hand from which the finger was severed you could state with certainty

167

whether the two were, or were not, once joined together. Here is the hand. You have the finger. If you will be so kind as to compare the two and let me know your judgment in the matter, I shall not trouble you again. In fact, you may keep both the hand and the finger until such time as my friend is released by the bandits and comes to claim them."

"Very well," said the doctor. "I will examine them and I will tell you. But I warn you also that if, as I suspect, there is more in this than meets the eye, I shall not hesitate to inform the authorities."

"By all means," said the Small General, swallowing hard. "Why should I, a most respectable person as you know, have cause to fear the authorities?"

"You know that better than I do."

The doctor, with the severed hand, disappeared into his room.

"I think," said Peahen, "that you are a great liar."

"I think that you——" retorted the Small General, and then decided not to complete the sentence.

There was no gainsaying the fact that the girl was very lovely, and it was a pity that under foreign influence she had grown so very impertinent. That, however, could be cured—easily.

"I have to tell you," said the doctor in a very formal manner, "that the finger and the hand were once joined together."

"You are most kind," said the Small General. "Now that the identity of my friend is certain, we will send the money for his release. As to the matter of the police, I shall tell them myself. Good day!"

A little more than an hour later a man calling himself an official of the *Yamen* called at the mission hospital.

"It concerns a statement made by a person named Sung," he explained to the American doctor, "regarding certain human parts which you have here. I am happy to be able to state that we believe we have caught the bandits. We shall, therefore, need these parts. May I ask you to be so kind as to hand them over to me."

"Certainly! I am glad to be rid of them."

"Throw them in the canal," said the Small General five minutes later, as his friend emerged from the hospital.

"Let us smash the jars first . . ."

"No, best of all, let us take them somewhere and burn them.

I do not like foreigners at any time, but I like them least of all when they begin talking of the police."

"The woman did not believe that I was from the *Yamen*. It would not surprise me if she has told the doctor."

"I shall deal with the woman in my own way," said the Small General. "She was once a most respectful and well-behaved girl. Contact with these ill-mannered barbarians has spoiled her. But she is young, and it may not be too late."

Then, as an afterthought, the Small General decided that it would perhaps be better to take the severed hand and finger to Chang who, with his passion for the correct way of doing things, might wish to have the American doctor's statement corroborated independently. There was no doubt that in many ways Chang was an asset to the Brotherhood, but there was also no doubt that at times his insistence upon trivialities was exasperating.

The Small General found himself wishing, too, that the face and personality of Peahen would not obtrude themselves so persistently when he was concentrating upon other and more important matters. Women, he reflected, and without very much originality, were incalculable creatures.

ᦵᧈ 4 ᦶᧈ

It was the first formal trial ever staged by the Brotherhood, and so that it should impress itself upon all those concerned, everything was done with some ceremony. The result was a foregone conclusion.

Sam-ling was clearly identified as the informer. A physician, member of the Brotherhood, testified unhesitatingly that the finger, the hand and the stump of Sam-ling's wrist had once been joined together. There was, too, the identification by Chang and the Small General.

Sam-ling, therefore, was as good as dead.

There was a little difficulty in establishing beyond doubt that the other two men were Sam-ling's brothers. But Brotherhood members came from Chinkiang and testified that to their certain knowledge the three were brothers.

But, as Chang pointed out, the fact that Sam-ling was the informer and the additional fact that the other two were his brothers, did not establish that the former had gained his knowledge from the two brothers. Merely to be the brothers of an informer was not in itself a crime, even though no doubt remained in the mind of a reasonable person that the three had conspired together. Inexorably Chang demanded that every link in the chain of evidence be completed before justice was done.

"Let us give these men justice as we hope to have justice ourselves," he declared. Those present who had shouted the loudest against the three brothers became silent and thoughtful, as every man pictured in imagination his own trial.

"We are agreed, however," Chang said, "that Sam-ling's life is forfeit. We are justified, therefore, in using whatever means seem best to us to learn from him whence he derived the knowledge which enabled him to turn informer."

It is better to draw a veil over the things done to Sam-ling before he confessed that his two brothers had betrayed the Brotherhood. He tried, with a stoicism worthy of a better cause, not to implicate them, but it was not long before he reached that state of shattered nerve and sapped will which permitted the truth and only the truth to pass his lips. Life was only a dim spark in a mist of searing agony when Sam-ling gave up the secret which he had striven to keep because he loved his two brothers, whose fate he sealed.

Over the weary weeks the five condemned pirates, hope long since fled, were overcome by their filthy surroundings and the animal-like life they lived in their half-world. They had almost forgotten the crime for which they had been condemned. Nothing had reality except the hideous discomfort, the periodical visits of their brutal and callous gaoler, and the sores which festered on their unhealthy bodies.

"You can end this when you will!" the gaoler jeered at them. "Confess your guilt and a sharp sword shall flash for you. There is a visitor coming to see you in an hour. Magistrate Chang is coming to enquire how long your filthy carcases are going to remain here."

Chang came with another man who, dressed in a sober silk gown, would never have been recognised, except by his intimates, as Red Tiger. He had to come because the condemned men would not trust a stranger. With a haughty gesture Chang dismissed the gaoler, who showed a disposition to linger.

It was some minutes before Red Tiger was able to convince the condemned men that he was who he was.

"Listen to me carefully," he whispered to them through the bars of their cage, almost vomiting at the vile stench which came to him. "Tomorrow morning you will tell the gaoler that you are ready to confess. The day afterwards you will be free men. You will be brought before Magistrate Chang, who stands here with me now. Confess, and your friends will do the rest."

"Is this a trick to hurry us to the execution ground?" they asked fearfully.

"It is a trick," said Red Tiger grimly, "but you are not the victims of it. I do not betray my children."

"I do not care whether it is a trick or not," one of the condemned men said when Chang and Red Tiger were gone. "I will confess, for I would rather kiss the executioner's sword than remain here another day or hour."

"To what do we confess?" asked another. "I cannot think clearly. . . ."

"Just confess!" said another wearily. "Who will care what it is you confess?"

"So you have had the good sense to confess!" jeered the gaoler. "Sooner or later, all my lodgers confess." He chuckled obscenely. "Then we are come again to the question of how much your friends and relations will be able to spare for the executioner. He is a reasonable man. For three dollars each you will have a quick despatch, but in these hard times he cannot do it for less. Whisper to me the names of some good friends who will help you. . . ."

One of the condemned men beckoned the gaoler to put his head closer to the bars. With eager greed he did so, to be rewarded by a great clod of congealed filth which took him across the mouth and nose. There followed the first laughter from behind the bars which had been heard during the interminable weeks of their imprisonment.

"Not even if ten times the fee were offered to me," said the gaoler, when he had cleansed himself, "would I allow you to escape one hundredth part of what awaits you tomorrow on the execution ground. I shall be there to watch. I go now to see the man who wields the sword, to make sure that he brings the bluntest he possesses, and when he hacks your stupid heads from your worthless bodies I shall be there to laugh. . . ."

The gaoler's triumph was short-lived. On his way to his lodgings his feet were kicked away from beneath him, while a sack dropped neatly over his head. When it was removed he found himself in an underground chamber. Near him were shackled the brothers Sam.

"That makes four!" said Red Tiger. "Where shall we find the other? We need five for tomorrow. . . ."

"What is to happen tomorrow?" asked the gaoler, having a great fear that he already knew the answer.

"We have the informer," said the Small General, ignoring the gaoler's question. "We have his two brothers, who betrayed us. This thing"—he pointed to the gaoler—"makes the fourth. It is

172

very just that they should die. I have a fifth candidate in mind."

"And who may that be?" asked Red Tiger.

"A small Japanese who has a big mouth," said the Small General.

Just as Soochow has always been one of the chief, if not the chief, centres of Chinese learning, so this fair city of the canals and lakes became over the centuries the home of the dramatic arts. Wherever one may go in China, whether to the far north, where the plains of Mongolia merge with the steppes of Siberia, to the south where the moist heat of Kwantung leads to the steaming jungles of Tongking, or in the west, where the pan-handle of Kansu reaches out into Central Asia, wherever there is a theatre there one will find men of Soochow.

Sung's younger son, child of the Young One, whose frail beauty earned for him the ironic name of Rose Petal, left Sung's island early to join his mother in Soochow. The soil did not call him. Under his mother's roof he associated almost entirely with actors, many of them, through his mother, blood relations. Hers had been for many generations a theatrical family and, therefore, because of the low esteem in which actors were held almost universally, of negligible social status.

Rose Petal had inherited his love of the theatre and a certain talent from his mother. These had been fostered, no doubt, by constant association with those whose talk was always of the theatre. Be that as it may, the lad was undoubtedly talented and had already, with considerable success, done female impersonations.

The Small General and Rose Petal, though as poles apart in thought and tastes, had a high regard for each other. The former admired his younger brother's wit and delicacy, while the latter looked to his elder for the protection and advice he always received.

The Small General recollected a story which his young brother had told him several days previously and it was this recollection which had sent him off to find Rose Petal. The latter, it appeared, had won a wager by appearing in a restaurant one evening dressed as a woman and, so excellently had the impersonation been done, that strangers, seeing what they believed to be a most attractive harlot—for no decent woman would have thus conducted herself

173

—had made amorous advances. Among these had been Watanabe, the successor to Matsudara, the Japanese manager of the Fureno Trading Company's branch in Soochow. The upshot of the evening had been that the Japanese had been saddled with the cost of an expensive meal and plenty of wine for more than a dozen guests, while Rose Petal, the object of his attentions, had disappeared immediately the bill had been paid.

The Small General found his younger brother at the Young One's house.

"Do you think," he asked, "that this Japanese still believes you are a woman?"

"Without doubt he does," was the laughing reply. "He has offered large bribes to the servants of the restaurant if they will reveal to him my address. I have made a complete conquest."

"It is not complete—yet," said the Small General, "but it soon will be. You have not forgotten, I hope, that it was a Japanese bullet which slew our father? Nor yet that it was Japanese money which lured an informer into betraying the five men of the Brotherhood to the executioner?"

"I have not forgotten," said Rose Petal. "What is in your mind?"

"This is in my mind, that you go to the restaurant and tell one of the servants that he may eat the bribe of the Japanese by informing him that you are to be found every evening at the 'Golden Duck'. When you have done this you will array yourself like a beautiful harlot and a table will be prepared for you. He is a lover of the theatre, this Japanese?"

"He says that it is his greatest regret that his father would not permit him to be an actor. . . ."

"He will have the opportunity tomorrow to play a part before the largest audience which ever delighted an actor's heart," said the Small General.

In a relatively junior capacity Watanabe had represented the Fureno interests in various parts of the world, including France, Germany and South America. In these countries the hissing little Japanese had never found the smallest difficulty, provided his pockets were well filled, in arranging long series of liaisons graced by the name of amours. These had been to Watanabe the one great compensation for his exile from Japan.

174

Then he had come to Soochow, where only the most degraded of women would have anything to do with a Japanese. It had hurt his pride, and when the pride of a Japanese is hurt he tends to suffer moral collapse. Women had often spurned his loudly declaimed protestations, but they had never before spurned his money. It was unthinkable, but nevertheless an unpalatable fact, that these Chinese, women of a race he regarded as so vastly inferior to his own that they might not be mentioned in the same breath, wanted neither his protestations nor his money.

Watanabe's heart leaped, therefore, when the restaurant servant told him, in exchange for several dollars, where he might find the lovely creature who had caught his eye. So it was with jaunty step that he entered the door of the "Golden Duck" to make one more onslaught upon her. The girl had become an obsession with him and, even if he had to pay more than he had ever paid before, he was determined to possess her. It was his intention to wear the girl on his sleeve in the presence of his countrymen, if only to prove that the most beautiful creature he had seen in Soochow had succumbed to the fatal Watanabe charm. To his colleagues, of course, he had never admitted that these conquests all over the world were of a strictly commercial nature.

The Small General found it hard to believe, as he looked at Rose Petal, that he was not looking at a lovely woman, but he took his seat at her table and prepared to see the tragi-comedy through to the end.

The Japanese took a seat at a nearby table. He was behind the Small General so that he could ogle Rose Petal in comfort.

In a little while the Small General, using some plausible pretext, left the room. Watanabe chose this opportunity to come to the table, where he demanded when and where he could see the charmer alone. As he spoke, the Japanese fingered a thick wad of notes suggestively.

"There is a private room at the end of the passage," whispered Rose Petal. "Wait for me there. It will not be long. Hush! He returns. . . ."

When the Small General returned to the table Watanabe was back at his own and before many minutes had arranged for the use of the private room.

"Here," said the Small General to Red Tiger, as Watanabe rolled down the steps under the private dining-room, "is the fifth man. It is just that he should accompany the others to hell, for if an informer merits death, how much more worthy of death is the one who offers the reward."

Red Tiger threw his head back and shouted with laughter. It was the type of grim jest which appealed to his rugged humour.

They stripped Watanabe of his fine clothes and shackled him beside Sam-ling, his two brothers and the gaoler, while a party went, with a key provided by Chang, to release the five condemned men.

When the informer, the gaoler, the two traitors and Watanabe were garbed in the unspeakably filthy garments which the five pirates had worn ever since their confinement, there was little to choose between the two batches of men. Only the gaoler (and he could not) would have been able to expose the imposture.

It is not uncommon in China, as in other countries, to drug men into stupor before sentence of death is carried out on them. So the dense crowd which surged all over the execution ground below the Great Pagoda, and the soldiers who were there to maintain order, saw nothing unusual in the spectacle of five nearly insensible men being led out to die.

Soochow was *en fête,* for the execution of five pirates was a spectacle not to be missed. Most of the spectators agreed that it was a pity the men were so heavily drugged that they would give no sport, for condemned men frequently lost their stoicism as the crowd roared its execrations.

The first to be despatched was Sam-ling, the informer. Next came the gaoler, but as his head rolled in the dust the executioner failed to recognise it. Watanabe was the last. Like his predecessor, Matsudara, he affected gold teeth. These were exposed in the shrunken grin on his face as his head joined the others.

"How did the gaoler come to miss those gold teeth?" asked a wit in the crowd.

"I can use them," said one of the soldiers with a laugh, running forward as he spoke and trying to hack the gold teeth out with the point of his bayonet, "and one thing is sure, that he will never need them again."

"It is a very pleasing thought," observed Red Tiger, who witnessed the incident, "which makes one believe that there is, after all, justice in the world: this Japanese monkey offers one thousand dollars reward to tempt traitors. Now the trail of the traitors completes the circle, so that here, rolling in the dust, we see the head of the man who offered the reward. See! The head of the Japanese has been kicked so that it lies between those of the brothers Sam. As to these, I find it a great pity, for I knew their father, who was a most worthy and upright man. He will have no compassion on them when they present themselves. . . ."

"It is well that it has ended thus," said Chang. "The five piratical patriots are now become five martyrs. For, since the people believe that it is they who have been executed, the effect is the same. Here, too, is a perfect example of the great truth that nobody is so vile that he cannot, by a twist in the wheel of fate, be put to high and honourable uses. Those five heads yonder, rolling in the dust—one of a Japanese, one of an informer, one of a brutal gaoler and two of traitors—may yet serve China well. It remains for us who live to exploit them shrewdly."

Since nobody came forward to collect all that was left of the five beheaded men, and public decency demanded that now justice had been done the things be put out of sight, the Small General threw some silver to the coolies so that it should be done quickly.

"Now," said Red Tiger, "we must go to rejoice with our liberated brethren."

"We will go," agreed the Small General, "but I shall not rejoice with any real enthusiasm until they have ceased to smell so abominably."

The five men, so recently liberated from the dire fate which threatened them, were not inspiring. Suffering had dulled their senses to the point where they were little more than animals. It was sad that they were even unable to appreciate the best joke of all: that their late gaoler had been decapitated by the very same headsman on whose behalf he had so solicitously demanded fees.

China has never been a happy country for sentimentalists and for the best of reasons. There have been many good and kind people, Chinese and foreign, who have devoted their lives to the alleviation of individual human suffering, but when they have come to the evening of their own lives, all the effort and toil has seemed very small in the retrospect. China herself has always managed to defeat her own people. The great rivers which deposit rich silt by tens of millions of tons and give life to the millions who live in the river valleys, give that life abundantly with one hand while taking it away with the other. Because of such a simple and unpredictable event as the too-swift melting of the snows in Central Asia, billions of tons of water will swirl through the Yangtsze Gorges from Chungking to Ichang and, where the river widens, will inundate without warning areas as large as the smaller countries of Europe.

To those who have spent their lives trying to save lives, a few hundred or a few thousand lives as the case may be, there is a sense of futility too great to be resisted when China herself drowns a million men, women and children between the rising of one sun and the rising of the next. Before such catastrophes, these good kind people ask themselves of what avail is puny individual striving. As well to try to bail out the Yangtsze itself with a teacup.

As these things have been going on for a very long while, so has grown the tendency to regard human life as very cheap.

Every Chinese, except the numerically negligible rich and educated, who in all lands can devise means to circumvent some natural laws, realises that his own fate is as precariously poised as that of a grain of seed rice. Such knowledge has bred a certain acceptance of, and humility before, natural laws. This attitude of mind the West, with its passion for labels, has called fatalism. But it is sure that since every Chinese knows that his own life hangs by a tenuous thread, whose strength or weakness is beyond his control, he has learned over the centuries that it is the path of wisdom to accept the dictates of fate without undue cavilling.

Having learned to smile at his own dire fate, it is surely not unreasonable that he should fail to be vastly impressed by the fate of others.

The Chinese crowd which mills and surges around the executioner who is about to perform his grisly office is infinitely less vile, for example, than the morbid western mob which fills a street outside a gaol when a hanging is about to take place. The Chinese mob says in effect: "Here is one poor devil at the end of his troubles. There is a lot to be said for a quick clean death like that. Better far than starvation."

There it is: of China's reputed population of 450 odd millions, perhaps one per cent, or less, gets all it wants of the best things of life, including food. The vast preponderance of the remaining ninety-nine per cent perches precariously, from cradle to grave, upon the hair-line which divides "nothing" from "not enough".

Death, therefore, does not seem so very terrible. There are even times when the unknown mysteries of death seem preferable to the known horrors of life.

The Chinese, judged by western standards, are cruel and callous. One might with equal logic apply the standards of the birds to the fishes and, having done so, call them backward because they do not fly. It is not the Chinese who are cruel and callous: it is China. China gives and takes life with a prodigal hand. To most of her people death is no more awful than birth: to many, less, for birth is the beginning of misery, while death is the end.

A medical missionary once summed up twenty years of toil and striving in China in these few graphic words: "I suppose I have saved a couple of hundred lives, no more. I have prolonged the lives of two or three thousands, and as I did so I wondered, even then, whether I was not performing a great disservice. If I were to labour here for ten thousand years I would not have time to redress the harm done in one day by the Yellow River in flood. There was a time when I was horror-struck by the way the Chinese laugh at death, but now I see that their true greatness is that they have not forgotten how to laugh their way through life."

❧ 5 ❧

THE Small General had remembered that he was also Sung of Sung's island. For many months the reins of the island's affairs had been in the hands of a cousin and, since it is proverbial that no man can tend another's land as well as its owner, he had decided to return, even if only for a short spell. Nor was it easy to make the decision for, in the loose way in which men think of such things, he believed that he loved China. But he *knew* that he loved his island home. This last was a small, compact and well-known love, easy to compass and understand and therefore easy to love, just as a soft and furry kitten is easier to love than the infinitely more useful cow.

The human unit in China is the family rather than the individual. Just as the head of the family is traditionally entitled to exercise authority, so the family itself is entitled to expect that its head will study the interests of all. The Small General was now head of the family, although still a young man, and he was conscious that he had neglected that family too long.

The activities of the Brotherhood were satisfying in an entirely different way. They gave him a sense of importance in a larger field. He had learned from Chang, too, that mere hooliganism, the all too frequent means by which the Chinese were wont to protest, achieved precisely nothing except the piling of chaos upon chaos. In moments of self-analysis he tried to learn just how much China meant to him. It was not easy for, he had to admit it with shame, he did not know China. In public he had deplored the wresting of the southern provinces of China by the French, the realignment of the Burma-Yünnan frontier to the advantage of Great Britain, and the seizure of Manchuria, first by the Russians and subsequently by the Japanese, who had also annexed the former German territory in the North. But these things were to him exactly what they were to the vast majority of Chinese people—a jumble of words and geographical expressions, which

180

meant almost nothing, except that in her dealings with all foreign powers China invariably secured the thin end of the bargain. The Small General had met in Shanghai two or three men from Shantung, burly giants, who had struck him as extremely uncouth. He had met a few Cantonese, too, and regarded them as rather foxy and unpredictable. Try as he would, he found that the barriers of ideology between himself and these remote countrymen were too high to permit of any real feeling of kinship or affection. The only language he had had in common with them had been the stilted Mandarin Chinese, which did not come naturally to his, or their, lips. While almost all educated Chinese spoke Mandarin, they *thought* in the dialects they had learned at their mothers' knees.

"You are right in your decision," Chang said, when the Small General told him of the matter. "Without the soil and the family there is no China. How can the whole be healthy if the parts are neglected? Take with you that old man Red Tiger, who will bring us all into sad disrepute if he is not watched. His faith in violence is, I fear, too profound now to be shaken. He has a scheme for stealing all the rifles from the soldiers of the garrison. He is a worthy man, but I find his ideas are too exuberant for me."

It was not hard to persuade Red Tiger to come to Sung's island, for the pirate was very old and more than a little tired. Furthermore, he loathed the life of the city with an abiding loathing.

The Small General went to take his leave of Lok, his father-in-law, from whom he expected to hear unpalatable truths. The marriage had not been a success. A great shame had been put upon Lok's daughter, for it was not seemly that a girl once married should spend nearly all her time under her father's roof. A married woman is as a rule dead to her own family, becoming a part of her husband's. She had finicking ways, this daughter of Lok. Accustomed to luxury, she hated the simplicity of life on Sung's island, whether her husband were there or not. The cousins, who made up the life of the island, disliked her cordially and were at no pains to disguise it.

The Small General was fond of Lok, who was now too old to do anything but sit at home and indulge himself with laughter and good living. The laughter in the circles of the Brotherhood was at times too grim, while there seemed no appreciation of good living.

181

As he went by water to Lok's house, the Small General hoped that he would find the old man in good humour. The talk would then be easier.

On Lok's hospitable table that night were shrimps fried in batter, a salad of ducks' tongues, and an elaborate dish of which ducks' livers were the chief ingredient.

Not for a long time had Lok laughed so heartily as when his son-in-law told him the story of Rose Petal's impersonation of a woman, and the substitution of the Japanese on the execution ground for one of the five pirates.

"How your lamented father would have laughed!" chuckled Lok. "It is ten thousand pities that he was not spared to enjoy the joke. He played some very pretty tricks on the Japanese himself, but none so good as this one. . . ."

"The Japanese at his office have issued a statement to the newspapers that this Watanabe has been called to Tokyo on urgent affairs. They have done this to save their faces, but having said this they will not be able to withdraw when they learn the truth, as they are bound to learn it, for the whole city is laughing at them."

"I had no appetite for my food until you came," said Lok, through tears of pure mirth, "but see now what a meal I have eaten! The last time I drank so much wine was with your lamented father. What a witty fellow he was! How he would have enjoyed this! There was a time when I thought him very simple, just a country bumpkin. Yes, he was simple—like a fox. But one could always endure his little jests because there was no malice in them. Many the joke did he play on me and, even now, I am not so sure that all of them *were* jokes. You will make just such another as your father. Why did you not tell me of all this before? I would have had chair coolies carry me to the execution ground. I may be old, but I am not too old to enjoy a merry jest. To have seen the head of that Japanese rolling in the dust would have been worth all the jostling of the crowd. Tell me, did he still hiss . . . ?"

The Small General was glad that he found Lok in jocular mood, for it gave hope that the old man would not be disposed to talk about his daughter who, her husband realised with annoyance, had not even come from her quarters to greet him.

Now was the time, if ever, to tell Lok the little joke about the secret of Sung's island.

"A little before he died," said the Small General, "my respected father charged me with the task of telling you the inwardness of a small jest of his. You will recall, doubtless, the time, many years ago, before I was born, when you came to our island to discuss with my respected father the question of the miraculous yield of silk?"

"Shall I ever forget it? But you do not suggest, I hope, that this was one of your estimable father's jokes?"

In carefully chosen words, so as not to humiliate Lok more than the facts would humiliate him, the Small General told him the story of how three silk cocoons were grown where only two should have been found.

For a little while it looked as though the story were going to strain Lok's sense of humour beyond its capacity. The old man's eyes narrowed at certain parts of the tale, particularly where reference was made to the handing over of Lok's fine houseboat on the instructions of the Silk Goddess. When the tale was done Lok appeared to be suffering greatly. He sat quite silent, his chin resting on his breast-bone and his eyes closed, as though in profound meditation. Then, it appeared, he was seized with violent hiccoughs, which shook his whole frame and made his belly quiver like a jelly-bag.

But the Small General's fears for Lok were groundless. The old man had been trying, for the sake of the shreds of his dignity, to suppress the laughter which would not be suppressed.

"Cruel young man!" he spluttered. "Cruel, cruel young man! To think that you waited these years to tell me such a tale! I might, who knows, have gone to join my ancestors with the jest untold, and for that I would never have forgiven you."

Lok's mirth became infectious. The Small General could not restrain his own.

"Cease laughing at once, you disrespectful puppy!" bellowed Lok in agonised tones between great gusts of laughter. "How can I restore my dignity when a youth who could be my grandson sits before me cackling thus? O estimable Sung! O joyous, mirthful and altogether depraved Sung! Even from your grave you reach out a long hand to make merry again at my expense. Simple country bumpkin Sung! How you must have laughed within you!

How you must have longed to share the jest with others, though heaven be praised that you did not! And, Sung old friend, you sired a son who inherits your cunning, you fox! He spends the evening with an old man, who is his father-in-law. He is uncomfortable because he knows that he is a bad husband and a worse son-in-law. But he waits until the old man is so full of wine that it is spilling out of his ears, and then regales him with merry stories, well calculated to keep the conversation off awkward topics. He is so like you, Sung old friend. That is just what you would have done if similarly cornered. But because he is your son, Sung, I will forgive him. Although it is her own father who says it, the girl has a viperish tongue and is empty-headed to boot. Because of these things, Sung, and because we both loved a good jest, we will forgive him, will we not?"

The old man's gusts of laughter echoed through the house so that servants pulled aside curtains to make sure that all was well with their master.

"The next time you come to make a mock of an old man with an overladen bladder," said Lok as the servants prepared to carry him off to bed, "see to it that he is not seated in the centre of a priceless Peking carpet!"

Before the Small General returned to Sung's island there remained one item only of unfinished business. Peahen, he had taken pains to ascertain by bribing a servant at the mission hospital, finished her turn of duty for the night at ten o'clock. She lodged in nurses' quarters, situated in the hospital grounds, some two hundred yards from the hospital itself.

As Peahen, tired after a long day's work, descended the hospital steps, the Small General emerged from the shrubbery which had concealed him. Realising that the least noise would bring others on to the scene, for a hospital never sleeps, he put one hand over Peahen's mouth to stifle her cries, while with the other he adjusted over her head a bag he had brought for the purpose. Then, slinging her over his shoulder like a sack of rice, he carried her to his houseboat—the identical one which Sung had been given by Lok—which lay in a canal some three hundred yards distant.

The girl's extreme lightness gave the Small General a shock. Before lifting her on to his shoulders he had braced himself for the strain he expected, only to find that there was no strain.

How like these damned foreigners, he mused, to fit a girl out with clean white clothes every day and give her nothing to eat!

The Small General did not enjoy the task he had brought on himself, but when stealing a woman, even one he had previously owned, it did not accord with his ideas of dignity to employ others. This was, he felt, a peculiarly personal undertaking.

On reaching the houseboat Peahen was soon comfortably ensconced in a closely curtained room, where a woman, the wife of the *laodah,* sat on watch to prevent any screaming before they were clear of the city.

On deck, under the canopy of stars, the Small General found that he was glad he had done this thing. For many weeks Peahen had haunted his waking and sleeping thoughts, and after all, he pleaded with himself for justification, who had a better right to her than he had? The American doctor might have had some rights, but these, the Small General had ascertained by careful enquiry, had never been exercised, though he did not deceive himself into believing that the exercise of those rights would have been contested very seriously by Peahen. Too often had he seen the look of adoration in the girl's eyes as they followed the young American. Where the attraction lay, the Small General was unable to see, but that it existed he was sure.

It was very peaceful lying on the deck of the houseboat as it was rowed slowly through the night, the only sounds the swish of the *ulohs* and the creaking of the wooden hull. Occasionally, as they passed beneath a graceful camel-back bridge, a soft greeting would come from some sleepless soul, waiting wearily for the dawn. But there were very few to mark the passage of this luxurious craft and its restless people.

The distance from Soochow to Ta Hu was a little more than fifteen miles and thence, across the open water to Sung's island, a further ten. By dint of great effort, which would mean maintaining a speed of some three miles per hour, it would be possible to arrive at the island as the dawn was breaking. The Small General had a fancy to do this, so he took a spell at the oars, giving each of the four rowers a half-hour of rest.

Happily there was no night mist over the lake, so it was easy to set a course by the stars.

The first gleams of light were suffusing the eastern sky as the houseboat drew into the wooden jetty. The only sign of life was a young cousin, rubbing the sleep from his eyes, going to tend the ducklings who were as yet too young—the time was very early Spring—to go out on to the mudbanks. It was not hard for the Small General, hearing their shrill piping, to conjure back the early dawns when he, too, had come out on a similar errand.

"Let her sleep!" he said softly to the *laodah's* wife, who had relaxed her vigil. "Go to the house when the people are awake and find some decent clothes, for I do not like the ugly garments they gave her at the hospital."

The Small General strode across the land, through the neatly pruned mulberry trees, to his father's grave, which adjoined that of his forbears. Before any disturbing influences could intrude upon his mood, he wanted to make his peace with his ancestors for having neglected for so long their, and his, island home.

In his nostrils was the bitter-sweet tang of freshly-turned earth. Song birds greeted the dawn from the tree-tops, while out on the lake were the raucous cries of flighting wild duck, out from marshy nesting places among the reeds to find food. It was all very right and proper to be back among small and simple things which he understood, and of which he had been a part since earliest childhood. This was, had he but known it, the China of his dreams and schemes, where those ancestors, beside whose graves he knelt, expected him to breed stalwart sons to carry on the work they had begun.

Somehow, the Small General realised, it was expected of him to raise the level of the island by dredging silt from the lake bottom, nor did he relish the idea, for he was soft with living in the city. Although Sung had left him a sizable fortune, it did not accord with his sense of the fitness of things to hire labour for the purpose. Just as stealing a woman was a personal matter, so too, he felt, was the carrying out of an hereditary obligation. Such things could not in decency be delegated, however great the temptation.

The Small General drew great exaltation of spirit from his brief communion with the past. Going into the house, he cast off the silk gown of the city and, from an old cupboard, withdrew his somewhat tattered but serviceable working clothes of blue cotton such as the lowest coolies wore. These were a link with reality, with the only real thing he knew and understood, part and parcel of that prime chemistry which translated pig dung and silt into

186

silk cocoons, and drew from the soil the good things which had made life possible for the Sungs and tens of millions of families like them.

All through that first day at home the Small General guided a pair of water buffaloes as they pulled a primitive plough through the rich silt of the rice field. Even the ache of tired muscles, which for many months, concealed by rich silks, had not been used, could not kill the sense of power which this simple task gave him, nor dull the surge of happiness at homecoming.

When he returned to the house there was no sign of Peahen, who was in the women's quarters chatting to his cousins, some of whom she already knew. In the kitchens the Old One still ruled supreme. With Sung's death, her day was done, but there had been nobody to challenge her precarious status.

Between the Old One and the Small General there had always been one of those warm and friendly understandings which do not require words. Even her hideous features could not kill the warmth of her welcoming smile. Perhaps she longed to lavish upon Sung's son the affection which, had she ever been given the chance, she might have shown towards the father. A fine basket of Mandarin fish had been landed during the day, so this time it was for the young master of the house to choose two of the best and fattest to be cooked for him, even though the choice were only a gesture, for there were plenty for all.

"I am glad," said the Old One, "that there will now be in the house again someone who understands a well-cooked dish. These others eat like ravening creatures, but so long as they have plenty it does not matter what it is."

"I have told the cooks in the best restaurants in Soochow and Shanghai that they should come here to take lessons from you," said the Small General, watching while a slow smile came to the Old One's face, though it appeared more like the expression which comes to a mouth full of unripe gooseberries.

"What about—her?" The Old One jerked a thumb towards a curtain behind which Peahen's voice could be heard.

"It will arrange itself," was the casual reply.

"Nothing to do with a woman arranges itself," said the Old One. "It is for you to do the arranging. You brought her here, did you not? Why? What purpose had you in mind? That she should help me in the kitchen?" The Old One cackled at her witticism and went back into the kitchen quarters. "It was not so when I was a girl. Men knew then what to do with a pretty girl."

The Small General knew, too, but there was something about Peahen's new-found dignity and poise which held him at arm's length. The men of China do not know how to treat a woman with reverence, for it has never been their way. Their treatment of women—merely by western standards, which are relatively new—seems bad. A man-child is welcomed in a family because there will come a time when he will *produce* food. A woman-child is less welcome because of the certainty that she will consume food. The marrying-off of a daughter, even a well-loved daughter, is sometimes—often—a blessing, because there will be one mouth the less to feed from the family rice bowl. There is no lack of affection for the woman-child. But every Chinese family—the rich always excepted—has been faced for centuries by the sobering truth that any fool can reproduce his species, but any fool cannot feed his progeny. A man-child will one day become a producer. If the women of China have tended to become humble and self-effacing, it is because the cold hard facts have taught them to realise that their very existence can, in certain circumstances, be a tragedy to those who brought them into the world.

Despite these things, the men of China are like the men of every other land on earth: the more elusive and unattainable a woman, the more ardently they desire to possess her.

The Small General could have understood, even if he had not liked it, if Peahen had given herself to this American doctor. He was equally sure that she had given herself to no man. What he could not understand was that, in the unsexed atmosphere of a hospital, filled with impersonal suffering human beings, Peahen had found happiness of a sort. He was not analytical enough to realise that, cheated of earthy things, men and women can derive their chief joy in life by a species of selflessness, between which and martyrdom there is but a thin dividing line. From the resignation which had come with this sort of life Peahen had acquired the serenity which was so perplexing.

It was true, also, that the Small General's high-handed seizure of Peahen was beginning to frighten him a little, now that he began to contemplate it in cold blood. He had worked all through the day with an almost ferocious energy, largely because the more he sweated the less time there was to think. He had left thinking behind him in the city. Now he was back on the land of his fathers sweat was more important than thought. Nevertheless, the situation was somewhat disturbing to contemplate.

As a temporary measure, because the house was overfilled with cousins and visiting cousins from the mainland, Peahen elected to sleep in the infinitely more comfortable quarters of the houseboat, where her presence would incommode nobody.

The Small General watched her walk down the pathway and along the jetty, carrying a lantern. For a little while a light gleamed from a side window of the boat and was then extinguished. He wished she had spoken to him, even in anger, before going to her bed. He was at a great disadvantage, for it was customary—almost universally so—for marriages (and within this term must also be included the state of concubinage), to be arranged through intermediaries, usually parents and sometimes brokers. There was, therefore, no system of what the western world terms courting laid down as a precedent. If the Small General had been an Italian—like his father!—it would have been so simple to go down to the jetty, strum a guitar and sing something from the operas. But he was not. He was instead a Chinese, whose life ran in grooves, deeply scarred by the centuries during which all thought and forms and ceremonies had been evolved until they had become static. One married a woman of parental choice, meeting her for the first time often on the day of the ceremony. One acquired a concubine by much the same means. One bought a woman, or in extreme cases, stole one. But one did not woo a woman, for within the meaning of that term it would be necessary to do things which, to a Chinese man, would involve humility and self-abasement, neither of which were seemly to show to a woman.

It was very evident, however, that there was no sleep that night for the Small General until this matter had been settled. Aside from everything else, he was beginning to feel more than a little foolish. His cousins and the women of the household had shown a disposition to titter when Peahen had gone off to the houseboat alone. Although the lights in the house were extinguished, he knew very well that behind every shutter was a pair of watching eyes, watching the master of the house to see how he would conduct himself in this crisis of his affairs. In the act of carrying off Peahen in this manner, other intentions were implicit. Not only his own, but the girl's pride was now involved. The Sabine women would have been entitled to feel aggrieved if, after their forcible abduction, their abductors had left them alone to do a little plain sewing.

Conscious of the eyes upon him, the Small General walked slowly down the garden path, along the jetty and across a narrow gangplank on to the deck of the houseboat. The door of the main saloon was, contrary to his expectations, open. At the far end of this were Peahen's sleeping quarters. He tried the door, half hoping that he would find it bolted. This also was open, so he had no choice but to enter.

The darkness was opaque. The only sound was that of the girl's gentle breathing, but it was not the breathing of a sleeper. It was good that she, too, had been unable to sleep.

"You are angry with me?" he asked after an almost interminable silence, or so it seemed.

"No, I am sorry for you!"

It seemed beneath his dignity to enquire why she was sorry for him and for some minutes he fought against asking the question, but at length he did so.

"Because you were so foolish as to come like a thief and take me by force. You had only to ask me and I would have come. . . . I have been waiting for you. . . ."

❧ 6 ☙

IN THE House of The Three Bamboos in Tokyo, the reinforced concrete edifice which housed all the far-flung enterprises of the Fureno commercial empire, eyes and thoughts were turned anxiously towards China, for it was upon China's 450 millions of people that the continued existence of this commercial empire very largely depended. The rest of the world, looking with alarm at the gigantic flood of cheap manufactured goods which poured in an unending stream from Japan's factories, looms and mills (a high proportion of which were owned or controlled by the Fureno interests), raised tariff walls in self-protection. China alone could not do this, for China's customs were under international control and China was bound by most-favoured-nation treaties with the principal powers. If China's tariff were to be raised against Japan it would have to be raised against the other powers.

As Japan cut the prices of her goods, so did tariff barriers rise almost everywhere, with the result that Japan, like other great industrial countries, found that it was very much easier to make goods than to sell them. In order to exist Japan had to sell goods, sell them in vast volume, or the economic structure of the mushroom empire would collapse. So, as tariff barriers rose all over the world, Japanese pressure in the China markets increased in much the same ratio. Deep-laden ships sailed from Yokohama, Kobe, Osaka and a dozen other ports to Shanghai, Tientsin, Canton and the up-river ports of the Yangtsze, freighted with a vast miscellany of cheap goods—mostly rubbish—which China had to buy in order that Japan might live. Had the pressure of Japan's industrial exigence remained purely economic it is probable that history would have been written differently. But to support the sales efforts of her bagmen Japan began in the late nineteen-twenties to rattle the sabre, making it abundantly clear that she regarded China—admittedly her natural outlet by reason of proximity—as something akin to a vassal state, due before long to be swept into the orbit of Greater Japan.

For a long while every foreign merchant settled in China—British, American, German and Japanese—had been dazzled by his own arithmetic. The smallest sum of money, when multiplied by 450,000,000, the reputed population of China, assumes gigantic proportions. It explains why China for more than a century has been the victim of foreign greed; why foreigners have bought and suborned Chinese statesmen; why eager bankers have poured vast loans into China's insatiable maw, knowing as they did so that the people of China would reap no benefit, although they would be expected later to honour the bill when rendered. When the Empire collapsed in 1911 from its own decay and corruption, the statesmen who had led it on its downward path were glutted and heavy with loot. With the coming of the Republic, which inherited the empty coffers of the Empire, the situation was hopeless from the beginning. The Chinese knew it and the foreign parasites knew it. To the foreigners the chief difference between the Empire and the Republic was that, whereas under the former régime the people of China were being squeezed and robbed by a small number of large thieves, under the Republic—perhaps as a symbol of democracy—the suffering millions of China were exploited by a larger number of relatively small thieves. Long before the Republic had existed for two decades everything portable had been stolen and every negotiable immovable asset had been hypothecated. (Bankers prefer this word to the simpler "pawned", as it saves them the social stigma of hanging three brass balls over their premises.)

There was a tendency, therefore, among foreigners to regard China as a sucked orange, capable of no further exploitation. This is understandable, since the world has for so long thought of wealth in terms of gold and silver, because a banker-dominated civilisation has fostered the confusion which exists between the symbols and tokens of wealth, and wealth itself.

But one great asset remained to China and this the greatest of all: the energy and the patient industry of her 450,000,000 people. No juggling with figures in foreign ledgers could take away this.

The Western powers found themselves unable to exploit this wealth because a short while previously slavery, that is to say, the actual physical and legal ownership of human beings, had been outlawed. There were, of course, more ways of killing a cat than choking it with butter, but it was a definite advance in thought which rejected the idea that one man might own another.

But in Japan slavery had never died. It had always taken another form; agricultural serfdom had merely been replaced by industrial serfdom. The ruling classes of Japan had never ceased to regard the masses as an asset to be exploited for the benefit of the few. It was, therefore, no great revolutionary change of heart which suggested to the rulers of Japan that one of the first steps towards world domination must be the enslavement of China's millions.

In the long run there would come a time when bayonets would have to be used. They knew that. But the time was not yet ripe. When the final assault upon China came, the Japanese knew they would have to reckon with the Great Powers and they were not ready for that either. Armaments of all kinds would have to be piled up, and these cost money, which could only be obtained by selling more goods. So Japan set out on the commercial conquest of China, and in the van of her commercial army was the House of The Three Bamboos.

Although the Japanese have earned for themselves the reputation of being somewhat devious-minded, in some ways they are amazingly direct in their approach to pressing problems. In Fureno warehouses throughout China vast stocks of miscellaneous merchandise had piled up because of the Chinese boycott of Japanese goods. This was a pressing problem of the first magnitude and the Fureno method of solving it was as direct as anyone could wish.

Enormous numbers of labels, stencils, transfers and tags were manufactured in Fureno factories, each of which bore, in Chinese characters and English, the simple legend: "Made in China". These, affixed to the appropriate articles, would surely satisfy the most ardent patriots in China!

With a similar simplicity of thought a small town in Japan, engaged in the manufacture of matches, had been named Sweden —officially. Only the most unreasonable people could possibly object thereafter to matches being labelled "Made in Sweden".

But the Chinese Maritime Customs were not, in the Japanese view, reasonable. It was deemed wiser, therefore, that in consigning these labels, stencils, transfers and tags to China, to send them under diplomatic seal to Peking, thence to be distributed, under the seal of the Japanese Legation to Japanese Consuls, Consuls-General and Vice-Consuls throughout China. As machine-guns, pistols and ammunition, morphine, heroin, cocaine and other narcotics had for a long time been consigned to China by the same method, it will be realised that this further arrangement required no departure from routine.

In the course of a short time a large case of these "Made in China" markings arrived at the Japanese Consulate in Soochow, whence they were distributed to the principal Japanese business houses in the city, chief among these being, of course, the Fureno Trading Company. For a few weeks the entire staff was busy affixing transfers, tying tags, brushing stencils and sticking labels on to a vast assortment of goods in the warehouse. These included brushes of all kinds, enamel-ware, textiles, made-up garments, umbrellas, rubber goods in great variety, knives, lamps, combs, celluloid articles, soaps, perfumes, tools, shoddy machines, cameras, drugs, lacquer-ware, and so on.

Contact between Japanese importers, as with other foreign importers, and Chinese merchants and shopkeepers, was through the customary intermediary, the compradore, who combined the functions of commercial traveller and guarantor of customer accounts. The Fureno compradores all over China—very wealthy men most of them—employed their own staffs, saw to the selling and distribution of goods, and bore all credit risks themselves. This in return for a substantial commission based on turnover.

Now Soo-loong, compradore of the Fureno Trading Company in Soochow, had for a long time been greatly troubled by the boycott of Japanese goods. Not only were Chinese merchants declining to buy Japanese goods, but they were showing a marked reluctance to pay for those which remained unsold in their warehouses, which they dared not exhibit in their retail shops for fear of dire consequences.

"I am a man of business," Soo-loong was wont to say when taxed with being unpatriotic, "not a politician."

And because Soo-loong was a very wealthy man, able to afford the very best protection, his critics had to be content with the answer. The bodyguard of Japanese and Japanese-trained gunmen who accompanied him everywhere were not only very quick on the trigger, but were not subject to Chinese law. Complaints against them were heard and judged by the Japanese Consul who, since he employed a similar bodyguard himself, was sympathetically inclined.

In daytime Soo-loong and his bodyguard were a trifle conspicuous, so for some weeks he met his customers at night. Some of them dined at his magnificent house. Some met him in private rooms in discreet restaurants and tea-houses, others in less reputable resorts.

One of these customers was Fung-li, the foresighted shopkeeper who, when torrents of rain descended upon Soochow, had a fine stock of Chinese-made umbrellas, upon which he made a most satisfactory profit. The boycott troubled Fung-li also, for in his warehouse he had large stocks of quite unsaleable Japanese merchandise, none of which he dared offer for sale. Fung-li, flattered by the invitation to Soo-loong's magnificent house, accepted it with alacrity, finding there a score or more of his competitors who were in very much the same predicament.

"I trust," said Soo-loong to his assembled guests, "that we are all true patriots."

There was a chorus of assent.

"Some men are born to be statesmen," he continued with apparent inconsequence, "others to be poets. We were born to be businessmen. We do not presume to tell those in high places how to conduct affairs, nor question the farmer's wisdom as to the time or the manner in which he plants his rice. We are ordinary, simple men of the market-place. We buy, we sell. We do not say 'This one has a right to sell his goods and that one has no right.' For us it is to allow the goods themselves to speak. If they have merit they will sell, provided always the price be within the means of the buyer. Every one of us here tonight"—he looked around the room—"has behind closed doors great stocks of merchandise, things for which the people of Soochow are crying out. But there are those who say that the people shall not have them. Why? Because they come from Japan. It is foolish and unjust to deprive the people of what they need. If the goods were too dear, or if they had no merit, I would remain silent. But it is not so. Does a cloak shed the rain any the less if it come from Japan or America? Is a floor any the less clean because the brush which sweeps it comes from here or there? We, as patriots, must end this foolishness. Nor shall we do so for greed of gain, but rather that the poor shall have what they need at the lowest prices. . . ."

Soo-loong led the way into another room.

Here was an exhibition and demonstration of how to convert "Made in Japan" goods to "Made in China" goods, by means of the labels, stencils, transfers and tags, so carefully manufactured in a Fureno factory. Here too were large banners, some of paper and some of silk, bearing the legend "Only Chinese Goods Here". These, too, were made in Japan.

Fung-li's eye was caught at once by a neat transfer which would help him to clear his stocks of Japanese umbrellas. Here was a chance to save a great loss and, at the same time, to be a patriot.

"There is no charge for these small tickets," observed Soo-loong, realising that his guests were interested. "Take as many as you require now and when you need more they will be sent to you. When your shelves and your warehouses are empty, the new goods we shall send you will be properly marked before they are delivered. We have a special factory for this in Shanghai."

"But supposing," said a waverer, "that the Brotherhood got wind of this. What would happen to us?"

"The Brotherhood! What is this Brotherhood but an association of lawless young students and loafers? Do not let it trouble your thoughts. But in case anyone should question you—it will not happen, of course—here are blank invoices of the New China Trading Company of Shanghai, who will in future consign all goods to you. See! 'Guaranteed that all goods sold by us are "Made in China".' What could be clearer?"

"Nevertheless, the Brotherhood has sharp eyes and ears and there are strange things told of the fate of those who cross its path. . . ."

"Those are tales to frighten children," said Soo-loong heartily. "Now my friends, come with me to where a feast is prepared. Let us no longer talk of business. We are good friends who seek to work in amity. I hope that my poor hospitality will seal our friendship. . . ."

When he returned home after the feast Fung-li could not sleep for all the rich food he had eaten and the old wine he had drunk. He passed the night in his warehouse, therefore, transforming his "Made in Japan" stocks into "Made in China".

"Heaven smiles upon me!" he said at dawn, noting with pleasure that heavy rain was falling from leaden skies and feeling sure that his competitors would have slept through the night. Routing his sons from their beds, he set them to work carrying "Made in China" umbrellas and raincloaks from the warehouse to the shop, on the window of which he affixed a handsome silk streamer bearing the legend "Only Chinese Goods Here".

The new Baron Fureno, grandson and namesake of the Tenjo Fureno who had created the great Fureno commercial empire from nothing, had all his grandfather's ruthless drive and energy, added to which was an impatient modern insistence upon efficiency in every department of the House of The Three Bamboos and all its widely scattered ramifications. At the time when the founder of the Fureno fortunes had built up the great business house there had been no competition as the world now knew competition. It had been one thing to erect this vast economic structure, but utterly different qualities and, more particularly, qualifications, were needed to hold it together.

He wondered, as he looked through the reports spread out on his desk, how his grandfather would have coped with the Chinese boycott and this mysterious organisation calling itself the Brotherhood of the Grand Canal, which were exercising such a malign influence upon Japanese interests in ever larger areas of China. Grandfather Tenjo had always believed in direct action. Throughout his life he had gone for what he wanted, regardless of the obstacles in the way, whether those obstacles had been physical or human.

Great things were at stake now. Not only had the world situation made the continued existence of the Fureno edifice precarious, but it was undermining the foundations of Japan itself. Fureno enterprises already employed more than a million workers in metropolitan Japan alone, while the Fureno Bank had commitments in a great variety of undertakings which employed as many more. If the House of The Three Bamboos toppled, Japan itself would revert to the status of a third-rate power, and would be compelled for several generations to forget the fantastic dreams which had spurred on her builders and to which all her economy had long been harnessed.

Meanwhile, an organisation calling itself the Brotherhood of

197

the Grand Canal stood in the way of the fulfilment of all those dreams. It had to be swept away, with all the other rubbish and detritus of decadent China.

The young Baron Fureno believed in bribes, as his grandfather had believed in them. "A bribe secures you an accomplice," the latter had said, "while a threat often makes for you an enemy."

Baron Fureno arrived in Soochow *incognito*. He came because he wanted to see conditions for himself. Soochow was, relatively speaking, a not very important trade centre. He came there because his information was that in this ancient city of the canals and lakes was the nerve-centre of the Brotherhood of the Grand Canal.

In the outer office of the Fureno Trading Company, Baron Fureno's sharp eye detected an elderly Japanese clerk in the act of tearing across an envelope bearing an unused postage stamp, and throwing the pieces in a wastebasket.

"For how long," Baron Fureno enquired politely, "has the House of The Three Bamboos been giving you your rice?"

"In three days," replied the clerk, "I shall have served this honourable house for twenty years. To mark the occasion I am giving a small feast in my house. . . ."

"In three days time," said Baron Fureno, whose identity was not known to the clerk, "the rice that is in your bowl will for two days have ceased to be Fureno rice. Your name?"

"My name is Fureno!" was the proud reply.

"You are not fit to bear it!" Baron Fureno pushed past the bewildered clerk who was, remotely, a cousin, and walked unannounced into the manager's office, now occupied by a young Japanese named Chizumi, since the unexplained disappearance of Watanabe.

In the forty-odd years since Soo-loong had joined the Fureno Trading Company as compradore he had known personally two bearers of the title Baron Fureno. He liked the third even less than he liked the others for, being a most courteous person himself, he liked courtesy in others.

On learning that the young Baron Fureno was to call on him during the evening, Soo-loong arranged to receive him with considerable ceremony, which good manners dictated was due to a man in the former's high position. There was no humility or genuflexion in this attitude of Soo-loong's: merely the courtesy one important man owed to another.

In the Chinese conception of good manners the drinking of tea, polite enquiries regarding health, and a few words about the weather or the crops, are deemed necessary preludes to business discussions. To a less degree the same is true of Japan. But as Baron Fureno saw things, these were mere survivals of mediæval-ism, which had no place in modern life.

"I am a busy man," said Baron Fureno a few moments after his arrival, pushing away untouched a teacup of egg-shell blue and texture, "and I consider this sort of thing"—a waved arm brought the elaborately set tea-tray within the scope of his displeasure—"a waste of time among business men. It belongs to the past."

"Like good manners," said Soo-loong gently. "Do you not find the manners of the young abominable?" he added with more tact.

"Soo-loong," said Baron Fureno, "I am come here to discuss with you a way to smash this Brotherhood of the Grand Canal."

"I am happy that you plan a long stay in Soochow," replied Soo-loong adroitly.

"It is to your interest as much as mine to see it smashed," continued the Japanese, on whom the last remark had not been lost. "Every day you become less wealthy by reason of its activities. Nevertheless, no matter what it may cost, I will find the money to smash it, and if we cannot smash it let us buy it."

"It is possible that you could buy the men," said Soo-loong sagely, "but how would you propose to buy the idea, without which it is nothing?"

"Idea? What idea?"

"The idea that grows every day in China, that Japan seeks to do us harm. It is not my idea, of course, but it is very widely held."

"The only way to combat an idea," said Baron Fureno impa-tiently, "is with a better idea. . . ."

"And the better idea?"

"That Japan is China's true friend. Let me get to the men behind the idea and I will take care of the rest. The men who gave birth to one idea can give birth to another—my idea. Who are the men behind this Brotherhood that causes so much trouble?"

"If I knew the answer to that question," replied Soo-loong,

"it is probable that I should not require an armed guard when I go abroad."

"There are ways of finding out. . . ."

"But I am not sure that this old man wishes to know. Knowledge of that kind might prove—unlucky."

"You are afraid?"

"If I were timid I should have severed my connection with your company ten years ago," said Soo-loong. "Nevertheless, the wise man is always a little fearful of things he does not understand. I hope that I am a wise man."

Now Soo-loong knew a great deal more about the Brotherhood of the Grand Canal than he was prepared to admit. He knew, furthermore, that his own name stood high on its black list, which was the chief reason why he used a bodyguard. He had a very fair idea that the disappearance of Watanabe had had something to do with the Brotherhood, though exactly what he did not know. Mention of Watanabe's name, he had noticed more than once, had evoked laughter. Soo-loong was worried. He was a man nearing seventy years of age. He had contemplated retiring from active affairs very soon, just so soon in fact as his personal liability for bad debts caused by the boycott of Japanese goods was ended. He was doing everything in his power to help merchants get these goods off their shelves so that they should be able to pay for them. He was old. He was very rich. He wanted to enjoy his last few years in peace and comfort.

The Fureno connection had been very useful, but it had now served its purpose. It galled him that lifelong friends became unaccountably myopic when he saw them in the streets, that his name had been omitted from the guest-lists at important functions. It had even reached the point where they no longer canvassed him for charitable subscriptions. Soo-loong did not like this implication that this money was tainted. It irked him, too, to think that his sons were being forced to bear the stigma which attached to the name of a man who worked with the Japanese.

To walk out of the Fureno office and declare himself silently anti-Japanese would be too crude and would convince nobody. If he were to rehabilitate himself in the eyes of his fellow citizens he would have to do something spectacular.

Long before Baron Fureno's arrival in Soochow he had reached these conclusions, but was undecided as to method. His talk with the young Japanese provided just one more instance of the way in which small and trivial things turn the scales of decision. If Baron Fureno, with some recognition of the respect due to a man twice his own age, had behaved courteously when they met, Soo-loong might have been influenced by the fact that he had eaten Fureno rice for a long time; might have decided that he would draw a red line in the books and go quietly into retirement.

"I will make certain enquiries," Soo-loong told Baron Fureno, "and if you will honour my poor house tomorrow night I may have news for you."

"I believe," Soo-loong told himself that night before sleep claimed him, "that I see a way of becoming a patriot without too much loss of 'face'."

There had been a time when Soo-loong and Lok-kai-shing were great friends. There had never been any open rupture. Even now when they met in public they exchanged cordial greetings, but the old intimacy had gone. Without actual knowledge Soo-loong —like Magistrate Chang—suspected Lok of knowing a good deal about the Brotherhood, if not of being one of the guiding brains. He had better means than Chang of knowing how violently Lok disliked the Japanese, for he had long ago negotiated with Lok the sale of the latter's mulberry plantation to the Fureno interests for many times its true value. He remembered Lok's attitude during the negotiations and his final remark when the deposit was paid and the contract signed. "You are too good a man," Lok had said, "to be working with the enemies of our country."

It had grieved Soo-loong that after this he and Lok had drifted apart, for he valued Lok's friendship highly and missed their convivial evenings together.

Lok was, of course, a member of the Brotherhood. Indeed, he was one of its governing council, and his money had been largely instrumental in its founding. He abstained from meetings, except those which took place at his house, because of his great age and infirmity, but his active brain and encyclopædic knowledge of men and affairs were invaluable. It had grieved Lok to observe Soo-loong's departure from grace. The latter, in Lok's view, should have severed his connection with the Japanese some years previously, at a time when it had become plain to all Chinese that Japan sought China's ruin and reduction to the condition of a vassal. But a friendship of half-a-century dies hard. Except for Lok's intervention Soo-loong's house would have been dynamited months before and its owner killed.

"I tell you," Lok had said to his colleagues of the Brotherhood, "that Soo-loong alive will yet be more valuable to us than Soo-loong dead."

How much of this was founded on prevision and how much due to Lok's affection for his erstwhile friend lay between Lok and his conscience to debate. But Lok's plea had carried the day and the life of Soo-loong was spared, for not even the forbidding bodyguard could have saved him from what was planned.

It was no great surprise to Lok when a servant announced that Soo-loong wished to see him. He was glad, too, for his soul rebelled at the thought that, sooner or later, if his old friend persisted in his folly, the hand of the Brotherhood must reach out and destroy him.

"It has been a long time—too long!" said Lok in greeting.

They drank tea in silence for a few minutes. It was Soo-loong who broke the silence.

"I will come abruptly to the purpose of my visit," he said, "nor will I try to deceive you, old friend, by making unworthy motives appear worthy to you. I am a man wearing a heavy load strapped to his shoulders, and who better, I asked myself before coming, to help me ease the load than Lok?"

"Who better, indeed? The Great Sage says it is only when winter comes that we know the pine and the cypress to be evergreens. In the winter of his adversity I am flattered and honoured that my old friend Soo should come to me."

"I will not disguise from you," said Soo-loong, "that in the service of the Japanese I have grown very rich, nor yet that love of wealth blinded me to other loyalties. But even as I say this, I plead that I have done little harm, if any. I know these people of Japan better than you know them, Lok, and better than most of my countrymen know them. I shall cease to sell their goods to-morrow, but the day after they will go on selling them through another and another and another. If need be they will bring an army to help them sell their wares. . . ."

"The other great foreign powers would surely not permit that," said Lok. "It would be the end of them in China. They would lose so much 'face' that they could never hold their heads high again. . . ."

"The Japanese will choose their moment well. They seize opportunity as a hungry dog snatches a piece of liver. I tell you also that the Brotherhood is defeating its own purpose by giving to the Japanese the opportunity they require. . . ."

"The Brotherhood, Soo? Why talk to me of the Brotherhood?"

"Because, old friend, I am prepared to cut off my right hand if you are not somewhere woven into the pattern of the Brotherhood."

"Even if I were—which I neither deny nor affirm—I could not admit the fact," said Lok. "But continue. I am interested."

"Violence is the weapon of the strong," said Soo-loong. "China is weak. To offer violence, therefore, is folly, for there is always the certainty that it will be repaid a hundredfold by the Japanese, who are very strong. Furthermore, violence is not the weapon of a cultured people. Any coolie loafing beside the canals can throw stones. But brains in the heads of cultured people will prove better weapons. That is all we have left to us—our brains and our culture. We have no government worthy of the name. Our army is a pitiful rabble and our navy is a joke. It is foolish to rely upon the other foreign powers, for they, too, are still robbing China of the last remnants of her wealth and dignity. . . ."

"You speak as a man who has devised a plan," said Lok.

"Less than two hours ago," said Soo, "there came to my house one Fureno, the man in whose hands rests control of the House of The Three Bamboos and, many believe, the control of Japan and her policies."

"You are fortunate in having such illustrious persons under your roof!"

"He is an uncouth young animal, devoid of manners or scruples, but he wields a power whose immensity should make wise men pause. It is not fear which causes me to speak thus, for you and I, Lok, have reached the age when there is no fear—of men and their power for harm. . . . This Fureno came to me with a proposal. I am now one to whom has been delegated the task of learning who are the men at the heart and centre of the Brotherhood of the Grand Canal. Having learned their names, it will become a matter for discussion between him and me to-morrow night whether it be more expedient to crush and destroy the Brotherhood or—to buy it."

"And which view is yours, Soo?" asked Lok, a quizzical smile playing about his lips.

"I have no view, Lok. I am come to tell you of what was said. I agreed to make enquiries. I wanted a little time to think and to talk of this matter with you. I am not seeking from you an admission that you are one of the Brotherhood. I have known that for a long time, as far as a man may know anything without facts to guide his knowledge. I did not refuse to touch the matter, because I knew that if I refused another would not, and that other might allow the glitter of Japanese gold to dazzle him."

"Do you permit me to pass on your words to others—others who might know something of the Brotherhood?"

"I permit you, Lok, to do aught that seems best to you, having regard for the welfare of our land. But before you do so I want to know from your own lips whether I have convinced you of my sincerity of purpose—that I have withheld nothing."

"I believe, old friend," said Lok slowly, "that you are sincere and will keep faith with me—and others. But I believe also that it may well be that your change of heart has come too late to be of service—to you. I make no promises. . . ."

"I will not conceal from you," said Soo-loong, "that I would like to live a little longer, to enjoy some of the ease and comfort which great wealth brings. But I am not come here to plead for my life. I am concerned that when I go to join my honourable ancestors I shall leave behind me an honoured name. It is for my sons that I desire this. It is late, as you say, to become—a patriot, but there has never been a time when Japanese gold would have made me connive at the destruction of—old friends."

"Go now to your own house," said Lok. "It is possible—probable that before the night is out you will have certain persons call there. I do not know who will come, nor do I know whether they will come in peace. But whatever the outcome, nothing I can do will be left undone to ensure that if you go soon to join your ancestors you will do so with an unspotted name."

"I did not ask more," said Soo-loong with a quiet dignity. "Whatever the outcome, old friend, it has been worth much to me to drink tea with you, for a cup of tea at the hands of an old and trusted friend is better than a banquet at the hands of a stranger!"

7

"IT IS my opinion," said Red Tiger, who could always be trusted to take the bloodthirsty view, "that we should allow Soo-loong to betray a few names—those of our enemies, of course—to the Japanese, who would then pay him—us a large sum as a reward. The Brotherhood needs money. . . ."

"But that does not help us to sit in judgment upon Soo-loong," said Chang, who found Red Tiger rather childish at times. "We are judging him now."

"We can kill him," said Red Tiger. "It would be a pleasure to strangle him. I will attend to it myself if . . ."

"Soo-loong is right in one matter," said Chang in rebuke. "The Brotherhood already deals too much in violence, thereby inviting violence. We need more subtle weapons."

"A sharp knife and a knotted cord have always been subtle enough for me," declared the old pirate. "I say we should kill those who trade with the Japanese."

Holding a dagger by the point, Chang passed it, hilt to the front, to Red Tiger. "It grieves me to see you kill yourself, my friend," he said, "but it is apparently your judgment that all who trade with the Japanese merit death."

"They should have their hearts cut out!" snorted the pirate. "But why give me this knife? I have a better one. . . ."

"I give you the knife," said Chang, "so that you may execute your own judgment—upon yourself. The spectacles through which you are looking at me now were made in Japan. So was the very knife you have just drawn from your sleeve. The cup from which you have just drunk your tea also came from Japan, as did the matches with which you just lit your pipe. Farewell, Red Tiger, I am overcome with grief that you cannot remain with us."

The laughter which followed this sally discomfited the old pirate, but it saved the life of Soo-loong. Chang's adroitness with words made the thought of killing seem rather foolish to those who heard him. Chang had an uncomfortable gift for being right, which at times his colleagues found hard to stomach.

"It is time," continued Chang, knowing that he had carried the day, "that we called a full meeting of the council. Soo-loong's story changes many things."

"Since he took his new woman to Sung's island," observed Red Tiger, glad of the chance to divert attention from himself, "the Small General's place has been empty."

"He has remembered that he is a farmer," said Chang indulgently, "and perhaps he wants to be sure that there will be sons to carry on when he is gone."

"If she is not with child by now," said Red Tiger somewhat coarsely, "the Small General Sung needs my help. I will go to him and tell him he is needed. I too am remembering that I am a pirate and that there is little need, it seems, for me and my kind. I am too old to learn a new trade. When there is killing to be done, send for me. Until then I will remain under the Small General's roof."

With the departure of Red Tiger from active participation in the Brotherhood's councils—though there were some who missed his forthright way of translating words into deeds—it was easier for Chang to persuade his colleagues that violence as a long-term policy was bound to fail.

It took the twentieth century some thirty years to reach Sung's island, where almost every article in daily use was either identical with or a counterpart of those which had been used for centuries. Oil lamps had been a concession to the twentieth century although, ironically, they barely survived the nineteenth in other parts of the world. Not only were the same tools used, but the same methods. If one of the older Sungs who lay buried behind the mulberry plantation had been able to return in the flesh, he would have noticed no material changes. The method of pruning mulberries had been standardised centuries previously. The shapes and patterns of ploughs, tools, cooking and eating utensils, dress, the rotation of crops and the type of fishing nets in use, were identical with those shown in paintings and writings of several centuries previously. Scarcely any new words had passed into the vocabularies of those who lived on the island, just as very few new ideas had crossed the few miles of water from the mainland to cause unrest. Nor was Sung's island unique in these respects. The twentieth century had come to the great cities of China, which were acquiring a veneer from the West. But neither the twentieth century nor western habits of thought and living had touched more than the bare fringe of Chinese life. The farmers—who *are* China—lived and worked in a way indistinguishable from that of their forbears of several centuries previously. Methods of maintaining the fertility of the soil had been stabilised by forgotten generations, while the daily needs of farmers and their families were unchanged in any material respect.

The Small General, whose ideas had been coloured by wider human contacts, found these things very admirable and, at times, very irritating. After a month of toiling like any coolie, dredging the lake bottom by hand, filling barges with silt and carrying the silt ashore to be spread on the land, he realised that in the West there had been better ways evolved of performing such tasks.

Filled with impatience and contempt for such antiquated methods, the Small General went to Shanghai and brought the twentieth century to Sung's island. This importation took the form of an efficient oil engine and suction pump, which performed in rather less than six hours more than he had been able to accomplish in a month of back-breaking toil.

"But," protested one of the cousins, "the oil consumed by the engine in one hour costs as much as a day's labour by three men."

"Granted," said the Small General, "but the engine does in a full day as much work as could be performed by sixty men working for twelve hours."

"We have not got sixty men," said the cousin.

"Also, by means of the engine, water can be pumped to any part of the island in time of drought."

"Men have carried water here for a long time. I think this engine is a foolish waste of money."

"Men should not have to work like beasts of burden," said the Small General, "especially when machines do the work better. Our rice land here is very small, but if it were larger there is a machine which can cut and thresh rice."

"By bringing the engine here you have put a great shame upon us all," said the cousin sullenly. "Like you, our roots are here on

Sung's island. We know that by bringing this engine here—this engine which you say does the work of sixty men in one day—you wish to send some of us away. . . ."

"That is not true!" said the Small General hotly. "This is your home as much as it is mine. I brought the engine here to save you all—and myself—from needless toil. The engine is your friend, if you will let it be."

What purpose could there be in buying an engine which did the work of sixty men, if not to save the wages of men by ceasing to employ them? Otherwise, there was no sense . . .

Peahen brought with her another facet of this many-sided twentieth century—her absurd foreign notions about excessive cleanliness. Everybody knew that a slight touch of pink-eye cured itself after a few weeks, but even though the dark brown fluid which Peahen dropped into the eyes of children did cure their eyes in a couple of days or less, there was no getting away from the fact that it hurt them abominably, as witness their screams.

The Old One, who was very attached to Peahen, took issue with her in many matters where hospital ideas of asepsis conflicted with the traditional ways of doing things. Without being invited to do so, Peahen took upon herself the duties of island midwife. The piles of clean towels, the pails of scalding water and other surgically clean equipment she brought to her first accouchement, evoked hearty peals of laughter from almost every soul on the island.

"There have been plenty of babies born without all this fuss," said the Old One, trying not to laugh, as she did not want to hurt Peahen's feelings.

"Plenty of them died, too," retorted Peahen, "and their mothers."

"These things may be very good in the hospital," said the Small General, "but the people here do not like it."

"They are ignorant and dirty!" said Peahen. "You are very wise in some matters, but where the healing of the sick and the preventing of disease are concerned, you are like a child. This is one matter—perhaps there are others—where the foreigners are wiser than we are."

Whenever discussions of this nature took place between them, the Small General recalled to mind the unbelieving way in which the American used to peer at him over the tops of his spectacles. Even the memory of this made him angry, blinding him to reason.

"I am a little weary of hearing how wonderful the foreigners are," said the Small General. "All I can remember of them is that they have brought much misery to our land, and that, next to the Japanese, they are our worst enemies."

"It has not taken you long to forget that it was the skill of a foreigner which restored to me my sight," said Peahen sadly. "Is that nothing?"

"For that," was the sober reply, "I will forgive them much. Until you came here, although I did not know it, I was as one dead. Now I am alive and very happy."

"I did not come here," said Peahen. "You stole me, like a thief in the night."

"Nevertheless, I noticed that you did not struggle much . . ."

"A weak woman is foolish to pit her weakness against a strong man. A woman has other weapons. This man who was carrying me off might have been a bandit. . . ."

"So! Although you did not know it was I, you failed to struggle! Whom else were you expecting to carry you off?"

"How should I have known?" asked Peahen. "Soochow is a very great city and there were many who came and went. How was I to guess that you were foolish enough to steal by force that which was already yours?"

Then they would go off together to watch the suction pump as it raised small mountains of mud, to make new soil for Sung's island.

"In a very little time," said Peahen one day, "there will be no further need for the engine, for there will be more new soil than you will be able to spread in two years."

"That is true," said the Small General, fearful lest the engine's only friend on the island, barring himself, were wavering in her loyalty, "but there will always be the need for water in time of drought."

"Supposing," said Peahen thoughtfully, "you were to put a row of strong stakes into the mud, between the two points of the little bay yonder, and the engine were to pump water and mud into the space enclosed. Would not the water then run off, leaving the mud? After a little while would there not be land where there is now water? Land on which much food could be grown?"

"You are right!" was the enthusiastic reply. "By these means Sung's island will not only be raised higher, but it will be made larger."

"One day will you tell our son that it was I, his mother, who found the way to make his heritage larger?"

"Our son is not yet born," said the Small General wistfully. "I want a son. I want many sons. With my engine and the pump I can make the island grow so large that there will be land for all of them. It would be a very fine thing in my old age to sit yonder by the house, to watch my grandsons ploughing where, when I was the Small General of the ducks, was only shallow water where the baby ducklings fed."

"It would indeed be a fine thing," agreed Peahen. "Would I also be permitted to watch your grandsons?"

"They would be your grandsons, too. . . ." Then the Small General realised that Peahen was mocking the egotism which, because he was a Chinese and she was a woman, came so very naturally to him.

The wiseacres of the island had already noted that Peahen had not what they considered the proper degree of humility in the presence of the Small General who, even though he was still wearing the nickname given him in youth, was nevertheless the head of the Sung family and as such entitled to a certain deference. This new woman, with her strange ideas about so many matters, good and beautiful though they admitted her to be, had a painful lack of reticence. In a certain queer fashion they bracketed her mentally with the oil engine and the suction pump: strange, new, disturbing things, which intruded themselves upon a way of life which had proved entirely satisfactory for centuries. Peahen and the engine were, by implication, a criticism of those who lay in the ancestral graves, who had been very well able to live full lives without the aid of noisy stinking machines, and women who were forever boiling towels and bandages. New things and ideas struck a blow at reaction, which has its roots deeply bedded in ancestor-worship. How can one introduce new ideas and new ways of doing things without the implication that the old ideas and old ways—the ancestral ways—were imperfect? Not only Sung's island, but all China, looked backwards rather than forwards for guidance, while those few who realised that, while China had stood still, the rest of the world had advanced in many ways, were judged guilty of impiety.

There was a blight that year which swept through the mulberry plantation, shrivelling the precious leaves and reducing to less than half the customary yield of silk cocoons. In varying degree the same blight hurt the mulberries within a radius of more than a hundred miles of Sung's island. It was one of the periodical afflictions of the silk grower.

"It is the accursed engine!" said the wiseacres.

"Do not talk like fools," said the Small General. "How can an engine bring a blight. Look!" He held a blight-infested branch of mulberry by the exhaust pipe of the oil engine. "So far from bringing the blight, the smoke kills it."

But they were unconvinced.

The unprecedented amount of silt over the land, sucked up by the pump from the lake bottom, unquestionably did bring a plague of mosquitoes that year. The pests bred and multiplied in the pools of sludge which lay everywhere. Furthermore, perhaps because of all the decayed animal and vegetable matter, in which they bred, their stings were highly poisonous.

"It is the accursed engine!" said the wiseacres.

"If you will try not to scratch the stings," said Peahen, "I have here a medicine which will kill all the poison."

But most of the sufferers came for relief too late and a dab of antiseptic upon running open sores did very little good.

"It is nothing to do with the engine," insisted Peahen. "It is because of the filth under your fingernails when you scratch that you suffer so."

"She says we are filthy!" they muttered.

"The mosquitoes sting me just as often as they sting everyone else," Peahen told them. "But you will notice that after one dab of medicine the redness disappears."

"Perhaps it is not the engine, after all," they said among themselves and sometimes within Peahen's hearing. "It is the new woman of the master who has done this thing. In order to prove that her stupid ways of doing things are the right ways, she has poisoned simple mosquito stings on us and on our children. Mosquito stings did not hurt us before, so why should they hurt us now? It is either the accursed engine or the new woman."

Red Tiger came to the island at a time when there were many

laid low by a fever akin to malaria and, although he secretly sympathised with the attitude of the people, loyalty to the Small General, son of his friend Sung, compelled him to dilate upon the wonders performed by western medicine. The people were not convinced, but in their awe of Red Tiger they quietened their murmurings.

"How go the affairs of the Brotherhood?" asked the Small General.

"The councils are full of wind and long words," replied the pirate. "I am a man of action and they have little use for such as me. There have been many new members of the council. They come from afar. They eat noodles* and I do not understand what they say. But a time will come before long when there will be some good killing. Until then I shall sit here and grow old. Lend me two cormorants and I will earn my keep by catching fish for you."

"This is your home," said the Small General. "There is always a place for you here."

"I see that your new woman still has a flat belly," observed the old pirate with his customary bluntness.

"Nevertheless, appearances are deceptive," said the proud father-to-be.

"Good! Then you will return soon to Soochow where they are asking when you will come? They think that your place is there."

"A farmer's first duty is to his land," said the Small General a trifle unctuously.

"I merely tell you what is being said," said Red Tiger. "They say that you are either one of the Brotherhood, or you are not, and if you are that your place is in Soochow. There is talk of big things afoot, but so far as I have been able to see, it is only talk. I say that we should kill every Japanese in the land. That is the sensible way of doing things. Long words will not frighten them away. That is sure."

With Red Tiger's arrival on the island the Small General spent less time with Peahen, who, contrary to ordinary Chinese custom, ate with him at the same table. Sticklers for the old ways objected to this arrangement, but it was nevertheless quite common in informal households. To have allowed Peahen to sit at table with Red Tiger would, however, have been an affront.

* In effect, they came from extreme North China where rice cannot grow.

The Small General had a growing faith in this slender girl's wisdom and appraisals. During the years when it had seemed that she would be condemned to perpetual darkness, she had evolved for her own comfort a gracious philosophy. Contact with western thought in the hospital had given her a wider horizon. It had impressed her also with the amazing efficiency of the West beside the monumental inefficiency of China.

The Small General had reached much the same conclusions independently. He could not understand why it was that Chinese craftsmen, who individually were fully as skilled as any foreigners, made such a poor showing collectively. All individual tasks were performed well, but collective tasks seemed to end in abysmal failure.

The Small General talked of these things often with Peahen and he found that from these talks there emerged a certain clarity which had not been in his mind before.

"I find myself wondering sometimes," said Peahen, "who and what I am. All I know is that I was found floating in the river. My father might have been a Mandarin and my mother a princess, or they might have been just poor peasants. It is possible that my mother did not know who was my father, or my father that he ever had a daughter by her. These matters are mysteries which will never be made clear to me. If I had ancestors they are lost to me as though they had never lived. How, therefore, can I feel respect for them? How can I believe that they were good and wise? I do not even know from what part of China I came. It is possible that I had been floating on the river for many days. With you it is different. You knew your father. Your ancestors are here beside your home. This island was fashioned by their hands. They are, therefore, alive to you still. Sometimes I am happy for you that this is so, but sometimes, although I am an ignorant and uneducated woman, I believe that this knowledge puts chains on you, and then I am unhappy for you. . . ."

"You may spare your pity!" said the Small General, bridling.

"You speak often," continued Peahen, "of being a patriot, of freeing China from the usurped power of the foreigners. When you say such things of what are you thinking? Of all China that you have not seen? Of an idea? Or of this little island which is yours? Would tears come to your eyes if word came to you that Peking had been destroyed by a great fire?"

"I do not know," was the slow reply.

"Would you feel impelled to wreak vengeance on the person who started the fire?"

"I do not think so. . . ."

"But if a stranger were to come here and were to cut down ten mulberry trees, your rage against him would be terrible, would it not?"

"Of course! This is my island. It is my home and the home of my ancestors. . . ."

"Peking is home to great numbers of people, just as it is the home of their ancestors. Are they, because they once lived in Peking, less worthy of respect than yours, who lived here on this small island? I mean no disrespect to your honourable ancestors —you know that. I do not even know the answers to my own questions, but I am sure that if one could find the true answers to these, many obscure things would become clear to us. . . ."

"You addle your head with too much thinking," said the Small General, impressed despite himself. "You will be saying next that respect to our ancestors is wrong and unworthy."

"No, I shall never say that," replied Peahen, "because I do not know. Nor is it likely that I shall ever know."

"You will feel differently when our son is born," said the Small General, trying to dismiss these revolutionary ideas as the whimsies of a pregnant woman.

"I do not think so," said Peahen with a quiet confidence.

"Then when the next and the next are born . . ."

"I would be happier at the thought of breeding many strong sons," said Peahen, "if I could see what sort of a land their China will be when their time comes."

"It will be nothing if there are no strong sons to till the soil. That, at least, is sure. For the rest, their home will be here. This is their China!"

"I am not sure that it is large enough," said Peahen, a stubborn look coming to her face.

The Small General was not sure that he knew what she meant.

8

ON THE twenty-seventh day after Peahen was delivered of a fine healthy son the infant's head was shaved and his proud father bestowed upon him the name of Patriot. The ceremony may be performed any day up to thirty days after birth, and in this case the twenty-seventh was chosen because, according to the advice of an astrologer, the stars were highly favourable. Neighbours and friends from far and wide were invited to the feast which followed, for the birth of an heir to Sung's island was an important event on and around Ta Hu.

Never before in the island's history had such an assemblage of boats lain beside the jetty and in the sheltered bay which formed a harbour. Even the aged Lok, although his own daughter was the rightful wife of the Small General, was present. A husband may divorce his wife for seven reasons: barrenness, lasciviousness, jealousy, talkativeness, thievery, disobedience towards her husband's parents, and leprosy. While she had given her husband no child, Lok's daughter had a valid defence against the charge of barrenness: she had not seen the Small General for more than two years. She could, it is true, have been divorced for talkativeness, but to have done this would have been a needless affront to Lok who, while he regarded his daughter as a pampered, empty-headed chatterbox, was none the less jealous of his family honour.

Because he was born of a concubine, there was no slur on Patriot's parentage. Quite regardless of this previous marriage, he would in the fullness of time inherit his father's name and fortune. The Small General was deeply touched by Lok's presence, which was due in varying degree to three reasons. Perhaps it is uncharitable to say that Lok dearly loved a cruise on the water in his sumptuous houseboat, the only means of travel available to him. Servants carried him on to the boat at one end of the journey and off at the other. The journey to Sung's island, also, would refresh his memories of many happy days spent there in the time of the elder Sung. Thirdly, due to his great age, he wanted to relinquish all his activities concerning the Brother·hood, which was now passing through great changes. He wanted to tell the Small General of what was happening and what, in his own good judgment, was likely to happen, for he bore a deep affection for this son of his old friend Sung.

"It is a dangerous name that you have given to this son of yours," said Lok when the other guests were departed to their homes, "for in these days it is not healthy always to be a patriot. There is always the chance, too, that when he becomes a man he may prefer—like his father—to be a farmer."

"It is not that I prefer to be a farmer," said the Small General. "I *am* a farmer. Fate and birth willed it so. I am also a patriot, for I love deeply the land where I was born and I would suffer much to protect it."

"You may yet do that," said Lok gravely. "Although I am old and inactive, still I manage to keep my finger upon the pulse of the world. Things do not go too well for China."

"There is too much talk and not enough killing," observed Red Tiger, waggling his beard.

"There will be plenty of killing before many years are gone," said Lok, "enough even to satisfy you. But it may be our people who are killed. The clouds are gathering and the storm will break. I shall not live to see it, but I am not too old to recognise the signs."

"All is in good order here," said the Small General. "I will go to Soochow."

"You will find many changes," warned Lok. "Whereas the Brotherhood numbered a few hundreds, now it has grown to hundreds of thousands. Therein lies our greatest danger. Out of a very small number, remember, there were two traitors, and perhaps a dozen more on whom no reliance could be placed. It follows that, even though our numbers grow to millions, the proportion of traitors and unreliables will remain constant."

"But does not Chang realise this truth?"

"Chang is a good man, a loyal patriot and a great scholar. But he is also an official by training and inclination. He has never had to battle with drought, like a farmer; fight for his fortune when the silk market fluctuates, as I have fought. He is, like all

217

officials, remote from the problems and perplexities of the common people. When an edict is issued that such-and-such must be done, the official likes to assume that, because it is the law, such-and-such will be done. His further actions are based, therefore, on the assumption that such-and-such has in fact been done, whereas, in truth, word of the edict has not reached the ears of more than a small number of those affected."

Peahen, hovering in the background with Patriot at her breast, heard this and many other talks. She determined that when the Small General went to Soochow, she and her son would accompany him.

The Council of the Brotherhood had swollen to more than a hundred members, who were drawn from all parts of China and also from countries abroad where large Chinese communities existed. From the Chinese in Singapore and Malaya, the Netherlands East Indies, San Francisco and Manila, came also large contributions of money.

The task of forming the Council had been an extremely difficult one. Its members, obviously, had to have a common language if their deliberations were to be completely understood. The nearest to a universal language which exists in China is Mandarin Chinese, the language of the official classes, the scholars and the upper classes generally. The prime task of the Council was to organise a trade boycott against Japanese goods and services. It was manifestly necessary, therefore, to secure the support of the small shopkeeper class, who did the bulk of the retail business of the land, but who, as a class, were far from distinguished for their scholarship. Equally was it true that the best brains of China were more likely to be found among those who spoke Mandarin Chinese than among those who did not.

The task was, therefore, to find men who did not hold their scholarly noses so high that they were unable to see trade at all, and yet to escape from the narrow vision of the small shopkeeper, able for the most part to see nothing but trade.

The Small General, though not of the upper classes, spoke Mandarin Chinese. It had been a tradition among the Sungs to do so for many generations. Sung, his father, had always insisted that the more formal aspects of family life and observance were discussed in this appropriately more formal tongue. Many, but not all, of the Sung women had learned Mandarin. Among these was Peahen, with whom the Small General spoke in Mandarin when he did not wish others, servants and the like, to understand. But it was true of the Small General, and of many others who had become members of the Council, that this language of the scholars did not come to the lips with the fluency and ease so highly desirable.

When his name was called in the ante-room of the underground Council Chamber—the only safe meeting-place which was at the same time large enough—the Small General stepped forward to take his seat, finding himself a few moments later in an utterly changed atmosphere from that which had ruled in the days when Red Tiger and his trusted lieutenants had been the Brotherhood's chief driving force.

All around him the Small General heard a babel of strange dialects from a gathering drawn from every part of China and beyond, wherever Chinese in large numbers had settled. The Council was not yet in session. Those present were broken up into small groups, each quite oblivious of the others and talking earnestly in the dialects which came most naturally to their lips.

Seeing in a corner Kung, the President of the Thieves' Guild, the Small General made towards him, glad to find a familiar face. At that moment there came into the Council Chamber a group of communists from Western China who, perhaps to illustrate their solidarity, entered bearing a banner and marching in military formation. Their arrival was greeted by some with scowls, others with haughty looks, and by some, tactlessly, with open laughter.

A few feet from Kung and the Small General sat a group of young men clad in the smartest European-style clothing, set off by rather loud shirts and flowing silk ties. These were chatting amiably in English. Nearby was a group of huge weather-beaten men from Shantung, whose ponderous movements contrasted sharply with the alertness and vivacity of others from Canton and other parts of South China. From British Hongkong there came a tall young man who, though beyond all doubt, of Chinese blood, carried himself with an air which suggested other influences. His clothes, although nobody present knew it, were made in Savile Row. He wore, also unrecognised, the tie of a famous British public school. There was a pained look on his face as he glanced at the communist banner and at one of those beneath it who, with a fearsome dagger he had drawn from its sheath, was paring his fingernails and, as occasion demanded, using the point as a toothpick. Even more strange and bizarre was a solitary man from Turkestan in the far West, who did not even look like a Chinese. His sweeping black moustache and tight-waisted gown of russet colour would have attracted far less notice in the bazaars of Baghdad, Teheran, or beside the Caspian Sea.

A hush came over the motley assembly as a door at the far end of the chamber opened and Magistrate Chang, looking every inch the scholarly aristocrat he was, entered majestically, carrying a portfolio in his left hand and in his right a beautifully carved ivory fan, pressed to his stomach. Everyone rose to his feet, which courtesy Chang acknowledged with courtly bows.

"For the first time in my life—I admit it with shame," said Chang when he had reached the small platform erected for him, "I find myself in a gathering composed of representatives of the whole Chinese race. All our many differences—differences of environment, of outlook, of language, even of appearance"—he looked around him as he spoke—"are sunk and forgotten in this, probably the greatest, crisis in our beloved country's long and honourable history. . . ."

Chang surveyed the assembly, quickly noting the many blank and uncomprehending faces turned towards him. His speech was too scholarly, too full of flowery idiom.

"There are not a dozen present who understand him," whispered Kung to the Small General. "He must bring himself down to earth."

". . . The people of Japan have shown themselves our enemies. They seek to strangle us economically. In the past the looting of China has been easy. All the great foreign powers have in turn taken advantage of our weakness and disunity. Precious territory was wrested from us. Our statesmen were corrupted by foreign gold. These things were bad enough: the worst of the foreign powers of the West did not seek to destroy our national existence, nor our sovereignty over *all* Chinese territory. But the monkey men of Japan will be satisfied with nothing less than this. . . ."

"He must descend the ladder of scholarship even further if he wishes to carry his hearers with him," whispered Kung, a scholar himself, who had learned better than Chang how to talk to a mixed gathering.

"The Japanese," continued Chang, "have stolen our language. They did this when they ceased chattering in the trees. They never did succeed in learning how to speak our tongue, so they took the written word and gave it their own monkey sounds.* Next they stole our philosophy and as much of our culture as they were able to absorb, twisting and perverting it beyond recognition. We did not protest, for no amount of alien thieving could lessen the worth or the extent of our ancient culture. The making of silk, the lacquer arts, pottery, the making of paper and the art of printing: these and many others they stole from us in turn. Perhaps even the art of walking erect they learned here in China. All these, from our plentiful storehouse, we could afford. But now they say to us—these things who have come down from the trees—that we may not buy, or refuse to buy, such goods as we need and reject those we do not need, regardless of whence they come. We, from whom they stole all that they have and are, must become their vassals, their slaves. . . ."

Once in sentencing a criminal to five hundred blows of the bamboo, Chang had chosen such exalted diction that the wretched man, crouching at his feet, had believed himself the object of laudatory remarks. Now most of those present understood Chang, and the few who did not joined just as heartily in the applause. To these last, willing friends descended the ladder of scholarship even further, explaining all in simpler terms.

"When these monkey men find, as they will find," continued Chang, as the cheering died down, "that we shall not submit to dictation in order to keep the wheels of Japanese factories turning, they will come here with guns and aeroplanes and all the other weapons they have stolen from the barbarians of the West. . . ."

"The British would never permit that," said the delegates from Hongkong and Singapore in unison, as though they had rehearsed it.

"The Americans would never permit it!" shouted a Manila-born Chinese.

"Nor France!" echoed a Saigon-born Chinese.

* It is a fact that written Japanese was "borrowed" from China, while the spoken tongues bear no resemblance to each other.

"Nuts!" observed a Chinese delegate from San Francisco, *sotto voce*. "That guy ain't never heard that Uncle Sam has built himself a navy!"

Before very long Chang found it impossible to make himself heard for the interruptions. Soochow has always been a centre of learning and culture, so Chang, a magistrate of that proud city, was unable—even in the doubtful event that he were willing —to temper his flowery metaphor to the culture-shorn lambs who, for the most part, comprised his audience. As Chang thought of these matters, the fight was as much for Chinese culture as for the rights of Chinese to buy what goods they pleased. But he could not reconcile it with his conscience to fight and plead for Chinese culture in the accents and phrases of the uncultured.

The arrival of the servants of the "Golden Duck" with food brought acrimony to an end. Good food is a serious business among all classes of Chinese, wherever they may be, as it always is among peoples whose history has been one of famine and privation. The arts of the kitchen, like so many other arts, probably originated in China. There was an established and highly civilised cuisine in China (which still exists, virtually unchanged) at a time when Europeans were glad to gnaw wild meat when they could find it, and when cooking was no more than the charring of meat to give it savoury smells.

Just when the sounds of hearty eating and the clattering of dishes were enveloping the chamber in their harmony, there came from one of the tables a shrill uproar. One of the delegates from Canton, it appeared, had just discovered the loss of his wallet which contained all his funds and his return ticket.

"Not only is Soochow a city where much nonsense is talked," said the unfortunate man, "but its people are thieves and assassins!"

Happily, the remark was made in the Cantonese dialect, which not six persons in the room understood.

"It seems there is work for you," said the Small General to Kung. "One of your children has forgotten the courtesy due to a guest."

"Where did you last see the wallet?" asked Kung, hurrying over to the scene of the uproar. "Give me a description and details of its contents."

"I last saw it when I was setting out for this place from my room in the Lotus Blossom Hotel. The wallet was of red leather, stitched and embroidered at the edges with silver-coloured silk. It contained . . ."

"Have no fear!" said Kung calmly. "Within two hours it will be returned to you. If it would please you, the thief shall be punished in your presence—provided the thief be a Soochow man."

"It would please me greatly!" snarled the man from Canton.

Four of Kung's men were already in and about the chamber. They were there as a precaution, lest any of the visiting delegates had original ideas on the subject of *meum* and *tuum*.

"I saw the wallet stolen barely ten minutes ago," one of his men told Kung. "Yonder is the thief! He has it concealed in the right-hand hip pocket of the trousers he wears beneath his gown. Shall I seize the man?"

The thief was one of the delegates from Nanking, a city on the Yangtsze, where usurped power was in the hands of a government which, according to popular belief, was planning to sell all China to the Japanese.

"No, do not seize him," said Kung. "Bring Foo-li here at once!"

Foo-li was a pickpocket, a master of his craft. It was said of him that he could steal the whiskers off a cat. He was a merry fellow, too, and enjoyed playing pranks when not at work. His favourite prank, which had caused some of the best free-for-all fights ever seen in Soochow, was to mingle with a gathering of highly respectable business men. He would then in turn take all their valuables, putting these in other pockets. He would feel for his own watch and exclaim: "I have been robbed!" All his victims would proceed to verify that their own valuables were safe, and the uproar which followed the production by one man from his own pockets of the watch of another, the wallet of a third and so forth, rewarded Foo-li amply for his trouble.

Kung pointed out to Foo-li the delegate from Nanking, describing the wallet and its location. "Bring it to me as speedily as you can," were Kung's instructions.

If Foo-li had a fault—barring, of course, those obvious ones attendant upon his chosen vocation—it was this love of a merry prank. Foo-li exceeded his instructions. In order to remove the wallet from the Nanking man's pocket it was necessary to slit his silk gown with a knife. This was mere child's play. Having re-moved the wallet, he determined to put to the test a theory which he had long entertained: that a man with a live rat tightly buttoned into a hip pocket should afford first-class amusement to the beholders.

In order to make the rat temporarily quiescent, Foo-li squeezed between his fingers the vein, or artery, which led to the creature's brain, cutting off the blood supply. A few moments after the rat had been comfortably placed and the pocket re-buttoned, Foo-li handed the wallet to Kung and retired to a spot from which he would be able to enjoy the coming spectacle.

The rat recovered consciousness slowly. The pocket was warm and comfortable, so there seemed no immediate urgency. The delegate from Nanking ate a hearty meal. Like most persons who practise the ancient art of pocket-picking, he was of the lean and hungry order of men, quick and restless in his movements. His appetite was prodigious. But there came a time when, filled to repletion, he leaned back in his chair, subjecting the rat to a cer-tain pressure. The rat, resenting this, sought a way out of the confined space, finding none. The delegate from Nanking, mean-while, felt certain movements in the region but, because he be-lieved the stolen wallet to be there, did not draw attention to the curious sensations. A rat is not for nothing a member of the rodent family, whose outstanding habit is that of gnawing.

With a wild shriek of pain and fear, the delegate from Nanking leaped upon the table, scattering crockery far and wide. Foo-li laughed joyously. Others joined in the laughter as the stricken man, the rat gnawing at his buttocks, tore wildly round the chamber. . . .

Kung, meanwhile, had paid a hurried visit to the Lotus Blos-som Hotel. For the sake of Soochow's good name he had arranged with the owner, an old friend, to subscribe to the story that the missing wallet of the Cantonese delegate had been found in his room.

When Chang finally recalled the gathering to order, the dele-gate from Nanking was missing, the delegate from Canton was full of abject apologies for his stupidity, while everyone else in the chamber was in a less critical frame of mind, owing to the twin panacea of good food and much laughter.

Therein lies perhaps the greatest virtue of the people of China: nothing can stem the tide of laughter, which sweetens the grim business of existence. Despite the rigid formality of most aspects of life and the constricting effect of ancient ritual, despite plagues, famines, floods, wars and poverty—China has never forgotten how to make merry. That is the one great quality which the imitative Japanese have never been able to filch from China. The agile men of Japan take themselves too seriously to learn laughter. As becomes those who claim descent from the gods, they are too intense and self-important for mirth.

But mirth alone will not weld into a single-minded instrument all the widely differing mentalities of a gathering such as that met in the underground chamber.

Another delegate from Nanking argued that his city, rather than Soochow, be chosen as the headquarters of the Brotherhood, since Nanking was now the capital of China. On reasonably valid grounds the claims of Hangchow and Hankow were advanced. All these were hotly contested by the delegates from Peking, while the Shanghai delegates argued that although their city lacked antiquity, it had surely established itself in the eyes of the world as China's most advanced city, the volume of whose trade and commerce surpassed all others.

"The Brotherhood came into being in this ancient city of Soochow," said Chang when the uproar had subsided. "Here for the moment its headquarters remain. But whether we decide to remain here, or to go elsewhere, it is not seemly that we should quarrel about such a trifle. I, for one, would agree to the headquarters going to any one of the cities named. It is not the location of our meeting-places which will decide the great issues at stake, but the wisdom and unity of our councils, the self-sacrifice of us all as individuals. We are met together to devise means whereby we hope to make Japan's position in the trade of China too costly, too embarrassing and too hazardous to be maintained. These monkey people must be made to realise that China is the arbiter of her own fate, that neither economic pressure, nor threats of force, can make us swerve from our chosen path. . . ."

"Death to the Japanese!" came a roar from the delegates.

"We are at least agreed upon two matters," observed Chang with a thin smile. "We love good food and we hate the Japanese. The former is a general human attachment, while the latter is

225

purely negative. Unity cannot be achieved around the base of a negative banner. Do we love China, our native land? Or does every little cock here crow only for his own dunghill!"

"I am a merchant, an importer and exporter," said a man from Shanghai. "I say to you all, with knowledge of what I say, that we have set ourselves a hard task. The people cry out for certain goods, which they must have in vast quantities. Our industry in China is, thus far, too backward to supply the demand. The cotton and woollen piece-goods from England, for example, are too costly. Yet the people must be clad. Where, unless it be Japan, are we to find these things?"

"We must make them ourselves," said a delegate from the Province of Szechuan in the West. "In our mountains there is pasture for sheep. In our valleys there is land on which cotton may be grown. . . ."

"How long, think you," asked the man from Shanghai, "will it be before Szechuan will find the wool, the cotton, the machines and the skill to supply one million, to say nothing of 450 millions, with clothing? A decade? Not less. Meanwhile, do I understand rightly, the people must go naked? There are vast cotton mills in Shanghai already. . . ."

"Which are owned in large part by the Japanese," came the voice from Szechuan.

"Every person present here knows only too well," said the Shanghai man, "that not one hundredth of the goods displayed in the shops of China as 'Made in China' are in fact of our own make. I will make a wager with any person here that he cannot go out into the city of Soochow this minute and buy—anywhere— a garment of cotton which is not, wholly or partly, of Japanese make. . . ."

A silence greeted this remark, for everyone present knew that the man from Shanghai spoke the truth.

"I go further," said the man from Shanghai. "I have in my hand one hundred dollars. I will make a gift of it to any person now present if he will establish to my satisfaction that nothing he is wearing was made in Japan."

"My son accepts your challenge with the utmost respect, sir!" said a woman's voice. "Since the hour of his birth he has worn nothing which I did not spin with my own hands. He bears the given name of Patriot. . . ."

The Small General turned with amazement, to see Peahen emerging from behind a screen, bearing their son in her arms.

"What an outrage for a woman to dare to address us in this fashion!" said an elderly man from Hangchow. "Has her husband never taught her respect?"

There were similar mutterings all over the chamber, chiefly from older men, whose ideas of woman's status had not been touched by the modern tendency to a nearer approach to equality, great as was the gulf which still remained.

All heads were turned towards the slender figure of Peahen as she walked towards the platform where Chang stood. She held herself proudly erect. The ghost of a smile hovered across her lips, while from her eyes there burned the fierce light of fanaticism, so unlike their customary serenity.

"Do nothing!" whispered Kung to the Small General. "Her voice may achieve something. The others would bicker and argue until they achieved nothing. Stranger things have happened than that a woman should succeed where men have failed. . . ."

As Peahen carried her son across the chamber in the crook of her arm, it seemed as though the infant smiled up into her face approvingly.

"You have either said too much, woman, or perhaps not enough!" said Chang, standing down from the platform in her favour. He had not, be it said, the least idea of her identity.

The man from Shanghai crossed the floor.

"Small son of China," he said, bowing deeply as he handed the infant a sheaf of banknotes, "you have taught us all a lesson. Through the mouth of your gracious mother we ask you to address us."

It became easier then for those with reactionary views to keep their places while a woman addressed them. Peahen rewarded the man from Shanghai with a quick smile and a bow of thanks.

"I am but an ignorant woman," began Peahen to an audience which was now, for the first time, quite silent, "a woman of China —all China. As an infant they found me floating upon the great bosom of the Yangtsze and no man knew whence or how I came. For that I am glad. For you, sir"—Peahen indicated a bearded old giant from Shantung—"I have love and respect, for it is possible that you are my honoured father, or even my grandfather. It might be so. As a good daughter should, therefore, I honour and love all men of China, lest by failing to give love and respect where they are due, I fail in my duty to my unknown father.

"From behind yonder screen I have heard men push the claim of this and that city as the headquarters of this Great Brotherhood. As each name was uttered, whether Hangchow, Peking or Shanghai, or any other, my heart went out in turn to each. May I not be a daughter of any one of those cities? Who am I, therefore, to dare to withhold respect and love for any one of them, for in any one of them may rest the honoured bones of my ancestors. They may have been princes, or they may have been humble peasants, these unknown ancestors of mine, so to princes and to peasants and to all the grades between I must in duty bound show love and respect, until at length I find that every man and woman and child of China comes within reach of my love. Any one of these may be brother, sister, aunt or uncle. . . . Alone in this room, therefore, I am able to say that my love and my loyalty do not go out to one village or city of China, or to one family, but to all. I have heard many tongues spoken in this chamber today, any one of which may be the tongue I did not learn at my mother's knee. So, perforce, even though I do not understand them, I respect one as much as another. . . .

"The people of Japan, I have been told, speak only one tongue in all the land. They give their allegiance to *all* Japan and not to any single part of it. The people of Japan are strong, while we are weak; they are united while we are divided. One day the people of Japan, so it is said, will attack us. If we are united on that day we shall resist them. If we are divided, we shall fall.

"All else is empty talk, is it not?

"If in this chamber you can achieve unity, nothing else matters. The rest will be accomplished by the force of unity. Go back, all of you, whence you came, taking with you a new idea: that your city, your province, your mother tongue are utterly without significance except insofar as they are a part of this, our beloved China. If you will do this it is the first step to unity and it will not be in vain that an ignorant woman has dared much— perhaps the anger of her man who sits among you—because her tongue has uttered the things which were in her heart.

"I go from you now. I go because this small son must be fed— fed at the breast of a woman of all China. See! He seeks my breast, nor does he care whether the milk comes from Canton, or from Peking. It is enough for him that it is the milk of China."

Peahen fumbled among the infant's clothes for the money which the man of Shanghai had given him.

"He gives it—to China!" she said, handing the notes to Chang, to whom she bowed. Before her audience had found their tongues, Peahen disappeared behind a screen at the end of the chamber to feed her son.

Patriot, at nearly eight years of age, was now the Small General of the ducks, thrilling, as his father and grandfather had thrilled, to the sense of power and importance which went with this command. It was almost sundown when, the ducklings having swept the mudbank clear of everything edible and a great many things which were not, headed for Sung's island and home. For many reasons Patriot was glad. It had been a long hot day. He was tired and hungry. All day, from the direction of Shanghai, had come the dull booming of guns—the guns of the Japanese. Even the old Mandarin drake, who was almost exactly the same age as Patriot, was nervous and excitable. He had communicated his nervousness to all under him, so that by the end of the day, every time the sound of the guns came across the water, several thousand small heads were cocked towards Shanghai.

The waterfront of Sung's island was now very much changed. Where a bay had been was now some five acres of brilliant paddy-green rice, the miracle accomplished by the foreign engine and pump which was now at work on the far side of the island, sucking up from the lake bottom the rich mud which was daily increasing the size and value of Patriot's heritage.

There was now an almost landlocked harbour on the island. On this evening it was full of houseboats and fast sailing *sampans*, for many guests had come. Even the ducklings returning from their feeding grounds, now had a special little waterway which led right to their night quarters. All they had to do was to swim under a narrow bamboo gate which, when the last straggler had passed through, was dropped for the night. This obviated the mad scamper across the foreshore, morning and evening, which had resulted in so many small ducklings being trampled under the great flat feet of the army.

The day marked (although Patriot was not aware of the fact) an emergency meeting of Number One Branch of the Brotherhood of the New China. Hence the assembly of craft in the harbour. Sung's island had been chosen as the meeting-place because of the events around Shanghai. Who knew whether guns would not be roaring around Soochow before long?

Having already washed himself in the lake, Patriot slipped on a new silk gown so as to be properly clad when going to pay his respects to the guests.

The small Patriot was very hungry. He wished, vainly, that it were possible for him to eat his evening meal before presenting himself to the guests, for the savoury smells coming from the kitchen were well-nigh unendurable.

Among the guests was the venerable Lok-kai-shing, seated in his own chair, which had been carried up from the houseboat. He had not left his own house for more than two years. He greeted Patriot warmly. Turning over in his mind as he did so was the thought that, but for events which did not now seem important, he would have been the grandfather of this straight-limbed and well-poised lad. Kung, the aged President of the Thieves' Guild, was there too, and Magistrate Chang, looking more dignified and aristocratic than ever. He was wearing his advancing years with much grace.

A chill fell over the assembly as the light breeze brought from the direction of Shanghai the sound of another tremendous burst of gunfire. It brought also from the kitchens the smell of frying fish.

"This is the day when the silkworms are hatching," said Patriot, calling through the kitchen shutters. "It is written—my respected father told me so—that the smell of frying fish is unwelcome to the young worms."

"It is also written," said the Old One, as she did so slipping into the boy's eager hand a large piece of duck meat, "that guests may not be sent away hungry."

"That also is true!" said the lad pensively. "My father told me so. But he did not tell me which was the more important, silkworms, or guests."

"One wonders," observed the Small General, smiling to his guests and asking their indulgence for this young son, "whether the silkworms hatched today will ever spin their cocoons."

"I was just about to tell you something most important," said Red Tiger, who was now very old and infirm, "but since you seem to prefer chattering about the smell of frying fish, it shall remain unsaid. . . ."

"You promised me that you would tell me about how you killed a traitor—when you were a pirate. . . ."

"I was never a pirate!" said Red Tiger virtuously. "I have been a patriot ever since I learned to walk. How can you suppose, if I were a pirate, that I could have enjoyed the friendship and esteem of distinguished and honourable persons such as Magistrate Chang here?"

"Nevertheless, the Old One told me that you were once a pirate."

"I have nothing more to say," said Red Tiger.

Once again there came across the water the thunder of the guns.

"It is the end!" said a voice.

"It is the beginning," said the Small General. "It had to come, whether today, or next year. Let us be thankful that it has come at a time when we Chinese are nearer to unity than we have ever been in our history."

In the kitchen, where she was helping the Old One to prepare food, Peahen smiled happily. It had been hard to live down her outburst in the Council Chamber years before; harder still to avoid the limelight which she did not want for herself. Strangers in plenty had acclaimed her, but she cared very little for their opinions. It was enough that the Small General, father of Patriot, was now high in the national councils of the Brotherhood. She did not want her man known by the reflected glory of his concubine, which might so easily have happened. Since then she had tried to make amends for her outburst by giving the Small General three more sons. Now she was content to forget that it was she who had lit the torch which her man now carried so proudly. In that knowledge was enough joy for her.

With an ear cocked to what passed outside, Peahen continued with her task of slitting and gutting the fish which the angry cormorants had caught that day. She was very happy—happier than she had ever expected to be in those far-off days when she lived in a dimly lit world of her own.

"Before you go to bed," she heard Kung say to Patriot, "I will tell you a story—one that you must never forget. It is not only for the ears of a child," he added to those around him.

"If it is a good story," said Patriot, "I will never forget it."

"It is a good story," said Kung. "It concerns my illustrious ancestor, the Great Sage himself!"

The aged President of the Thieves' Guild, whose claim to descent from Confucius rested on very slender evidence, ignored the smiles around him.

"A very long time ago," he began, "my illustrious ancestor, Confucius, was on a journey. Beside the road he came upon a woman who wept bitterly.

" 'Why do you weep, woman?' he asked.

" 'Upon this very spot,' replied the woman, 'my father-in-law was killed by a tiger. A short while later,' the woman continued, 'my husband also was killed by a tiger. Today, and it is more than I can bear, my son—here on this spot where we stand—was killed by a tiger.'

" 'Then why, woman,' asked my illustrious ancestor, 'do you not remove yourself to another district?'

" 'Because here,' the woman replied, 'there is good and just government. Who knows what kind of government I might find elsewhere?'

" 'Remember that,' said my illustrious ancestor to his disciples, who were with him. 'This woman utters a great truth when she says that bad government is more to be feared than a tiger.'

"Will you remember that story?" asked Kung.

"It is a good story," said Patriot thoughtfully. "I will remember."

"It is indeed a good story," said Magistrate Chang, who had been an attentive listener, even though he questioned the authenticity of the teller's pedigree. "It is vastly important that you should remember. Do you hear the thunder of the guns across the water?"

"It has been in my ears all day," said the lad.

"You hear the thunder of the guns," continued Chang, "because for a very long while our native land, China, has been badly governed. The guns roar because of the mistakes of yesterday—mistakes made by me and by other old men. It is too late to repine and to weep. Our day—the day of all the old men who

232

failed—is gone, swept away by the guns you hear now. Tomorrow belongs to you, do you understand? Yours will be the task of helping to govern the New China which will one day emerge—tall, serene and erect—from the wreckage of the old. When that day comes I want you to carry with you the memory of that poor woman, who feared bad government more than she feared the tiger which had killed three of her loved ones. . . . Perhaps you do not understand today, but if you do not, your honoured father and gracious mother will help you to understand tomorrow."

"Soon I shall understand everything," replied Patriot, "for I am now—did my honoured father tell you?—the Small General of the ducks. Of more than three thousand ducklings I took out this morning only three were unable to swim home. These I brought back in the bottom of the *sampan*. They were very small and very tired. . . ."

"Here stands another, I suspect," said the Small General, "who is very small and very tired and very hungry. . . ."

"I beg to be excused," said Patriot, taking the hint, "for my mother has promised that I shall have a piece of Mandarin fish with my rice this evening. Then I will sleep, for tomorrow I must be with the ducklings a full hour before dawn."

"Tomorrow! That is right," said Chang. "Keep your eyes fixed always on tomorrow, while we who have passed our days contemplating yesterday will talk a little before we eat and sleep."

THE END